Britt...

Who's Fooling Who

Many, many blessings!

ALISHA YVONNE

Ebony Literary Grace

Alisha Yvonne

05-02-14

Who's Fooling Who

ALISHA YVONNE

Ebony Literary Grace
PO Box 18080
Memphis, TN 38181-0080

ISBN 10: 0-9746367-5-4
ISBN 13: 978-0-9746367-5-7

Library of Congress Control Number: 2011925690

First Printing: March 2011

Printed in the United States of America

10 9 8 7 6 5 4 3 2 1

This is a work of fiction. Any references or similarities to actual events, real people, living, or dead, or to real locals are intended to give the novel a sense of reality. Any similarity in other names, characters, places, and incidents is entirely coincidental.

1 Corinthians 13:4-7 (NIV)

[4] *Love is patient, love is kind. It does not envy, it does not boast, it is not proud.* [5] *It does not dishonor others, it is not self-seeking, it is not easily angered, it keeps no record of wrongs.* [6] *Love does not delight in evil but rejoices with the truth.* [7] *It always protects, always trusts, always hopes, always perseveres.*

Tempest

1

"**W**hat?" I screamed. "Stop talking to me because I'm not listening anymore."

I was pissed that Ace would even insinuate I needed to stay home rather than hanging out on ladies night. I looked forward to the times I could meet up with my girlfriends, Lynette and Tracey. We'd dine and party at various locations across Memphis just to have a breather from our men. Ace knew the monthly routine, but I guess he thought since he wasn't feeling well, this night should've been an exception. I stomped about the bedroom, letting his words go in one ear and out the other as I continued to perfect my beauty.

"I'm just saying, Tempest—" he started again.

"Just saying what?" I snapped my neck around, giving him the meanest eye I could.

I was done with ignoring Ace. He'd said far too much, and frankly, I didn't want to hear anything else he had to say. The bottom line was that I was going out, and this would be the beginning of me learning how to take care of *my* needs again.

Ace sat up in bed, covered at the waist. "I never asked for this illness—"

"Well, I damn sure didn't either," I shouted. I wouldn't let him finish his statement. "The man I married was happy and healthy. This . . . this . . . disorder has reduced you to something other than what I'm use to."

We both remained silent, staring at each other for a minute. I turned to face the mirror on the dresser. My hair and makeup was flawless. Linda at Hair Clinque had been able to recreate my favorite hairstyle, which was deep-waved, combed off my face, and hung halfway down my back. I kept my hair dyed jet-black because I admired the way the color brought out my butter-brown skin. I smiled as I played with my one hundred dollar hairdo, but my smile turned into a frown when I noticed a set of eyes on me.

I despised the reflection in the background—my husband, Ace Clinton Bynum. Although he still bore a striking resemblance to the actor Blair Underwood, he reeked of pity, and it was getting harder to look at him every day. I took a deep breath then quickly turned to face him again.

"Fibromyalgia . . . you think I bargained for that when we took our vows fourteen years ago? I'd never even heard of such a thing until it hit you."

"Well, neither had I, Tempest," Ace shot back. "But, I do recall our vows stating 'for better or worse…through sickness and in health.'"

"Don't flatter yourself, Ace. I can remember our vows perfectly. But, why don't you try putting yourself in my shoes for a while and see if you'd feel the same."

Ace tried to sit up, but quickly slammed his back to the headboard, apparently stricken by pain. "Mmph," he moaned, reaching to rub his lower back. "I've thought about it, and putting myself in your shoes, I know I'd be a better spouse given the circumstances. I meant it when I said I'd love you always and forever."

I placed my hands on my hips and twisted my lips before I could respond. "Contrary to what you believe, I do love you, Ace," I said, followed by a loud huff. "You just turned thirty-five yesterday, for goodness sake! Did you know when we got married that we'd be celebrating your thirty-fifth birthday by me feeding you cake in bed because you would be too weak to get up? I sure as hell didn't know."

"No, I didn't know, but I'm sure at some point you were told life is like that sometimes. You have to take the good with the bad."

"Do I?" I asked, snapping my neck at him. "Say what you want, but neither of us saw this Fi-bro-my-algia-thing coming."

"Would it have made a difference if you did know? Would you have still married me?"

I remained silent for nearly a minute. I stood blinking, carefully thinking of a way to say what I felt. "I don't know," I finally answered. "I just don't know."

"I think you do know. It took you too long to respond. That's okay. You don't have to say it."

I opened my mouth to speak, but then paused, took a deep breath and closed my eyes. After slowly releasing the air, I said, "I've dedicated the last two years of my life to taking care of you. I'm still young, and I'm not the one who's sick."

"Now, Tempest, you know that's cold."

"Is it? Ace, have you forgotten all I've done in the past twenty-four months? Bathing you, clothing you, cleaning up after bowel disturbances, cooking and feeding you when you're too weak to lift a fork to your mouth . . . need I go on?"

"I can't help that I'm sick, Tempest, and if you weren't my wife, I might not expect you to do so much."

"I know you can't help it. Your life is sad right now. Although depressive symptoms are a normal part of this illness, I don't fully understand your misery. However, I can't stress it enough that it's not fair my life has been taken from me, too." I looked at Ace sternly for a few seconds then marched toward the bathroom. "I plan to keep living."

Five minutes later, I returned to the bedroom to find Ace sitting in bed with a bitter expression. This was one time I was glad looks couldn't kill. Ace's eyes said they wished I were dead. He clasped his hands together and squeezed them tightly before dropping his head to stare at the burgundy and black, silk comforter. He shook his head as though he was dismayed.

I picked my two and a half-carat, diamond solitaire earrings off the dresser then stood in front of the mirror, humming softly as I put them on. I knew I'd hurt Ace with all I'd said, but I couldn't let him spoil my night. I continued to prance around the room as if he wasn't there. I meant every word I'd said. I loved Ace, but I was past ready to start living my life again.

Ace lifted his head. "What time you plan on coming back tonight?"

"Why?"

"Because I asked you. Just answer the damn question."

I tucked my black, beaded clutch under my arm. "I don't know, Ace."

"'I don't know, Ace'," he mimicked. He began to yell. "'I don't know' . . . always 'I don't know.' Well, tell me when the hell you're gonna know something. Every time I ask a simple question like how long will you be out, you don't know."

"Why are you asking anyway?" I yelled back. "You look like you wish I wouldn't return."

"To be honest, Tempest, I don't care. Stay out as long as you'd like. Hell, wait until morning before you come home. I really don't think I want to see you anymore tonight."

I laughed heartily. "Suit yourself, Ace. You're the one who's in pain and need assistance. You're only hurting yourself by telling me to stay away."

He moaned and reached for the spot on his lower back that ailed him. I shook my head as I watched the pitiful sight. Ace was a fraction of the man he used to be. I certainly didn't care to be in his company very much. I almost wished I could throw him away like yesterday's garbage, but I knew somewhere deep inside the eyes of the being lying in that bed was my husband—the true Ace Clinton Bynum—the man I promised to love and cherish forever.

Ace shifted his posture then looked at me. "Go! What're you standing there for?"

I smiled. "I have no earthly idea. I'm outta here." I started out of the bedroom.

"BITCH," he yelled.

I stopped then turned to look at him. "You're so sad, Ace," I responded, shaking my head. "So sad."

"Get out of here, bitch."

I walked toward the door. "You don't know what a bitch is, but I'll show you one. I promise you that."

I slammed the door on my way out. Ace had the situation twisted. I'd put the last two years of my life on hold, trying to care for him and his disorder, and the best he could do was let me know he thought the lowest of me. Hmph! Oh, he had to pay for that. It was time to bring his "bitch" comment to life.

Lynette

2

I t was eight o'clock in the evening and my girlfriend, Tempest, still hadn't arrived to The Roof Top at the Peabody Hotel for dinner with Tracey and me. I was a little agitated because I hadn't eaten since lunch, and it was really too late for me to digest anything, especially if I was going to try to follow my Weight Watchers plan. I didn't eat much at lunch because I wanted to save room for a few extra points in case I overdid it with food and alcohol during dinner. Thanks to Tempest, I had recently learned how to drink and couldn't wait to get my drank on. Tracey and I just chatted, trying to be patient.

"Girl, how did you get your curls so small and full like that?" I asked.

"Umph. You don't know nothing, huh? Girl, this is a straw set," Tracey answered.

"Rolled with real straws?"

She laughed. "That's possible, but Linda used the small hot dog rods to do this."

"You got extensions?" I asked just before Tracey sipped her glass of water. She set the glass down then smiled. "G'on tell the truth, Tracey. It's just me sitting here."

"Are you tryna be funny? Of course I got extensions. You know Linda be hooking it up."

"Talking about Linda Tompkins down at Hair Clinque? The same lady who does Tempest's hair? I didn't know you were still going to her."

"Yeah. For the most part, I do my own hair, but I can't do weave like Linda. Who does your hair?"

"I do, but I see it's time for me to start going to Linda. She's an excellent stylist."

"Yes, you really should. I wouldn't trade her for the world. You know I was thinking: we've got to be some desperate chicks to come all the way from Marion, Arkansas to get our hair done in Memphis."

"Hmm. I guess so considering it's about a forty-five minute drive. But a woman's gotta do what a woman's gotta do."

The live band started playing, so Tracey and I took a pause for the cause. The Roof Top was a very nice environment with an all-adult, mixed crowd. Everyone seemed to be enjoying the music and the atmosphere. I slid closer to Tracey so she could hear me speak.

"It's not like Tempest to be late," I said frustrated. "I sure hope Ace isn't feeling ill again."

"Why?" Tracey said, laughing. "You heard how Tempest was talking the other day. Ace could be about to take his last breath and she wouldn't miss coming to The Roof Top. The woman is fed up." Tracey rolled her eyes then smacked her lips.

"Oh, Tracey, don't say that. I heard Tempest, but surely she didn't mean everything she said. She and Ace have been together too long for her not to love him."

"She didn't say anything about not loving him. She said she's tired of centering her life on him and that illness, remember? She's drained."

I shook my head. "I just know if it were Lemont who was sick like Ace is, nothing would tear me from him."

Tempest walked up and sat down. "So I guess I'm the topic of discussion, huh?"

Tracey nodded then gulped her water before responding. "It's about damn time you show up. What took you so long? You were about to send this girl's system into shock," Tracey said pointing at me. "Her stomach has been talking louder than we have." We all laughed.

Tempest looked at me then grabbed my hand. "Girl, what happened to the Weight Watcher's plan?"

"I'm still on it," I responded. "But, I'm about to watch my weight go off the roof top if I don't hurry up and get something to eat."

Tracey beckoned the waitress over so we could order dinner and drinks. Tempest ordered Cran-apple with Grey Goose, and Tracey ordered Crown and Coke. Being a newcomer to the drinking scene and a practicing Christian, I stuck with what my taste buds had recently grown accustomed to—a strawberry daiquiri. As soon as the waitress left to take care of our order, Tempest took us back to the subject at hand.

"So, you think I'm a fool for walking out on my husband tonight, huh?" Tempest's face was eerily serious.

I was caught off guard with the question so I looked to Tracey for help, but she only shrugged at me. "Don't get mad, Tempest." I cleared my throat. "I don't know how to explain what I meant. I was only thinking out loud."

"Thinking I'm a fool, right? That's what I asked you."

"Tempest, you're about to blow a fuse over nothing," I answered.

She huffed. "Just answer the question, Lynette."

"No. I don't think you're a fool, but I do think you're a little inconsiderate."

"Inconsiderate?" Tempest rolled her eyes and began fidgeting in her seat—a sure sign she was gonna go off. "Well, let me get this out right now: I did walk out on Ace tonight. He's not feeling well—AGAIN. But, considering I only get to meet up with my girls a couple of times a month, I wasn't about to miss the opportunity to release. Call me what you want to, but you're right: I am about to blow a fuse. If you haven't walked a mile in my shoes, you can't really judge me."

"See. I knew it. You love to get mad over nothing. Am I not your friend? Aren't I supposed to tell you when I think you're wrong? Ace is your husband of fourteen years, Tempest."

"Shut up, Lynette. 'Cause you really can't afford to talk. Your shit ain't right at home either, so just shut up."

I banged my fist on the table. "Don't you tell me to shut up." Tracey grabbed my hand, but I jerked away. "She's got a lot of nerve," I said, turning to Tracey.

"Well, if you didn't know, now you know," was the opening to Tempest's snide remarks. "You're trying to judge me 'cause you can allow your husband to run all over you. Well, that's you. Yes, I'm fed up with not having a life due to my husband's sickness, but at least I'm learning how to take care of me. You, on the other hand, are okay with letting your husband tell you to do things you're totally uncomfortable with—buying heavy-ass weave to glue on your scalp, thongs that I'm pretty sure he has never noticed for the simple fact they get lost whenever you put them on, and I'm not going to even go there with the tattoo-thing because oops I forgot you're a Christian woman," she stated, gesturing quotes on the word Christian. "And for what? 'Cause all that still ain't keeping his ass at home. He's still creeping and probably dare you to say something else about it."

Tracey had heard enough. "Tempest, stop it. You're way out of line."

Tempest snapped her neck around to Tracey. "Why? Because I can call 'em like I see 'em?" We were all silent for a few seconds then Tempest ranted on. "You know what, Tracey? Your shit stinks, too. Lynette and I are just never close enough to smell it, but all marriages have their share of trouble. Ace is not my high school sweetheart, and we haven't been married for twenty-two years like the two of you have with your spouses, but we're going to be fine. Despite what you may think, I love Ace, and when he gets well things will be better between us. In the meantime, you two can just get off my back."

Tracey had turned beet-red. "Oh, I'm going to get off your back alright—off your back and onto your ass in a minute. Obviously you've forgotten who I am. I'm not as good a Christian as Lynette. I'll beat you down for talking out of line to me."

I leaned closer to Tracey and put my arm around her. "Tracey, calm down. The band is wrapping up and everyone will hear us over here in a minute."

"Lynette, you ain't gotta calm Tracey down. She's a bad bitch, but trust me, she ain't bad enough. If you like that straw set you're rocking, then I suggest you get yourself together before I take your li'l red ass by the head and mop the floor with you."

"Try it," Tracey yelled with all her might.

The band had just ended its final note, and if it hadn't been for the applause from the audience, Tracey's outburst would've been heard all across the place. Although Tracey was fuming, Tempest easily smirked as she went inside her clutch bag.

"Here," she said as she pulled out a twenty then slid it across the table. "Cancel my order and tip the waitress for her time. I'm leaving. I don't mess around with fake-ass women like you two."

"Did you hear that?" I asked, turning toward Tracey.

"Yeah, and I'm still trying to understand the 'fake' part," Tracey said, cutting in.

"Yeah, fake. The real Tracey and Lynette would listen to me and have my back on whatever, so when you hear from them, tell them to get at me because you two obviously aren't my real friends."

Tempest left quicker than she came. Tracey and I watched the back of her blaze off through the crowd. I couldn't have caught her if I had wanted to, and by the look on Tracey's face, she wouldn't have let me go after Tempest. Tracey's forehead looked hot enough to fry an egg on it.

"You betta talk to your friend, Lynette, and I'm not playing. She's gonna get hurt if she tries to talk crazy to me again."

"She's not just my friend, Tracey. She's your friend, too."

"I don't know about that—especially after tonight. I just don't know about that anymore. She gets mad too easily—and for what? Just because someone is trying to give her constructive criticism."

"You have to understand her position, Tracey. She's hurting. She and Ace had a beautiful marriage until he got sick. This is a drastic change for her. Remember you're the one who said to me she's drained."

"That still doesn't excuse her to talk to us like we're fools."

"I know, but you've got to find it in your heart to forgive and overlook her."

"Well, you have to pray for me. I told you: I ain't that good of a Christian yet. Take me and this situation up to the altar on Sunday because I'm about ready to wash my hands of Tempest after tonight."

"Trust me. I understand. She was the hardest on me, you know."

"Oh, she was extremely harsh with you. I don't think I could've sat there and took all of that."

"Well, it's over now. Let's just tell the waitress we don't need Tempest's order and try to enjoy the rest of the night. I didn't drive across the bridge for nothing."

"Me either, but I say we go back across the bridge later on rather than getting a room. I'm not in the mood to stay all night anymore."

"That's fine. I can call to cancel our room at the Radisson right now."

Tracey and I hung out until midnight—long enough to let the alcohol wear off—and then we headed back to Marion. It must've been God who designated me to drive us to Memphis because I certainly didn't anticipate having to go back home the same night. That one very weak daiquiri I drank had worn off before my meal made it to the table, so I knew I was in good condition to drive us home.

I dropped Tracey off around one in the morning then headed to my house, which was only about five minutes away. I tried calling Lemont to let him know to be looking out for me, but he didn't answer the house phone or his cell. Once I let the garage door up, I noticed Lemont's car was there. *Oh, he must really be knocked out,* I thought. I entered the house then stopped in the kitchen for a glass of water.

As I reached for a glass, I saw Lemont's cell plugged into the wall over the countertop, charging the battery. I was about to ignore it, but there was a flashing, red light that made me curious. I wondered how he'd managed to forget his cell in the kitchen because Lemont always kept his phone close to his side. I poured my glass of water then drank it before deciding to violate his privacy.

I set the glass in the sink then opened Lemont's cell. There was one missed alert, so I pressed to see what it was. To my surprise, I had opened a photo of a nude woman with a close and clear view of her twat as she held it open while laying spread eagle on a bed. There was a caption that read: EAT ME, LEMONT. I stood there in disbelief. I wanted to throw the phone against the wall and destroy it, but I needed to let Lemont know what I'd seen.

I headed upstairs to our bedroom to confront my lying, cheating husband. I wanted to cry, but the tears wouldn't come, and I didn't know why. All I knew was this man had just promised only a month ago that if I didn't leave him after having found out about his infidelities, he would change. He tricked me. He knew the month before I was ready to move on with my life. The twenty-two years I'd spent with him already had only reaped one outside child and a bundle of heart-breaks, which resulted in several miscarriages before I could finally have my own child.

I made it up the stairs in no time, but I stopped in my tracks when I heard an unfamiliar voice on the other side of my bedroom door. I stepped closer to eavesdrop. My heart fell to my stomach when I detected the voice to be that of a woman. She was moaning my husband's name as if he was serving her right. She even told him she loved him.

I stood in the hallway, trembling, not knowing what to do. The tears decided to come, and they were hot with anger. The hurt had disappeared. I paced for a few minutes then decided I needed to confront the sinners. Good thing I didn't know where Lemont kept his gun because I'm not so sure I wouldn't have lost my religion and carried it into the room with me.

I knew the door wouldn't be locked because Lemont wasn't expecting me back home, and our ten-year-old daughter, Victoria, was away at my mother's for the weekend. I made a mad dash into the room like a crazy woman. Lemont was caught off guard, but his whore was still moaning as if she didn't hear me come in at first.

"Oh my God, Lynette," he yelled, trying to alert his mistress to my presence. "What're you doing home?"

Disgusted, I threw his cell phone at him then ran out of the room and back down the stairs. I had to get out of there. I didn't know where I would go, but I needed to be anywhere but there.

Ace

3

My dearest Tempest, or should I say my wicked wife, took it upon herself to hire in-house help for me. There was never any discussion other than her telling me she had interviewed some people and she would be making a decision before the week was out. I didn't argue because if she was burnt out with having to come to my aid, I wasn't going to force her to continue.

For some reason, Tempest didn't stay out late the night before as she normally would have. I couldn't imagine what transpired to make her leave her girls on their ladies night. I heard her entering the bedroom only an hour after she had originally left the house. I didn't rise because I thought she'd forgotten something and would soon be back out, but to my surprise, she opened her dresser drawer and pulled out her nightgown. She went into the bathroom to change then came out and walked past me without acknowledging that I was awake. When she closed the door behind her, I assumed she would be sleeping in one of the guestrooms. I was right because she didn't return all night.

Tempest was up around seven the next morning, getting prepared for the nurse. By nine o'clock, she decided to assist me out of bed so I could take a bath and shave. Once I finished, I put on a fresh set of pajamas and prepared to sit in the recliner since Tempest had made up the bed. I was almost seated when Tempest entered the room with breakfast.

"Un-un, Ace. What are you doing?" she said, carrying a tray of food.

"I'm just going to sit here and watch television, if you don't mind."

"Well, I mind very much. You should be in bed," she said with a pleasant pitch.

"Excuse me?"

"Honey, I know we ended with a rough night, but it's a new day now. I understand you're still a little weak, so you should be in bed." Tempest set the tray on the dresser then came to assist me over to the bed.

Perplexed, I asked, "You made up the bed so I could climb right back into it?"

"Yes. I changed the sheets and everything. How do you feel since taking a bath? You feel pretty good?"

I slid into bed then pulled the covers up to my waist. "Well, as you said, I'm a little weak, but other than that, I'm okay."

"Good. You know our company is coming today, right?"

"Company? Oh, you mean the in-house help. Yeah, I remember. Is that why you're being so nice to me all of a sudden? You're excited someone is finally coming to relieve you, aren't you?"

"Ace, that's a mean thing to say."

"Keep it real, Tempest. You've been complaining the last few months about having to care for me. I imagine you've been singing happy-lleujah all morning about this caregiver."

Tempest rolled her eyes then strutted over to the dresser to retrieve the breakfast tray. When she turned around, the old

Tempest was back. It was as if she'd done a transformation right before my eyes. Her face was hard and her eyes spoke hatred as they glared at me. She slammed the tray on my lap.

"Here. Hurry up and eat so I can clean up the mess before this woman gets here. You don't want your first impression to be that of a slob, do you?"

"Whatever, Tempest."

She sashayed out of the room, slamming the door behind her. I tried not to judge Tempest because I could only imagine what it was she was feeling. I knew my illness had been tough for her to deal with. It seemed as though we went from being a blissful couple to damn near hating each other over night. Not having children made it easy for us to travel and handle the company we built together right after college. We'd been each other's backbones until God saw fit to stricken me—definitely a test, trial and tribulation.

Tempest returned about fifteen minutes later to take my tray. She didn't bother to ask me if I'd had enough to eat or how I was feeling. She just collected my dishes and left the room again. Surprisingly, she left the door partially opened—what she'd normally do so she could hear me calling if necessary. After about twenty minutes, I could hear her cackling and chatting with someone in the hallway.

"I tell you what. Why don't I finish showing you the rest of the house before I take you in to meet Ace," I understood her to say.

"Sure. That'll be fine," a vibrant feminine voice replied.

The phone rang. "Ace, honey, will you answer that?" Tempest said. "Our company is here."

I didn't respond. I just answered the call. "Hello," I said just after picking up.

"Hi, Ace. It's Lynette," she answered, sounding as if her morning had been just as gloomy as mine. "Sorry to disturb you. Is Tempest in? I tried calling her cell, but she didn't answer."

"You didn't disturb me, Lynette. Tempest is here, but she has company right now."

"Oh. Well, that explains why she didn't answer her phone. So, how are you doing today? I hear you weren't feeling so well last night."

"I had a few pains here and there, but I'm doing okay this morning. I'm just trying to take it easy right now—still lounging around. How about you? You don't sound like yourself, Lynette. Are you okay?"

"No. I mean, not really. But, I guess I'll be okay."

"You need to talk?"

She sighed. "Well, if you don't mind, I do have a question."

"Sure. Go ahead."

"If Tempest hasn't told you, I'm sure you've heard the rumors at the bonding company by now. Lemont is cheating on me."

"Lynette—"

"Before you say anything, Ace, I just want to say, I understand you men stick together and you probably won't tell me much. My question to you is why do men cheat? All I do is work and come home, take care of our child, tend to all Lem's needs and then some. How can he justify cheating on me?" Lynette began to cry.

"Lynette, I'm so sorry for you. I don't know what to say. Did you actually catch him in the act?"

She sniffed a bit more then responded. "Something like that. Last night when I came home from Memphis, I saw Lem's phone on the kitchen counter. I decided to look in it and found a nude picture of an unknown woman. When I went upstairs to confront him about it, I overheard him and another woman making love in our bedroom."

"Oh my God, Lynette. Are you serious?"

"Well, when I opened the door, ready to spit fire, I discovered Lem nude and alone in bed, but his mistress was on the speakerphone still stating her business. She hadn't heard me enter the room."

I wiped my forehead. Lynette had made me nervous for a minute. I figured if Lem was that stupid then surely he was somewhere dead after Lynette had turned his own gun on him. I tried to console her.

"Maybe it was just a voice from a 1-900 number. Did you ask him about it?"

"Not at first. I stormed out of the house and went to a nearby hotel for the night. After returning home this morning, he tried to pretend to be concerned about where I'd been, and then he confessed as to who the woman in the picture on his phone was, and he also said they'd been seeing each other on and off for months. I don't get it. I'm a big girl, but the woman in that photo was bigger than me. So what's wrong with me?"

"Lynette, perhaps it's not you at all. Perhaps Lem is the one with a problem. I'm not sure he'd appreciate me being in his business, so I don't think I should be the one to talk to him."

"I understand. I'm sorry for sharing all of that with you. I guess I just needed to vent. Tempest would've been the ear if she had answered her phone."

"That's okay, Lynette. It's just me. I'm not taking your business any farther than this bed I'm in right now."

"Thanks, Ace. I left Tempest a message. I suppose she'll call me back when she gets time."

"I'll make sure of it. Let me ask you something though. What happened to make Tempest come home so early last night?"

"Ace, that's a difficult story to tell right there. All I can say is Tempest got mad at us for the umpteenth time and left. Tracey and I know how to deal with her though."

"Oh. Okay. I was just wondering. I'll make sure she returns your call, Lynette."

"Okay. And you hurry up and get better. I'm sure your folks at the bonding company need you."

I smiled. "Well, you know Tempest is holding it down, right?"

Lynette laughed. "Yeah. If I know Tempest, she's cracking the whip."

I chuckled a bit. "Have a good day, Lynette."

"You, too."

We hung up then Tempest entered the room. I sat up then glanced around her to see the woman she'd hired. Tempest put on the fake smile I'd seen so many times before then introduced me.

"Faith, this is my husband, Ace Clinton Bynum," she said, moving out of the way so Faith and I could get a look at each other. "And Ace, this is Faith Winston, our new aid."

Faith's eyes enlarged as wide as golf balls. I had to do a double take myself. I couldn't believe the sight of the woman standing before me. Tempest noticed my surprised look then turned to ask Faith to excuse us.

"Um, Faith. I need to speak to my husband in private for a few minutes. Do you mind going downstairs until I call you back up?"

"Oh . . . um . . . of course not," Faith answered sweetly.

Faith took another glance at me then left the room. My wife closed the door behind her. I prepared my ears for a tongue-lashing after the expression I'd given Faith. Tempest walked over to the bed then sat down.

"Now, honey, I know Faith is not the best looking thing, but I couldn't help myself. Although she's," Tempest said, pausing to look at the ceiling, seemingly raking her mind for the right words. "Well, um . . . she's un-pretty, and that's putting it mildly, but she interviewed very well. She's more than qualified to stay here and help take care of you." Tempest put on a sly grin as she stroked her hair. "Besides, you didn't think I'd bring an attractive woman into our home, did you?" She laughed. "Did you see that hideous scar on her forehead? Too bad she doesn't have enough hair to cover that thing. It's a wonder how that

19

happened—my God, as if she wasn't ugly enough. Well, at least I don't have to worry about you falling for her, right?" Tempest laughed some more. I had no comment. Tempest rose then started toward the door. "I'll go get her so you two can get acquainted. Try to be nice, honey."

Tempest left the room, leaving me flabbergasted. Despite Faith's physical appearance, I felt Tempest shouldn't have said such cruel things. I prepared myself for Faith's return. I knew I'd need strength from above in order to get through a conversation with Tempest in the room. I heard the women coming into the room, so I said amen to the quick prayer I sent. Tempest was all smiles once again.

"Ace, honey, we're back."

I reached to shake Faith's hand. "How are you, Faith?"

"I'm doing well, Mr. Bynum. How are you?"

"Not too bad. I'm holding up."

Tempest interrupted us. "Faith, I can't thank you enough for taking on this job. You should find Ace easy to get along with, but in case you don't, just let me know. I'll be sure to straighten him out." She laughed. Faith giggled, too.

"Oh, I'm sure Mr. Bynum will be no problem at all."

"Call me Ace," I said, trying to make Faith feel comfortable.

"Okay, Ace." Faith gave a slight smile, hardly showing teeth.

"You know what? I'm just gonna leave you two to get more acquainted while I go out to do some shopping. Faith, I know you won't be officially starting the job and moving in until Monday, but I think this is an excellent time to talk with Ace so you can know more about what his needs will be."

"Sure. You've shown me the house, and I think I can pretty much remember where things are, so take your time if you'd like."

Tempest smiled so big, I thought she was going to injure all the muscles in her face. "Thanks," she responded. "I'll do that." She turned her attention to me. "Feel free to call me if you think of something you'd like me to bring back."

I nodded. "Call Lynette. That was her on the phone when you told me to answer it."

"Will do," Tempest sang as she exited my bedroom.

Faith and I were silent until we heard the chime of the alarm, signaling Tempest had exited the front door. We looked at each other simultaneously. I couldn't hold back any longer.

"Faith Yarbrough?" I stated.

"Clinton Bynum?" she responded.

"Faith, sweetie, what are you doing here?" I reached for her hand, and she gladly accepted. When I pulled her to me, she began to cry. "Sweetie, it's so good to see you."

Faith seemed at a loss for words because all she could do was hold me and cry. I couldn't believe it. My first love was actually with me, holding me, and consoling me. I knew at that moment, God had sent me an angel.

Faith

4

Ace Clinton Bynum—my first love—that's how I remember him. I lay on Clinton's chest for close to half an hour, weeping. The bad part about those minutes was the fact that neither of us could seem to speak. Clinton had dumped me just after our high school graduation, saying he was only doing what he felt was best for both of us. I was on my way to Clark Atlanta University, pursuing a career in journalism, and Clinton was headed to the University of Tennessee at Martin with a football scholarship. I'd heard over our entire senior year how Clinton's friends were hounding him about me. They felt he could do better than me. Clinton was a stunner—several notches above good-looking, and I didn't even come close to being bottom-runner in the pretty girls club. That was so many years ago, but fate had placed us in each other's paths once again. I just couldn't believe it.

"I didn't think I'd run into you again," I told him.

"This is incredible. Tempest has no idea what she's done."

I wanted to sit up and look at him, but he held me too tight. "You think she'll fire me once we tell her?"

"Think? I *know* she will. That's why we're not going to tell her."

"Clinton, we—"

"Sshh," he said, stroking my hair as I lay on him. "I need you here with me, Faith. Promise me you'll keep our past a secret."

He said he needed me, and the sound of his voice was convincing. I wanted to care for him, so my promise was solid.

"You have my word. She'll never hear it from me," I told him.

I flashed back to some of the days I'd had with Clinton. My parents and I moved to Memphis from Clarksdale, Mississippi during the summer before seventh grade. The kids I grew up with didn't tease me, but Memphis was something terrible to get use to. I met Clinton in the ninth grade, but we didn't become close until the eleventh grade. He approached me about tutoring him with calculus. He needed to pass with at least a "B" to maintain the necessary grade point average to graduate the following year with honors. I didn't have many friends, especially when it came to boys, so I figured helping Clinton would make me popular in some light. Little did I know our studying would payoff in more ways than I could've imagined.

While I gave Clinton lessons in calculus, he gave me lessons on love. Clinton was my first kiss, first touch, first everything. In the beginning I thought he was only using me, but I didn't care because of how good I felt when I was with him. To my surprise, when our twelfth grade year came around, Clinton let it be public knowledge I was his girlfriend. There was no shame in his game, and all the girls had a different reason to frown upon me—jealousy.

When Clinton took his friends' advice to end our relationship, I was devastated. He wrote me a long letter explaining how the miles and distance would eventually destroy what we had so we needed to sever things while we could still end on a pleasant note. That note was anything but pleasant in my mind. I was too hurt to even say goodbye to Clinton before I left for college. He stopped by my house, asking if he could at least see me off to the airport, but feeding off my pain, my brother knew just how to respond to Clinton—by slamming the door in his face.

True, I wasn't the best-looking woman in the world, but Clinton had always talked about how my inner beauty outshined everything. He made me love him, and I knew no matter how angry I was I'd always love him. Who knew seventeen years later I'd be the one he'd have to depend on. The lengthy silence must've given Clinton just enough time to think of the right thing to say.

"Faith, sweetie, I'm so sorry."

I rose to look at him. "For what, Clinton?"

"I was wrong when I broke up with you. I was young and dumb. My boyz were in my ear, and I didn't know how to be a man and tell them to shut the hell up. Besides, I didn't trust myself. I figured the time and distance between us would force me to cheat. I didn't want to do that to you. So . . . again . . . I'm sorry. It feels good to finally say those words to you."

"And here I am, Clinton—without a bitter bone in my body. Your apology is accepted." I smiled.

He placed a soft peck on my forehead. "You've always been a wonderful lady, Faith Yarbrough."

"I go by Winston now," I responded. "I got married several years ago, but now I'm divorced." I reached for his hand. "How did you get like this, Ace?"

"Life is whipping my ass, I guess. Besides breaking up with you, I kinda always thought I'd done things right in my years. But, maybe not. Fibromyalgia is not even as common in men as it is women. It's just strange."

"Strange things sure do happen, huh? I was supposed to be in TV broadcasting after college, but I didn't graduate. I ran off to Florida to be with a man who turned out to be a no-count, good-for-nothing woman beater. That's how I ended up with this scar on my forehead. Nine years after I married him, I found myself having to jump out of his moving car to get away from him. So not only do I have people referring to me as Ms. Celie from *The Color Purple,* but now I look like something from Star Trek, too."

"You do not," he fussed. "Don't ever let me hear you downing yourself again. I kissed your forehead so many times since you've been here because I see an angel—nothing remotely close to what you described. You are an angel. Do you hear me?"

A warm tear fell from my eye. "You haven't changed, Clinton. Except I guess people call you Ace now."

"Yeah. I think you better practice calling me Ace as well before Tempest figures something out. How'd you get into nursing anyway?"

I pointed at my forehead. "Well, I wanted to re-enter broadcasting school after I left my husband, but I didn't have the confidence to do TV with this scar."

"Nursing is a great career. I just remember it wasn't your passion. I'm sure that scar has a lot to do with your lack of self-esteem, but if you stick around me long enough, you're going to get over it."

I sighed. "You know . . . when I left my apartment this morning, I wasn't sure what to expect out of this assignment. Now, I couldn't be more happy about being here."

"Have you finished getting everything out of your place or are you going to keep it?"

"No need in keeping it. I'm going to be here every day starting Monday, remember?"

"True," he answered, stroking my arm.

"Besides, my parents are still around. I can always move back over there if plans change."

Ace gazed into my eyes. I wondered what he could be thinking. Seeing him again made me realize how much I missed him. Feelings I didn't know I still harbored began to surface. I wanted to tell him how I wished he were mine, but I couldn't. Ace was a married man, and I wasn't about to be a Jezebel by tearing him from his wife. He looked as if he wanted to read my thoughts. I smiled and squeezed his hand. He started out of the bed.

"Are you okay, Ace? Should I get you something?"

"No. I'm fine. I was just thinking I would be better company if I got out of bed for a while. Did you see the house?"

"Yes, Tempest gave me a full tour."

"So, did she show you which room would be yours? I'd like to see how she fixed it up for you," he said as he stood.

"She did, and just let me tell you, Ace: this is a lovely home. I'm so proud for you and Tempest."

"Thanks, Faith. Well, our home is now your home, so get use to it."

I grabbed his arm. "Here, Ace. Let me help you."

We went off, arm in arm, to the guest bedroom downstairs. It was an 18 x 20 room with wide windows, which gave a poolside view. There was also a full-bath in the room with a Jacuzzi bathtub and side shower. Out of all the five bedrooms, this one was the smallest, but I absolutely loved it.

"Do you like this one?" Ace asked.

"Are you kidding? Of course I like this one."

"But we have others. Did Tempest show them all to you?"

"She did, but this is the only one she offered. Really, Ace. I'm fine with this room."

He took my hand. "No, no, no. Let's go have another look at the other rooms first."

We headed into the den. It had hardwood flooring and a double fireplace like I once dreamed for my own home. I walked up to the mantel to get a closer look at an outdoor picture of Tempest and Ace. It was a summer portrait of a couple in love. Ace stood behind Tempest, resting his chin on her shoulder. Her hand stretched behind her, cupping the back of his head. Her smile was content and so was his. I couldn't help feeling jealous. As I strolled along the mantel, I secretly played a mental game of replacing Tempest's face with mine in all the pictures. I noticed there were no children. I turned to Ace.

"Where're your kids?" I asked.

"There aren't any. We decided getting our business off the ground was more important. Finances are great now, but she says she's not ready to buckle down and be a mom yet. What about you? Any children?"

I shook my head. "No, and I suppose there won't be any now."

"Why? You're mid-thirty-something like me, right?"

I laughed. "Yeah, that's a great way of putting it."

"You're not too old, Faith."

"Age isn't the issue. I'm not married, and I don't foresee a wedding happening soon, considering I don't have a man." I started out of the den. "C'mon," I said, gesturing. "I want to see the backyard."

The pool was amazing. It had a built-in waterfall and a Jacuzzi. I stood, admiring the scenery. Ace walked up to me and gave my back a once over with his hand. When I turned to him, he had a look in his eye I couldn't quite figure out.

"Why are you looking at me like that?"

He placed his arm around my shoulder. "I'm still wondering if I'm dreaming or are you really here?"

"I'm here, and you're not dreaming." Uncomfortable, I removed his arm and headed back inside.

We stopped in the kitchen for a glass of ice tea. Technically, I was still a guest, but I insisted Ace let me make my way around the kitchen. He took a seat at the table.

"Well, since I can't convince you otherwise—" he started.

"That's right 'cuz I do know what a refrigerator and a pitcher of tea looks like," I said, interrupting him.

"Okay, but what about cabinets and drinking glasses? Do you know what those look like? Huh?"

We both laughed. I shook my head. "Well, if I don't, you're in trouble."

I poured the glasses then took a seat next to Ace. He couldn't seem to stop staring at me. Something told me Ace was having dangerous thoughts about the meaning of my presence. Once upon a time, he wasn't the kind of man who'd cheat, but the years could've brought about a change. A what-if ran across my mind. My conclusion was that I didn't want to be that woman—the one he'd use to replace whatever he wasn't getting from his wife. I needed to make that known, but he spoke before I could.

"Faith, you have no idea what I'm feeling right now."

"Maybe not, but I'd like to know."

"I feel like we've been given another chance at closure."

I almost choked on my tea. "I'm excited to be here, Ace. I hated when my previous assignment expired because I had grown accustomed to the client. She had extended complications after giving birth, so I was hired to help for nearly a year. I had no idea what the next assignment would be like, but hey . . . here I am, and I'm happy. I just don't want you to think that because we have a history we can be more than friends. Above all, we need to respect the patient/caregiver relationship."

Much of Ace's glee drained from his face. He took another sip of tea then answered, "I understand." He cleared his throat. "Well, like I said: our home is your home now, so you're welcome to anything we have here."

I smiled. "That makes me feel good, Ace. You're just as kind today as you were years ago." I glanced around the kitchen. "Perhaps someday I'll meet the man of my dreams, and we'll share a home like this one."

"I'm sure you will."

I caught Ace staring at my head, so I called him on it. "You can't help it, huh?"

"What?"

"My scar . . . it draws everyone's attention."

"No . . . no . . . no," he said, grabbing my hand. "No, sweetie. I wasn't looking at your scar. I was noticing your hair. You still wear the short, curly natural I remembered from high school."

I rubbed my hand across my head. "Well, Ace, some things don't change. I wasn't able to grow hair back then, and I still can't grow any." I laughed.

"Your hair never bothered me. You still wear the large hoop earrings?"

"Yeah. I do when I'm off duty. You remember that?"

He nodded. "Girl, that do and those earrings made you eclectic and Afro-centric. I loved that about you."

"Hmm. Thanks, but you never told me that."

"There are a lot of things I never got to tell you. The little boy in me back then wouldn't let me." He sipped his tea.

I didn't know what he meant by "a lot of things" but I hoped I'd find out. "Well, time has brought us back into each other's paths, so perhaps I'll get to hear more real soon."

"I think so," he said, nodding. After a brief moment of silence, he said, "You know . . . I'm serious about you taking any room you like." He gulped the rest of his tea.

"The one Tempest chose is very generous. I believe I should be downstairs anyway. You and the Mrs. will need your privacy upstairs."

"Hmph," he huffed. "I hear you, but trust there is no need to be concerned for that." My puzzled look must've made him feel a need to explain, so he continued. "Well, with my illness—"

"Oh, Ace, I'm sorry," I interrupted. "I didn't mean to pry. I was just—"

He placed two fingers over my lips. "Sshh . . . I know. I remember your heart. All your intentions are good." He stood. "C'mon. I think I should go back upstairs now."

"Are you okay? Tired?"

"I'm starting to feel a little weak again."

I took his hand then lead the way. Just as we reached the bottom stair, he tugged my arm, forcing me to stop. I turned to him.

"Oh, I'm sorry, Ace. Do I need to slow down? I'm walking you too fast, aren't I?"

"No," he said with glassy eyes.

I was confused. "Then what's wrong?"

He pulled me close then wrapped his arms around my waist. My knees nearly buckled under me, and my guards unexpectedly came tumbling down. I snuggled my head on his collar bone as he held me tight. He loosened our embrace then gazed at me.

"Oh, God," I whispered.

"What's wrong?"

I didn't want to say it, but I knew I wouldn't feel better unless I did. "I still love you, Ace."

I had his undivided attention. "Then 'Oh, God,' is right." He paused for several seconds. "Because I still love you, too."

At that moment, we locked lips.

Tempest

5

"Lynette, what's up," I said into my cell just after she answered. "I heard you called me."

"Hey, Tempest. Yeah, I called. I wanted to check on you and rap to you a bit."

"Oh? About what?" I asked, walking out of Exxon. I got into my car then cranked it.

"About last night."

"Hold on a minute. I've got to reconnect my Bluetooth because I'm about to pull out of the gas station." I made the connection then continued our conversation. "Okay. I'm back. Now what about last night?"

"Girl, has gas gone up again? How much did you just pay for regular gas?"

"I drive luxury cars, Lynette. I'm in my BMW. Ace would kill me if I bought regular gas."

"Oh, well school me then. My Acura must really be mad at me. Regular is all I buy." She laughed.

"Anyway, I didn't buy gas."

"I thought you said you were at Exxon."

"I am. I mean, I was. Exxon sells more than gas, and don't try to get all up in my business. Just tell me what you were saying about last night."

"Okay, okay. Geez . . . anyway, after you stormed off, Tracey and I hung around until about midnight then drove back to Marion."

"Oh my gosh . . . nothing happened on the ride back, did it?"

"No. We were sober, and besides, I drove. You know I wouldn't have gotten behind the wheel otherwise."

"Okay, so what happened?"

"Gurl, I came home and caught Lem having phone sex."

"What? With who?"

"Some hussie he'd obviously been fooling with for a while now."

"You've got to be kidding me."

"No. Not kidding at all. I just want to choke him so bad. I do so much for our household and within our marriage. Why does he have to cheat on me? I guess it's time for me to wake up and move on, huh?"

"Nope."

"Huh? I just knew you would tell me I should be moving on."

"Chile, naw. You have a beautiful home. Why should you have to leave? Lem's ass ain't going nowhere, so why should you?"

"I'm not happy, Tempest. He's not being a man of God."

"I don't know about the man of God stuff but as for your happiness, you got to find your own. That's what I'm doing."

"What do you mean?"

"Honey, I've hired in-house help. I can afford it. It's time for me to start living my life again."

"You have a nurse or something?"

"Yes. She's a caregiver, or better yet, a lifesaver—the answer to my problem. I realized I'm not going to leave Ace—I worked hard for our home and the bail bonding business we own—so I figured I might as well find a way to live with him and be happy. Her name is Faith. I was showing her around when you called earlier."

"You actually trust another woman in your home with your husband?"

"Well, honey, she's an ugly duckling." I chuckled. "Besides, it's not like Ace is going to be able to do anything sexual with her, even if he wanted to. He's having issues getting it up right now."

"Hmm. I guess in that case there is no need to worry about Ms. Faith."

"Trust me. I'm not," I said, letting out a hearty laugh.

"So where are you heading now at twelve-thirty in the afternoon?"

"Out," I answered straight-forth.

"Out?"

"Yeah. Out. Last I remembered, I was a grown woman and didn't need to check in with anybody. You know something I don't? Has my adult status changed?"

"No. Forgive me for asking. You just try to be good."

"Oh, I'm always good."

"Well, don't let my small talk stop ya. I'm going to my prayer closet. Me and the Lord got some stuff to discuss."

"A'ight, girl. And just so you know, I ain't mad at you and Tracey about last night anymore. Tell big head, Tracey, I'll give her a shout tomorrow."

Lynette laughed. "Okay. Bye."

After hanging up with Lynette, I made my way downtown to the Madison Hotel. Valet took the keys to my BMW then I headed up to the mezzanine where I saw him with a drink in one hand and holding his cell up to his ear with the other. He looked up just as I stepped to him.

"Hey, man. Let me get back with ya later," Craig Dennison, my husband's former college roommate and frat brother, said just before closing the flip on his cell. "Mrs. Bynum." He nodded. "I see you decided to join me."

I couldn't help flashing all my pearly whites. "You doubted me, Mr. Dennison?" I reached to shake his hand, but he pulled me to him instead.

"Damn, you feel good." He held me around the small of my back.

"So, do you."

Craig's eyes let me know he saw something he liked. "It's been a long time since I've been able to hold you like this. You ran from me in college. I'm not letting you get away this time."

I closed my eyes and shook my head as he leaned over to inhale the seducing fragrance of Very Sexy by Victoria's Secret on my neck. While savoring the moment, I briefly thought back to our college days when I'd hang out in the break room of the football dorm and play cards with Ace, Craig and the rest of the gang. Usually, I was the only female out of the bunch, and once the card game was over, I'd retreat to Ace and Craig's room for the night. Ace feared getting in trouble for breaking curfew if I were caught leaving, so to his bed I went until morning.

I snapped out of my trance when Craig pulled back to look at me. "What?" I asked cool and calm.

"I just wanna look at you," he replied, sliding my hair from my eyes, wrapping it behind my ears.

"Well, are you just gonna look at me or are you gonna invite me to your room?"

Craig's eyebrows rose. He seemed to be at a loss for words as he began to stutter. "T-t-t . . . to . . . to my room?"

"Um. Yeee-uh. You heard me right. To your room."

The corners of Craig's mouth met his ears. I don't think I've ever seen a man grin so hard in my life. I smiled just as he began to lead me back downstairs, stopping in Grill 83, the hotel's elegant restaurant and bar, to set his glass on the counter-top.

"Would you like to order something before we head to the room?" he asked.

"Sure." I looked at the bartender. "I'll have a gin and tonic, please."

Craig did a double-take. The bartender nodded then headed to fix my drink.

"Girl," Craig said almost shouting. "You know that gin makes you sin."

"You mean just like in our college days when you and I use to creep into the men's bathroom while Ace was asleep?"

The grin returned. "Yeah . . . just like that . . . until you got soft on me and started dodging me. I never understood what happened, Tempest."

I sighed. "The guilt started weighing on me. I loved Ace, and—"

"You didn't love me?"

"Craig, let's not go there right now."

"No . . . let's, Tempest. You still owe me an explanation, remember? If I hadn't run into your brother the other day, I never would've gotten this opportunity to be with you now."

"Funny you should mention my brother, Kenny, the rat. Why did he have to play football his freshman year? He was too damned sneaky for his own good. He made it a point to catch us in the act back then. He was the one who talked me into making a choice between you and Ace."

"He did?" Craig seemed surprised. "Well, I guess if he knew, a lot of other people did, too. You can't blame him if he didn't want people to look down on his sister for playing between two football players, frat brothers at that. Anyway, how about answering my question? Did you not love me?"

Damn, I didn't want to answer him. I turned my back on him until I heard the bartender only seconds later. She asked Craig if she could fix him another drink, and he agreed.

"I think I need this one to be a double, Christie," Craig stated. She nodded then walked away.

"Christie, huh? I see you two have gotten acquainted."

"I play pro-ball, remember. This is the hotel my team frequents when we come to Memphis, and stop trying to avoid answering me. Did you not love—"

"Craig, we were good at creeping," I shot at him. "I could've grown to love you, but there was no time for that."

"What? So, in what little time we did have, somehow my heart managed to get wrapped up into what we were doing, but you could only value the sex?"

"Craig, I—"

"Save it," he interrupted. Christie slid a tall glass of black Russian toward him. He settled the tab then turned to me. "C'mon," he snapped. "Let's just go to the room."

The elevator ride was silent. We went up to the sixteenth floor, into the presidential suite. I marveled at the elegance. I had been to the Madison Hotel for my brother's wedding reception only two years before, but I didn't know there was more beauty to be seen. Craig caught me with my mouth opened.

"You might want to close that," he said, gripping the bulge at his midsection, "unless you want something to put in it."

"I see your language hasn't changed."

"What? I haven't cussed." He shrugged.

. "No, but your words to me weren't nice either. I remember you would act ugly every time things didn't go your way. I take it you're upset because I told the truth."

Craig took a gulp of his drink then set it on the table so he could put on a show for me. He unbuttoned his shirt, exposing a perfectly chiseled, chocolate chest and ripped abs. The elastic from his underwear sat just above the waistband of his pants, accenting the faint hairline leading to the monster I remembered between his legs. When he made his chest jump, I thought I was gonna scream. He took me back to when I loved to sit and watch him make his breast dance before my eyes. He beckoned me.

"Get over here," he demanded, extending his hand.

I set my purse and half-empty glass on the table next to his black Russian then went to him like an obedient puppy in heat. We locked lips the second I was an inch from his face. He tasted like kahlua and Bailey's Irish Cream, sending tingling sensations throughout my body. He hadn't changed. He still had that captivating effect on me. I caressed his hard body as he held the back of my neck, exploring my mouth with his tongue. When he began to lap my neck, I felt a heat between my legs that nearly set my panties on fire. Ace hadn't been able to arouse me in such a way in two years. My body craved Craig, and at that moment, I couldn't help thinking of how indebted I was to my brother for giving in to my pleas of letting me have Craig's number. Craig and I must've been having the same thought simultaneously.

"What do you think your brother Kenny is gonna say when he finds out you came to see me?"

"To hell with Kenny. Don't stop," I said, moaning, pulling Craig's face down to the split in my cleavage. "I have condoms in my purse." It seemed my stop at Exxon wasn't in vain.

Craig's tongue worked like a magician's wand. Juices began to magically flow down my leg. He held me around my waist as I began to tremble. "I got you," he whispered just before sliding his tongue in my ear and two fingers deep into my throbbing womb.

I clamped down on him and screamed as I erupted for what seemed like forever. Craig picked me up without bothering to remove his fingers then carried me to the bedroom. He placed me on the bed, and I watched as he threw his clothes on the chair, one by one.

"The condoms are in the little brown bag in my purse," I said pointing to my Gucci bag. "You can get them out."

Craig was silent as he undressed. I should've been removing my dress and thongs while he disrobed, but I felt paralyzed and out of wind. Craig didn't care though. He instructed me to spread my legs, and somehow I found the strength.

He started toward me with a naked penis. I panicked and tried to sit up to stop him. I was too late. He only had to use one hand to pin me to the bed as he tore my thong with a single tear. I screamed his name.

"Craig . . . Craig!"

"Yes, baby?"

"Where's your condom?"

I tried to get up once again, but my attempt was futile. Craig was inside me, raw-dawging me with long, hard strokes faster than I could make another move. I moaned and pleaded at the same time, pushing upward on his shoulders.

"Oh my god, Craig," I screamed, "where is your condom?"

"We don't need one," he grunted.

"Craig! Get up. Stop. Stop it. Please . . . no . . . oh God . . . NO." I began to cry.

Despite my pleas, Craig began to bang me even harder. The river that once flowed freely between my legs for him was now drier than the Sahara Desert. I became delirious as I screamed, inching higher into the bed. Craig stopped momentarily to pull me back to him, in a position to better thrust his hips. I dug my nails into his sides, attempting to defend myself. It didn't work. Craig seemed to have turned into someone other than who I remembered, so I soon realized he wasn't going to stop—even if I drew blood. I only hoped to slow the force he used to pound into me. I began to feel pain in my lower back and legs. I tried one more time to reason with him.

"Craig," I called. "Craig, baby, why are you doing this?"

He didn't answer me. Sweat poured from his forehead and dripped onto my face. It dawned on me what Craig's behavior was all about. He had decided to ruin what should've been a beautiful moment between us because of his pride. I should've just lied and told him what he would've preferred to hear—that he was the one I'd always wanted and should've married. My truthfulness had cost me, and now Craig was relentless. I knew I had to take my punishment like a woman. I just couldn't stop crying, which seemed to piss Craig off.

Surprisingly, he stopped. "Why are you crying?" he asked, fussing. I remained silent. "Huh? Ain't this what you want? Didn't you come here for this?"

I began to hyperventilate. He dipped his eyebrows, seemingly puzzled by my inability to breathe. I took the opportunity to beg his pardon. "Craig, I'm sorry," I huffed. I swallowed a few more pockets of air then continued. "You didn't let me tell you what you mean to me."

He used his arms to hold himself over me, glaring into my eyes for a brief moment then he let out a loud tsk before stabbing my womb once again. I bit my bottom lip and let the hot tears roll down the sides of my face until he was done. My six-month sexual drought was over, but certainly not worth the aggravation I endured—not to mention having to sit over a toilet in a hotel suite, draining semen that came from a man other than my husband. I couldn't wait to get the hell out of there.

As I headed toward the exit of the bedroom, I glanced at the floor just by the foot of the bed and noticed what remained of the thongs I'd worn. At first, I figured there was nothing to salvage, not even memories of what once was because I wanted to forget I ever knew Craig, but then I had to think again. I slow strolled over to the spot where the undies lay then kicked the straggly-looking things under the bed. Craig didn't budge. He lay naked on the bed with his legs crossed and hands behind his head like he was king. We quietly glared at each other until he broke the silence.

"Thanks for a good time, Tempest," he mocked with a smirk.

I shook my head. "No . . . thank you," I said, opening my purse to pull out the lotion bottle from the hotel's bathroom. "Not only did you bruise my vaginal walls when you raped me, punk, but I do believe this is your semen that just came out of me. Oh, and I'm sure there's more DNA up there where this came from."

He quickly sat up in bed and yelled, "You weren't raped."

"Hmph. You don't think so?"

"Tempest, go take your conniving ass home, girl. You can't prove our sex was nonconsensual."

"Let's see if you're saying the same thing once I leave the Rape Crisis Center and when the police come check my nail prints in your sides."

The moment Craig jumped off the bed, I ran out the room and down to the elevator. As I pressed the button, I noticed him heading toward me. I placed the lotion container into my purse and held on for dear life. Surprisingly the elevator door opened and a service maid walked off. The maid and I stood and watched Craig's ashy, black ass run back into the suite then peep out the door, calling to me.

"Tempest," he yelled. "C'mere. Tempest . . . c'mere, girl."

"Hell naw," I screamed. "This shit ain't over, Craig."

I hopped on the elevator, leaving the service maid standing in the hallway to wonder what all the ruckus was about.

Lynette

6

"Lem are you gonna go with me to my class reunion or *not?*" I asked just after stepping into the doorway of his office in our home.

"NOT," he snapped.

I walked in and stood over him. "Okay . . . so what was all of our discussion about? You promised we would start doing things together. Why can't you go with me to the picnic?"

"I'm not feeling no damn picnic today, Lynette. Why don't you take Vicki? Ten-year-olds love the outdoor sun, ya know."

"Vicki is spending time with my momma today, Lem. I told you earlier that Momma called to ask if Vicki could stay over another night. C'mon now. After last night the least you could do is hang out with me for a while today."

Lem got out of his desk chair, waving his hand by my face as he started out of the room. "I don't wanna hear that, Lynette." He stopped in the doorway and turned to me. "I already told you

I've put a stop to what me and that girl had. Phone sex is the most we've done in a while."

I stepped toward him. "Why did you confess, Lem? Why admit you've carried on an affair at all?"

He glanced at the floor briefly then looked into my eyes. "Because," he answered, pausing to take a deep breath. "I figured it was better I told you than someone else."

I shook my head because he'd confused me. "Someone like who? Who would know?"

"Your mother."

I thought I was gonna faint? "Momma? My momma would know about *your* affair?" Lem nodded then walked off. "Oh, no, Lem," I yelled, going after him. "You come back here. How in the world would my momma know about what you've been doing before I'd know?" I held on to his arm.

"Can we discuss this later?"

"No. I have to face my mother tomorrow when I pick up Vicki. How do I play this off? You need to tell me everything my mother knows."

Lem walked into the kitchen to fix himself a half-glass of Patrone. He gulped the liquor in nearly one swallow. I stood patiently, waiting for him to explain what I didn't know was possible. My mother lived in Forrest City, Arkansas, nearly an hour away from me, so I couldn't imagine how she'd know details of my husband's infidelity. Lem poured another half-glass before addressing my concern.

"You know how I use to play poker in the back room down at Mandy's Café," he stated just before taking another sip of his drink.

"Yeah. Now what?"

"Well, the woman I'd been seeing used to hang out with me there."

"What?" I slapped the glass from his hand. It crashed into the sink. "How would my momma know that?" I practically screamed.

"Lynette, look what you did. Glass is everywhere," he stated, raising his voice.

"I'll clean it up later. Tell me how Momma would know about your hussie."

"Your momma's friend, Ms. Ruthie, would play cards with us most nights. Hell, I hadn't seen Ms. Ruthie since we got married. I didn't know what she looked like until your momma showed up at Mandy's about a month ago and confronted me outside."

I gasped. "My momma went down to Mandy's?"

He pulled down a glass from the cabinet to fix another drink. "She gave me an ultimatum. She told me I had to stop frequenting Mandy's and to break off my affair with Tekeysia."

"Tekeysia, huh? Is she a young girl? I don't know many women our age named Tekeysia. Please don't tell me you're having an affair with a teenie bopper. You know we live in a small town, Lem. Oh, God. How could you do this to me?"

"She's not that young, Lynette."

"What's not that young?"

"Twenty-three."

"Twenty-three?"

I wanted to break down right there. I ran out of the kitchen and upstairs to our bedroom. I threw myself face first onto the bed and balled. I expected Lem to be right behind me, but once ten minutes had passed, I knew he wouldn't come.

After cleaning my face, I went downstairs to talk to Lem some more, but discovered he'd left. I called his cell.

"So you walked out on me, huh?" I said just after he answered. He was silent, but I knew he was there because I could hear the radio in the background. "Lem," I called.

"Yeah, Lynette."

"Aren't you ashamed of all the bad years between us? I mean, I love my stepson . . . at sixteen-years-old, he's the perfect man-child I could never birth. But, he was also born due to your adulterous ways. I'm tired, Lem."

"So what do you want to do, Lynette? I'm tired, too. Just tell me what you want to do."

I couldn't believe he was ready to give up on our marriage so easily. I couldn't help but wonder how this could be the same man I'd once said my vows to.

"So, I should just forget all the years I've invested in this marriage and forget about the child we had together so you can run around with tramps?"

A heavy sigh invaded my ear. "Look, it's not like I don't love you and Vicki. I've just got some things to straighten out in my head."

He really wanted out. Twenty-two years with the man of my dreams, and he wanted out. I smashed the cordless phone down on the floor then ran back upstairs to sulk.

Hours passed before I was able to collect myself. I thought about what Tempest would say if she knew the shape I was in. She'd force me to get up somehow and decide a way to make my life anew. I got off the bed and stood before the mirror on my dresser. The reflection was sorry, no pitiful to say the least. I glared into the red, swollen eyes of a cute yet overweight, medium-toned lady who had never learned how to be a woman.

I had belonged to Lemont Rapid ever since the tender age of sixteen. He was the most handsome man in all of West Memphis, Marion, and Earle, Arkansas put together. He was all the man I'd known sexually and ever cared to know intimately. He'd been my rock, my backbone, my shield . . . my everything. I trusted him with my life, letting him have total control over decisions for me and our child. I couldn't even pump gas if I wanted to. Lem wouldn't teach me. He made sure my tank was filled so I wouldn't have to see a gas station if I didn't want to. Lem even handled all our debts. My paycheck was direct-deposited into our joint account, and he'd make sure our bills were paid. I never even learned how to check our account balance. He was king of our castle, so I felt I had no reason to question his majesty. Lem's control had crippled me. I couldn't imagine life without him.

I thought back to our happy days—the honeymoon stage—trying to make myself feel better, but it didn't work. My cell began to vibrate on the dresser. I nearly broke my neck, running to answer it. I wanted the caller to be Lem, but it was Tracey instead.

"Hey, gurl," she said just after I answered.

"Hey," I responded, unable to mask my sadness.

"Lynette, what's wrong? You sound like you've been crying."

"That's because I have."

"Is everything alright? What's going on? I was expecting to see you here at the picnic by now."

"Tracey, I don't think I'm going to make it. I've got problems at home again, and I'm sick about it."

"Lynette, I'm sorry to hear that, but I really wish you'd reconsider. Your issues at home is nothing new, so there's no sense in sitting around letting whatever it is spoil your class reunion. You've been looking forward to this weekend. Have you not?"

"Yeah," I murmured.

"Alright then. Leave Lem and the problems you got with him at home. Come on out and enjoy yourself. Everyone keeps asking me about you, including Parnell Fender."

"Parnell's there?"

"Yes, and he keeps asking me when you'll be here."

"Why is he asking about me? I know we had a small crush in high school, but he knew back then I would end up marrying Lem."

"That's beside the fact. I think he just wants to fellowship and remember our youth together. Trust me. You'll feel better if you get out of the house. We'll discuss whatever the new issue is after the picnic."

"But I didn't get a chance to get my nails done."

"Who cares? You're married, remember? Parnell is too, so he can't have you even if he wanted you, and neither can anyone else. Now bring your butt out of that house, Lynette. Don't make me come over there."

"Okay . . . okay. Maybe you should come and get me."

"Whatever. I'm on my way."

Tracey hung up on me. I began to feel somewhat excited about seeing my old classmates. Parnell Fender and I had the hots for each other back in our high school days, but Lem swept me off my feet before I could really see what Parnell was all about. Once I was head over heels for Lem, there was nothing Parnell or any other guy could say to make me turn from Lem.

Tracey was at my door within half an hour. I jumped into the car with her and we were on our way. There was an awkward silence between us, and I could tell that Tracey thought so, too, because she spoke out of the blue.

"You know, Lynette, if it makes you feel better to talk about the situation between you and Lem, go right ahead. I guess it was kind of cold of me to suggest you leave it behind. I'll listen if you wanna talk," she rambled.

"No, Tracey. I think this time you were right. I always let Lem's actions consume me. He's gotta know how much I hurt over the things he does, so this time, I'm not going to give the devil what he wants—my joy."

Tracey reached over and felt my forehead. "Who are you, and what have you done with Lynette?" she asked jokingly.

I smiled. "Shocking, huh?"

"To say the least."

"Well, I know you and Tempest think I don't learn anything from you, but I do. I'm gonna have to find a way to keep my sanity and my joy."

"Oh goodness. Please tell me you're not going to start listening to Tempest's evil ass."

"A lot of things Tempest says make sense. She doesn't always have the best approach, but she's right when she says I shouldn't have to leave my home. Lem is going to be Lem, and I can't expect anything more or less from him. Why does that have to mean I can't create my own happiness?"

"I don't like how this sounds, Lynette."

"I'm not talking about going out to have an affair. I'm just saying, I need to rediscover Lynette—me and what I like."

"Okay. You scared me for a minute. I was just about to tell you to take a look at what I just came out of with Rick. We both ran around on each other for years. If God could fix my broken marriage, I know He can fix yours."

"I hear ya, sis. But when? I just keep asking when." I shook my head in despair.

Tracey and I sat quietly listening to Hallelujah FM for the remainder of the drive. I began to weep when I heard the introduction of "Encourage Yourself" recorded by Donald Lawrence and the Tri-City Singers. I knew the lyrics well, and they spoke straight to my spirit. I could sense Tracey glancing over at me, but she remained quiet, allowing me to have my moment.

As we pulled up to the park, I could see the place was packed. I scanned the area, trying to see if I could recognize anyone in the distance, but I couldn't. Tracey got out of the car before I did then leaned back in to fuss at me.

"C'mon, slow-poke. I see Milton Riley over there," she said, pointing. "I want to go speak."

"That's your old crush," I said, fiddling around in my purse. "You don't need me to go say hello."

"Forget you, Lynette. I'm gone."

She shut the car door then headed toward a table with a crowd of people around it. I watched her tip up on the guy she said was Milton then tap him on the shoulder. He seemed to recognize her right away, immediately embracing her. I shook my head, sighed then collected myself to go pretend I was happy in front of what looked like tons of old friends.

I got out of the car, pressing the lock button before shutting the door then turned to see my reflection in the window one last time before joining everyone. I attempted to suck in the hefty belly I'd gained over the years. *Oh, why didn't I just wear a girdle?* I thought as I began walking toward Tracey and the clan she was entertaining. I was nearly twenty feet away and could still hear her voice over everyone else. The closer I got, the more self-conscious I became about my weight gain, so I turned around to double back to Tracey's car.

I tried to move as quickly as possible without having being noticed, but I heard a male voice calling out to me.

"Lynette," he called. "Lynette Sabourne, is that you?"

I looked over my shoulder and saw Parnell running to catch up to me. My heart fluttered at the sight of him. He was tall, big-boned, toffee-colored and well-groomed—simply gorgeous. A wide smile enhanced his face as he got closer. I returned the compliment with a gleam equally as flirty as his.

"Lynette Sabourne," he called again. "Where do you think you're going?" He stopped just inches in front of me.

"I . . . I . . . um . . . I left something in the car. I was coming back," I said, pointing toward the car as I lied.

"Well, I sure hope so. I've been waiting to see you all afternoon." He paused. "Can a brother get some love? I've been outdoors, but I'm not sweaty," he stated, stretching his arms to me.

I stepped into his embrace. *Hmm, not sweaty at all. Smelling pretty darn good in fact,* I thought. He gave me one tight squeeze before letting go.

"It's good to see you, too, Parnell. How are you?"

"I'm great. In fact, better now that I see you." He smiled.

Lawd, have mercy, I thought as I began to swoon. I walked over and leaned on the car for support. Although there was a Spring-like breeze caressing my body, I began to perspire as though I'd just stepped out of a sauna. I began to fan myself with my hand.

"Excuse me, Parnell. I feel like I'm flashing. I'm not as young as I use to be, you know."

48

Parnell began to fan himself, too. "Well, it's not just you. It is warming up out here. You wanna sit in the car?"

"Um," I said, looking around him. "Well, I would, but this isn't my car. Tracey drove me here, and she's off somewhere with the keys."

Parnell reached into the pockets of his knee-length shorts. "I tell you what. My truck is right over here," he said, pointing. "How about we sit in my vehicle and cool off a bit while we catch up on old times." He held his arm up for me to grab it.

I smiled. "Okay."

My mind began to wonder as we started toward his truck. *Should I have chosen him back in the day?* I thought. Parnell was speaking, but I couldn't hear his words for admiring his strong, masculine arm. I shook my daze momentarily to hear what he was saying.

He opened the door and helped me in the truck. "I want to hear all about you and Lemont and your children, if you have any." He closed the door and walked around to the driver side.

I inhaled then released a relaxing sigh. *Lemont who?* I thought.

Tempest

7

I did just what I had promised Craig Dennison—drove to the Rape Crisis Center downtown. The Detroit Lions star running back chose the wrong woman on the wrong day. My cell phone kept blowing up, and of course the calls were from none other than Craig. Ignored them all. My mind was set on conducting a plan that would hurt him and his career. People really should be careful of whom they try to come up against. I'm sure when Craig made up his mind to attack me, he hadn't considered I might be one to retaliate with blows that would destroy him—and I'm not talking anything physical either.

Just after walking into the Rape Crisis Center, the receptionist addressed me. I closed the door and immediately went into victim mode.

"Ma'am . . . oh God . . . ma'am, you've got to help me," I panted, tears flooding my eyes.

"What's wrong?" she asked.

I turned to look at the door then back at her. "Help me . . . please. I've been raped and I think my attacker is right behind me. Please . . . you've gotta help me."

"Have you called the police?"

"No. I was driving very fast to get away from the man when I looked up and saw your facility, so I just pulled in here."

"Hold on a minute, ma'am," she told me, picking up the phone. "I'm going to get the police down here."

"Thank you," I responded.

I jumped at every little sound, pretending to be terribly frightened. I listened as the woman told police over the phone that I appeared to be shaken and that they were about to take me into a room to administer an examination. I couldn't help smiling inside. If Craig thought he was mad when I left, his anger was about to shoot to a whole new level. The woman hung up the phone and gave me her attention.

"C'mon back, ma'am."

"Thank you," I cried.

Once we were in the room, I was instructed to undress and then fill out some paperwork while waiting for the nurse to see me. I ran through the paperwork quickly, noting that I wanted my identity to remain anonymous.

The nurse came in to see me. She asked details of the rape and whether I knew the perpetrator. Instantly, victim mode returned. I don't know where I found so many tears.

"I know exactly who he is, but I can't tell you," I cried. "He'll get me."

"Listen, sweetie," the nurse said. "There are a team of us who will be here for you. We'll stand by you on this. You have to tell us who this guy is or otherwise, he'll do the same thing to some other woman."

I sniffed then wiped my face with a tissue the nurse handed me. "I hear what you're saying, but I can't say. I just can't. I'm so afraid. Besides, if my husband finds out, I don't know what I'm gonna do."

"Sweetie, I know you're concerned about your marriage, given the fact you were somewhere you shouldn't have been, but if you don't tell us who this guy is, there could be potentially hundreds more women who'll have to suffer exactly what you have. You don't want that do you?"

"No," I cried.

"Then let us help you."

I remained silent for a second then responded. "I can't." I began, crying harder than before.

"Alright, sweetie. Just try to calm down. We'll talk about this later. Right now I need to get you examined."

She asked me to lie back on the table then proceeded to scrape, blot and poke around in my vagina. She also checked the rest of my body for incriminating evidence. She took samples from under my fingernails and swabbed my mouth as well. *Craig, if only you knew,* I thought.

Once the examination was done, I got dressed and waited for the nurse's return. She came back into the room, offered a pill called the Morning After Pill, which was explained to me as a pregnancy prevention treatment.

"But how potent is it?" I asked. "Is there any chance I'd still end up pregnant?"

"It's an extremely large dose of the average birth control pill. It should work, but in the event you should become pregnant, the dosage will cause your body to reject the embryo. This is also known as a chemical abortion."

I couldn't stomach what I was hearing. "No thank you. I won't need the pill. I'm not fertile anyway. I'm thirty-five-years old, and I haven't gotten pregnant yet."

"Are you sure it's you and not your husband?"

"I'm sure. Well, now it's both of us who aren't fertile, but yes, I'm sure."

Just then a knock was at the door. "Come in," the nurse said.

A uniformed policeman opened the door. "Hi. I'm Officer Jones, and this is Detective Williams coming in behind me. We're here to take a report. Is this the rape victim?"

"Yes. Come on in, Officer and Detective," the nurse said. "This is Mrs. Bynum. She came in extremely shaken just before two o'clock this afternoon. I've been talking with her, and she's not comfortable releasing the perpetrator's name for fear of retaliation. She's also fearful that this will destroy her marriage, considering she wasn't supposed to be in the company of this gentleman."

The detective nodded. "Thank you. I'll take it from here," he said. He turned to me. "Mrs. Bynum, I hope you're doing okay in spite of the circumstances."

"I'm okay."

"Good. I understand you're reluctant to give up this individual's name, but I assure you, the law is on your side. We'll do whatever we can to protect you." He pulled out a pen to write on his pad. "Now . . . who is this person and where were you when the assault occurred?"

I proceeded to give him all the details of the rape, including the fact that the sex was almost consensual until he refused to wear a condom. The officer agreed that once I asked to stop, my attacker should have ceased. I didn't answer the who and the where questions, but that didn't keep the officer from reiterating how much he needed to know.

"Mrs. Bynum, I want to help you, but in order for me to do that, you're going to have to tell me everything."

I opened my purse and pulled out my cell phone, pretending to dial my husband. "Wait. I can't. I haven't even spoken to my husband."

I dialed Craig's number, listened for him to answer then hung up. I knew this would provoke him to call me back. I turned to the officer.

"My husband didn't answer. I just don't feel comfortable giving this guy up. He's famous and this rape case definitely stands to ruin his career. He may come after me."

My phone began to ring. I pretended to accidentally drop it on the floor next to the officer's foot. He did exactly what I figured he'd do—looked at the caller ID when he picked it up. "Craig Dennison," the officer exclaimed, glancing at the name on the phone. He and the detective then stared at each other.

"Craig Dennison, the football player?" the nurse asked.

"Um . . . um," I stuttered, reaching for my phone. "Um, yes, but I know what you're thinking."

"Is he the famous guy who raped you, Mrs. Bynum?" the detective asked.

"Um . . . I didn't say that. Why would you say that?"

The officer turned to the nurse. "Do you have DNA samples from her?"

"Yes, we scraped her womb, mouth and under her nails."

"Good," he said. "Mrs. Bynum, I hope you know that if we find DNA to match Craig Dennison, you won't have to press charges. The state will pick it up."

"But I didn't say Craig raped me."

"You won't have to," he said. "We're going to subpoena him for DNA samples, and with the name he has, expect this news to be all over the media."

I gasped. The nurse spoke up. "You won't release her name to the media will you?"

"No, we won't, but I can't promise how much longer we can keep her husband from finding out because we have to be in touch."

Oh, no! I hadn't thought of that. "Please, please . . . whatever you do, don't send anything to my house, and contact me by my cell if you must."

When my phone rang again, I took a look at it. "Is that him?" the officer asked. I didn't respond. "Why don't you answer it? He's not the one who raped you, right?"

I answered the call. "Craig, I'll have to call you back. I'm having a meeting with the police right now."

"You bitch," he screamed. "I know damn well you didn't report me to the police. Tell me you didn't."

"Craig, listen. I'm gonna have to call you back. This meeting shouldn't take much longer. I'll call you back as soon as we wrap up."

I hung up the phone. The detective and the policeman looked at each other as if they didn't know what to make of the call. After noticing the time on the clock on the wall, I was ready to get out of there. It was four o'clock. I'd accomplished all I had come to do.

"May I leave now?" I asked, jumping down from the table. "I appreciate this center very much."

"Mrs. Bynum, you stated you believed your attacker had followed you down here," the nurse said. "Would you like an escort home?"

"No," I was quick to say. "Well, maybe to the interstate, but after that, I should be fine. He doesn't know where I live."

The officer followed me out and to my car. I reminded him to only trail me to the interstate before getting into the driver seat. Once I noticed his cruiser next to mine, I pulled off, and he tagged along. I waved at him in my rearview mirror once I was ready for him to back off.

As soon as I saw the officer pull off on an exit, I redialed Craig's number. He answered on the first ring.

"Have you lost your damn mind?" he screamed into the phone without saying hello.

"Yes," I answered. "I'm crazy as hell. I bet you wish you had known before you decided to take advantage of me, huh?"

"Tempest, did you report me to the police?"

"I just told you I'm crazy. Do you really have to ask me that question?"

"Oh my God," he yelled.

"Well, you certainly are calling on the right one, because He's the only one who can help you now." I laughed. "And guess what?" Craig didn't say anything. "Craig," I called.

"What?"

"I said guess what."

"What?"

"I didn't even have to pull out the lotion bottle. I guess I better throw this heap of sperm I collected into the trash."

"What did I ever see in you?" he said. I laughed as he continued. "I must've been out of my mind to fool with you again. You were a sly bitch back in the day, and I see nothing has changed."

"Why thank you, Craig, but flattery won't do much for you now. I suggest you get the hell out of that room before they come hall your ass to jail."

"You told them where to find me, too?"

I didn't answer him. I just laughed. I turned up the radio as Craig began to scream my name. I snapped my fingers and sang the song on the radio, pretending not to hear him. Craig was screaming so loud he sound like he was going hoarse. Once my song went off, I decided to answer him.

"What do you want, Craig?"

"That's what I want to know from you. What do you want from me?"

"You hurt me, Craig. We were supposed to engage in something beautiful, but you let your ego get the best of you."

"I'm sorry."

"That's not acceptable."

"Then what do you want me to do?"

"Hmm. I don't know yet. Give me some time to think about it."

"How much time? Tempest, you know they'll be after me soon. I can't believe you did this to me."

"There are a lot of unbelievable things in this world, Craig, and the fact that you'd sexually abuse me is one of them. You hurt me, and now I hurt you. That's just the way it goes."

"It doesn't have to be like this."

"It does in my book. You have to understand getting revenge is how I operate. No one hurts me and gets away with it."

Craig sighed, sounding defeated. "So when do you want me to call you back?"

"I don't. I'll call you."

I hung up on him, and surprisingly, he didn't call me back. After pulling into my garage, I turned the ringer off on my phone in the event Craig decided to call. I entered the house, thinking Ace would be upstairs in bed, but to my amazement, he was sitting in the kitchen having a drink with our hired help. He seemed overly nice once I entered.

"Tempest," he sang. "How was your day, darling?"

When I looked at Faith, she smiled, seemingly awaiting my reply. I answered his question with a question. "What are you doing out of bed, Ace?"

"Strange, isn't it?" he stated. "This is actually my second time out of bed. It's been an up and down day for me health wise. I'm feeling fine compared to how I felt last night. You know how this disorder is with me. It chooses when it's going to control me. Oh, how I wish I was the decision-maker of when to feel good and when not." He picked up the bottle of champagne and held it up. "C'mon have a drink with us, Tempest."

I frowned. "What . . . this is some type of celebration or something?"

"Oh, Faith and I were just chatting. You know . . . trying to get familiar with each other."

I'm sure the creases in my forehead thickened. "There's not that much to be familiar with, Craig. All she needs to know is what foods you eat, the times you take your medications, and the other minor rules of the house. What else is there to get to know?"

"Well, I needed to explain the complications of this disorder, Tempest."

I shrugged and shook my head. "She's a nurse, Ace. Besides, she and I had already discussed your disorder during her interview." Faith was looking down at the table. I addressed her. "Faith, I know technically you don't start work here until Monday, but I would have been more appreciative of you having fixed some type of meal for my husband rather than sitting and having a drink with him."

Ace interrupted. "We were just discussing dinner, Tempest. What are you so uptight about?"

"You were discussing dinner, huh? What about lunch? Did you eat lunch?"

"We snacked," he answered.

I huffed and slapped my hands on my hips. "Faith, it was nice seeing you again. Thanks for keeping my husband company while I was out, but I'm home now. I can take things from here. I look forward to you moving in on Monday."

"But what about dinner?" Ace asked.

I bit my bottom lip and clinched my fist before answering. "She's a grown woman, Ace. I'm sure she knows how to find dinner on her own."

"I'll be fine, Mr. Bynum," Faith said, sliding her chair from the table.

"Ace," he responded. "Call me Ace, Faith."

Faith nodded then bid us good day. Ace's spirit seemed to change the moment she closed the door behind her. He re-corked the champagne then slid his chair back. I questioned his sudden somberness.

"Did you meet a new best friend or something, Ace? Just asking 'cause I swear you're not acting the same as when I first walked in here to find you two cackling."

He pushed his chair under the table then gave me an evil eye. "Can you blame me? Yes, it was good to have someone around to laugh with for a change. Not only do you not laugh with me, Tempest, but you hardly crack a smile anymore." He started to walk away but turned back. "I don't know if you had a bad day or what, but maybe if you just try pretending your day was fine, you'd feel better. I get sick of your mean ass."

As he walked away, I didn't bother responding. I wasn't intimidated by his new best friend. Ace had never been a cheater, and judging by the looks of his new confidant, he wasn't going to start even if he wanted to. The thought of him trying to perform was hilarious.

"What the hell is he gon' do with her anyway?" I said in a barely audible tone.

I began to chuckle, and then burst into a hearty laugh. My laughter was short-lived when I picked up my cell phone and noticed a text from Craig. It stated: WHAT'S YOUR PRICE? I didn't have a price—yet. Craig needed to squirm a bit more. He hadn't suffered like I wanted him to, so there was nothing to negotiate as far as I was concerned. A second text came through: HOW MUCH LONGER ARE YOU PLANNING TO TORTURE ME? I made sure to text him back: INDEFINITELY. I have to admit: giving him that response felt pretty good. Another smile crept on my face, and since my husband had just accused me of not being able to create an upside down frown, I turned my phone off then headed upstairs to show him.

Ace

8

Tempest was in and out of the house on Sunday. It seemed like every few minutes, her cell phone was ringing. She must've left out to converse with whoever the caller was— sneaky I'd say, but that was Tempest. There had been very few occasions when I was afforded the opportunity to hear conversations between her and her girlfriends. Off to another room she'd go, but this time, she was out the door.

After the last time of stepping out to chat on the phone, Tempest's cell stopped ringing. There had been back to back calls then suddenly there were none. I believe at some point she turned her ringer off. I refrained asking what she was doing or where she'd been. She made sure I had food and water within reach, so I really didn't have anything to complain about. Her distance and space gave me time to think of Faith—what was and what could be. That kiss Faith and I shared left her soft lips edged in my mind. I couldn't wait to see her again.

Monday morning, I was in a pleasant mood and having a pretty good day health wise. Tempest's demeanor hadn't changed much, but for the first time in a while, I didn't care. She could stomp around, cuss me out, or whatever. It wouldn't have made me any difference. Little did she know, she had done me a huge favor by hiring Faith to move in and care for me. What better company and care-giver than a woman I knew loved me?

I was like a big kid when the doorbell rang. I climbed out of bed and made my way downstairs. Tempest had gone to the door to answer it. Faith entered with two large suitcases.

"Do you need some help, Faith?" I asked.

Tempest interrupted. "Now what can you do? Your muscles are already weak enough."

"That's okay, Ace," Faith answered. "I'm fine." She headed toward her room.

"I wasn't talking about me," I responded. "I thought you'd lend her a hand, Tempest."

She gave me an evil eye. "Since when have you known me to lift anything heavy?"

"I only have a few more bags," Faith said in passing, heading back outside.

Tempest stood in the door, looking out at Faith with her arms folded. She seemed repulsed by something, but I dared not ask what was wrong. I went to another subject.

"Well, are you gonna offer to help her unpack?" I asked.

She did a double take. "Do what? Help her unpack?"

"Yeah."

Tempest laughed. "You know, Ace, sometimes you can really be funny. I like the fact that you've got jokes this morning."

I started to rebuttal, but figured what was the use. "I guess I'll have a seat in the living room since there's nothing I can do to help the woman," I said, walking away.

"No. C'mere," Tempest called. "You've gotta see this."

I went to the door as Tempest had requested. Faith had just unloaded her final bag and set it on the pavement. I looked at Tempest then shrugged. "What?" I asked.

"That shit can't stay here," she said.

"What? The woman only has a few bags. I think she's done well to limit her luggage considering she'll actually be staying here."

"That's not what I'm talking about, Ace."

"Then what are you saying?" I looked out again and noticed Faith struggling toward us with two of her bags. "Man, I really wish I could help her."

"Ace, are you listening to me?"

"Yeah, Tempest."

"That raggedy piece of metal she calls a car can't stay here."

Tempest had managed to shock me once again. I waited until Faith passed us and was out of sight before responding. "You can't be serious," I whispered. "She can't help what she drives. Besides, she's gonna need transportation to run errands and take me to my doctor's appointments."

"Then let her drive one of your cars. I ain't playing, Ace—that thing can't sit in front of our house," she said, pointing. "It won't fit into our garage, and do you know how bad that will make our property look?"

I sighed. "Fine. I'll have her added to my insurance, but you gotta be the one to tell her what to do with her car. I'm just not going to do that."

"You think I won't?"

I walked into the living room, shaking my head. Tempest went into the room with Faith. I could hear them chatting, but I couldn't hear all that was said. Faith came out of the room with a fed up look on her face. I silently prayed she wasn't thinking of quitting.

"I just have one more bag outside," she said as she passed.

Tempest was right behind her in the doorway. Faith dragged the last bag inside to her room then the two of them grabbed their purses.

"Where're you ladies going?" I asked.

"I'm going to follow Faith to the place she's going to take her car then bring her back."

My eyebrows rose. "Really? Already?"

"It's not a problem," Faith said. "I've called my parents and they've agreed to let me park my car in their garage."

"Will that leave one of their cars out in the open?" I asked.

"Yes, but really . . . it's not a problem."

"Okay, well let's get going," Tempest said.

Tempest handled things so fast, I could hardly keep up. They were out the door before I knew it. I sat in the living room, thinking for a bit then retreated to the den where my sixty-inch, plasma TV mounted the wall. It had been a while since I'd sat in the den and watched TV. As wonderful as I felt, I had to take advantage of being able to roam parts of my home without experiencing pain.

I'd been watching television for half an hour when the doorbell rang. That was odd considering we hardly ever had visitors, and I knew it couldn't have been the mailman with a package because he didn't drop off anything until late in the afternoon. I made my way to the door. I could see a tall, strong-looking male figure on the other side of the stained glass, but I couldn't make out who he was.

"Who is it?" I asked.

"An old buddy, Ace. Open up, man," the gentleman said.

The voice did sound familiar so I opened the door. I couldn't believe my eyes. "You've got to be kidding me," I said as I reached to shake his hand.

"Man, don't give me your hand to shake like we're strangers," he responded, pulling me in for a one-arm hug.

"Craig Dennison," I said. "Mr. Football Star . . . what it be like, bro' man? Come on in," I said, closing the door behind him. "I thought you got up in high places and done forgot about your people."

"Naw, man. It's just been hard on a brother when I'm in town. Moms want me here. Pops want me there. My younger brother wants me to kick it with him, but then I got old friends who argue it's their turn to hang out with me. I get pulled from every angle, and before I know it, it's time to leave and I haven't seen half the people I intended to."

"Well, I'm sorry you had to catch me in my pajamas, but nothing has changed with my health since we last talked."

"Oh, that's right. I remember you telling me about you being sick when we talked over the phone. Man, that was over two years ago, wasn't it?"

"Definitely been a long time ago. I sure am glad you found time to visit me. I didn't know you knew where I live."

"I didn't. That's the other thing. I had to hunt you down, man. You just don't know. I've been looking for your place since Saturday."

"I'm glad you found me. Come back here with me to the den. I was just watching ESPN."

Craig followed me. "Yo, Ace, man . . . you really do have a nice place here. I take it there're a lot of mofo's going to jail these days." He laughed.

"Man, when I was a little boy, my granddaddy told me the few businesses you could always count on staying open were hospitals, funeral homes and jails. I'm thirty-five years old, and I'm just now starting to believe it."

"Me, too," Craig answered, laughing. "I mean, sorry you didn't make it to the NFL, but you really don't have anything to complain about. This place is hooked up—almost as nice as mine."

"Ha . . . ha. Thanks for the compliment, but I can only dream of having a mansion like yours. I saw you on MTV Cribs."

"I started not to do that show, but then figured what the hell."

Craig took a walk around my den, stopping at Tempest's picture on the mantel piece. "Have a seat when you get ready, man," I told him.

"I will. I was just looking at your wife. She's still beautiful, Ace. What's the secret in keeping her so long?"

"Money," I answered abruptly. Craig laughed. "Oh, I'm serious. Man, if our business wasn't successful, Tempest might've left me long ago."

"Oh, c'mon. She loved you back in the day. You don't think she still does?"

I shrugged. "It's hard to say, man. I don't even try to worry about it anymore. We're sitting on too much cheese for her to want to leave, so I know she's not going anywhere . . . why sweat it? You know what I mean?"

"Yeah. You two got a lot of years between you, so no need in walking away from anything now." Craig picked up a few more pictures. "Speaking of Tempest, where is your lovely wife?"

Just then, I heard the door open. "Sounds like she's coming in now."

"Ace," Tempest called to me.

"I'm in the den," I answered.

"Ace who's car is that in—" she stopped just as she stepped into the den to see Craig.

"Look what the wind blew in, Tempest," I said.

This was the most quiet I'd seen Tempest in a while. Craig spoke. "Well, hello there, Mrs. Bynum. How's it going?"

She remained silent. Faith walked in and stood next to Tempest. "Is there anything I can get started on right now, Tempest?"

My wife seemed to be at a loss for words. She didn't answer Faith because she was too busy staring blankly at Craig. I wondered if she was star struck.

"Are you okay, Tempest?" I asked.

"Um . . . yeah. I'm alright," she answered.

"Well, Faith asked you a question. Are you going to answer her?"

She came around to herself. "Oh, Faith, I'm sorry. Did you need something?"

"That's what I was asking you. Should I start making lunch or do some laundry or what?"

"Um," was all Tempest managed to say before going back into a trance as she stared at Craig.

I interjected. "I tell you what Faith. You just got here, and you haven't even unpacked. Why don't you go square away your things then we'll talk about dinner later."

"That's fine," she answered then walked out.

I turned to Craig. "Oh, Craig, I'm sorry. I forgot to introduce you, didn't I?"

"Ace, man, you know I know your beautiful wife."

"Right. I didn't mean her though. I meant the young lady who just left. She's our new hired help."

"Aahh . . . so you are doing well for yourself."

"Oh, man, please. I'm sure you've got several hired aids around your place." I turned to Tempest. She was at a standstill. I wondered what would get her to budge. "Are you gonna sit down or what?" I asked her.

"Who? Me?" Craig asked.

"No. I was talking to my wife." I called to her. "Tempest."

"What Ace? No. I'm not staying. In fact, I think I'm gonna leave you guys in here to catch up on old times." She stormed out of the den, and then out of the house, slamming the door behind her.

"Man, when I tell you that woman keeps an attitude on her, please believe me," I said.

"I believe you." Craig laughed. "I know plenty of good-looking women just like her."

"Should I get Faith to fix you something to eat or drink?"

"Naw, man. I'm getting ready to get out of here. I've still got some more stops to make before catching my flight this evening."

"Damn. I sure hate you have to go. Here . . . take my number," I said, going over to the mantel piece to retrieve a business card. "All of my numbers are on here—office, home and cell. We're going to have to hook up soon."

"No doubt. We will. I promise to do better with staying in touch."

"Cool. Glad to hear it."

I walked him to the door and watched him pull off in a Mercedes Benz he'd obviously rented since he no longer lived in Memphis. Faith must've heard the chiming of the door as I opened and closed it because she walked up.

"Did your friend leave?"

"He's gone, and so is my wife."

"Oh—"

I pulled her in for a long passionate kiss. Once we caught our breaths, Faith took a step back.

"What's wrong?" I asked.

"Ace, this is wrong. We can't carry on like this. You're married. I want to be here for you, but we can't dismiss the fact that what we're doing is unethical, immoral and just plain wrong."

"I'm sorry, Faith. I just missed you since the last time I saw you. I . . . I . . . as much as I love kissing you, I promise not to do it again. In fact, I won't be coming on to you in any way anymore."

She smiled and nodded. "Okay. Now may I get you something to eat or drink?"

I looked at my watch. It was nearing noon. "You know what? I think I will take a sandwich now . . . but only if you'll have one with me."

"No problem."

We headed to the kitchen for lunch. Afterward, Faith went to finish unpacking, and I went back to my spot in the den. She joined me several hours later. I was very tempted to put my arm around her as we sat on the couch, but I remembered my promise and refrained.

A breaking news alert flashed across the screen. "Hmm, I wonder what this could be about," I said.

Tempest entered the house and stepped into the den. "What're you all watching?" she asked.

Faith answered her. "We were watching Wheel of Fortune, but a breaking news alert just flashed."

Tempest stood beside the couch, staring at the television just as Faith and I were. Action News 5 Anchor Joe Birch popped up on the screen.

"Good evening once again, everyone," Joe Birch said. "I'm returning to you with a shocking news alert. Detroit Lions, star running back, Craig Dennison, was picked up by Memphis police this evening as he dropped off his rental car to Hertz on Democrat Road in order to take his flight back home."

Footage of Craig in handcuffs, being escorted by police into the Criminal Justice Center aired as Joe continued. "Dennison is wanted in questioning for the rape of a Memphis woman, but the police aren't commenting on who and what her connection is to the star running back."

"I don't believe this," I yelled. "He was just at my house."

"Sshh," Tempest blasted.

Joe continued. "The woman was reportedly raped on this past Saturday in Dennison's hotel room, but police say they've had a hard time catching up with Dennison ever since the allegation. Memphis police aren't giving us much, except that Dennison is being hauled in for questioning and possibly a DNA test."

I was hurt. Craig was a good-looking guy and had plenty of money. He didn't need to rape anybody. I dropped my head in despair. I silently prayed the charge was false. Craig couldn't be guilty. He just couldn't be.

Lynette

9

I looked at my watch. *Two A.M.,* I thought. I wondered if I was seeing things, so I checked the time on my cell phone. "Two A.M.," I exclaimed.

Parnell looked at his watch. "Yes, it's two o'clock in the morning. Is something wrong?"

"Parnell," I said, just before wiping my mouth. "Two A.M.? Are you kidding me?" It was Tuesday morning, and we'd seen each other every day since the picnic. We'd gone to see a movie, and then we stopped at I-Hop for a bite to eat. "You know I have a husband to go home to. Why did you let me stay out so late?"

"I'm sorry, Lynette. I thought you were aware how late it was once we left the theater."

"No. I didn't know. The last time I remember looking at my watch it was ten o'clock."

"Right," he responded. "I recall you stating it was ten o'clock, but that was shortly after the movie was over. We drove around, talking for hours before we came here to eat, Lynette."

"Well, I'm sorry to rush you, Parnell, but I need to go home."

"No problem. I'll just get a to-go box for the remainder of my food. I really didn't mean to get you into any trouble. Has Lemont tried to call you?"

I looked at my cell again. "No. I don't see where he's made any attempts."

"See. You might be worried over nothing."

"You don't understand. My husband knows the only time I'm out late is girls' nite out—when I hang with my best friends. That time came and went on last Friday."

"Lynette, do you hear yourself?"

"What?"

Parnell beckoned our waitress. "Excuse me," he said to her just after she walked over. "We're going to need some to-go boxes and the check, please."

"Yes, sir. I'll be right back," she responded.

Parnell turned his attention to me. "I asked you if you hear what you're saying because you're telling off on yourself."

"What do you mean?"

"Lynette, I know my wife's daily routines just as you say Lemont knows yours. Now, had it been nine o'clock at night, let alone two o'clock in the morning and I hadn't heard from her since the day before, I'd be blowing up her cell phone and pulling my hair out." Parnell wore a low, faded haircut, so I couldn't help looking at his head after his comment. "It was a figure of speech, Lynette. Just a figure of speech."

I smiled. "I know. And I hear what you're saying. There are some problems in my household, but I don't feel comfortable addressing them right now."

"Understandable, but I do want you to know that if you ever need a shoulder, I'll lend you mine."

I nodded. Just then, the waitress walked over with our boxes and the check. Parnell and I began to pack our food to leave. I found myself concerned that Lem hadn't tried to call me.

He knew I would normally be home, in bed, resting up for work the next morning. I didn't mean for Parnell to figure out there were problems in my marriage. Quite frankly, I felt embarrassed for him to know, but what was done was done.

After getting into his truck, Parnell reached over and squeezed my hand. "You don't have to feel ashamed around me. Lynette, it's just me—Parnell Fender—the same guy from high school, but with just a little more weight and a few more years on me."

"Parnell, keep it real. You have a lot more than a few years on you." I laughed.

"Whew. For a second, I thought you were about to say I have a lot more weight on me." He laughed as well. "I'm glad you're laughing, Lynette."

"I'm okay. I trust God. I know everything is going to be fine."

"Glad to hear you say that. I really hope you're not in any trouble."

"Naw. I should be alright." I looked down at the box in my lap. "And at least I've got lunch to take to work."

"You mean you're not going to eat it once you get in?"

"No. I was only misbehaving when I ordered it. I should've told you I'm on the Weight Watchers Plan."

"Really? Well, so is my wife, and she's doing very well on it. I'm impressed by that, Lynette."

Great, I thought. *More wonderful news about his wife.* I turned my face to look out the window so he couldn't see my expression. During the time Parnell and I drove around before stopping at I-Hop, I learned more about his wife and family than I had cared to know. I mean, his wife was a top Avon sales representative, fluent in two languages other than English, and a Sunday school teacher. His daughter was a straight-A student, played the clarinet very well, and had been a girl scout for five years. Parnell was a man of many talents himself. He was in ministry and a leader at his church as well as a popular property investor in Dallas, Texas. That's only a fraction of the things I learned about him and his family. Given all Parnell shared, the Fender's seemed like the ideal, African-American family.

After pulling up to my driveway, which led to the garage, I grabbed my purse and the sack of food. "Well, Parnell, it's been fun."

"I enjoyed today as well, Lynette." He looked around then back at me. "How do you know if your husband is home?"

"Um . . . he should be here. I'm sure his car is in the garage," I said, knowing I was more than likely telling a lie. "I'm just going to go to the door around back."

Parnell opened his car door. "Oh. Well, at least let me see you to the door safely. It's pretty dark out here in your neck of the woods."

"You don't have to do that, Parnell. It's pretty calm out here in Marion. Really. I should be fine."

He got out of the truck anyway. "I hear you, but what kind of man would I be to let you disappear around a corner in the dead of the night, not knowing whether you made it safely in the house."

"Alright. If you insist."

After walking me to the back door, Parnell reminded me to call him any time I felt like it. He gave me a hug then told me good night. Shame on me, but I silently wished he'd sneaked a kiss in on me.

I opened my back door and noticed a flickering light in the den. As I walked closer, I saw Lem sitting in his Lazy Boy, pressing channels with the TV remote nonstop. He didn't even look up at me as I spoke.

"Hey there," I said. He remained silent. "What are you doing up?"

"Worried about you," he said, staring at the TV.

"Hmm. That's funny, considering I haven't got a call from you."

He looked up at me. "I don't have time to play silly games with you, woman. Are you trying to tell me that you deliberately stayed out late because you were trying to teach me a lesson?"

"No. That's not what I'm saying. I'm just saying that if you were so worried, your actions should have proven it."

"Well, I happen to like sitting up to nearly three o'clock in the morning, flipping through cable channels, Lynette. Didn't you know? This shit is fun."

"Lem, stop being sarcastic."

He was really confusing me. Just days before he made me feel like he wanted out of our marriage, but there he was acting as if he cared after all. He stood then clicked off the TV.

"Goodnight, Lynette." He headed upstairs to our bedroom.

"What do you mean 'goodnight?'" I asked, following behind him.

"In case you haven't noticed, it's way past my bedtime."

"How would I know that, Lem? You're hardly ever here at the same time when I go to bed."

"Whatever, Lynette, and please don't come in here arguing," he said, entering our bedroom. "'Cause I can go sleep in one of the guestrooms if you're planning on keeping me up."

"Puhleeze. I'm about to take a shower and get ready for bed myself."

"Good," Lem answered, dropping his robe to the floor then climbing in bed.

I went over and picked up his robe and hung it up before going to take a shower. While bathing, I had a notion I should put on something sexy and demand my husband take me. What we needed was to make passionate love to each other, remembering how much we fill each other.

When I stepped out of the shower, I dried off and went into my panty drawer to retrieve the negligee that grabbed his attention only a month before. Lem was snoring, but I had no doubt I could wake him. I put on my smell-goods, dressed in my little black seductive piece then went over to my husband's side.

"Lem, baby, wake up," I said, shaking him. "Lem. Wake up."

He rose, giving me a strange once over, frowning as if I'd placed something tainted under his nose. "What's wrong with you, Lynette?"

I stood so he could get a full view. "Nothing is wrong, honey. I just need you. That's all."

He looked me up and down then replied, "You done lost your mind, waking me up like that."

"Excuse me? I barely shook you."

He got up and retrieved his robe. "I knew you'd pull something like this," he said, pointing his finger at me.

"Like what, Lem? I'm not arguing with you, baby." I started toward him. "I just want my husband to make love to me. What's so wrong with that?"

"Lynette, you bring your good Christian ass up in here right at three o'clock in the morning and expect me to cater to you . . . woman, please."

"Lem, you come home at all sorts of times. What's the difference?"

"The difference . . . since you haven't notice . . . is I don't bother your ass. When I come in late, I shower and go to bed. I don't mess with you."

"You're full of it, Lem. Had I come home at a decent hour, you still wouldn't have made love to me."

"You know what? You're probably right."

I was angry. "Well, forget you, Lem," I responded, pushing his forehead backward with my finger.

Lem snapped. He gave me a harsh shove, which almost landed me on my butt. Had it not been for the dresser, I certainly would've hit the floor hard. I used the dresser to catch my balance, and out of reflex, I quickly jumped to my feet. I was dumbfounded. In twenty-two years, Lem had only put his hands on me once, and that was when we were only teens. Our marriage had never come to this. I was so stunned, I couldn't even cry. I looked into his eyes for some type of remorse, but it was no where to be found. I said the only thing I knew to say at the time.

"How could you?" I asked.

"You started it, Lynette."

"You don't love me anymore, do you?"

Lem looked over at the wall then at the carpet before responding. "I didn't say that."

"Then how could you?" I screamed. "How dare you use that type of aggression with me, Lem?"

He put his finger up to his lip. "Ssshh, before you wake up Vicki," he said, looking toward our bedroom door. "I told you when we first came in here I didn't want to be bothered, Lynette. That hasn't changed. I want to be left alone. Don't you have to be at work in a few hours? I'm going downstairs to the guest-room. Don't come bothering me, Lynette, and I mean it."

He walked out of the room, leaving me standing with my mouth open. One minute he seemed to care, but the next he seemed disgusted by me. The tears came, and good thing they did because crying was the only way I knew how to handle his treatment.

As I got out of that uncomfortable, little piece of garment, anger set in, and I nearly tore it to shreds. I tossed it into the garbage then put on my favorite pair of cotton pajamas. I kneeled beside my bed then said a prayer.

"God," I called out loud. "I know there has to be some-thing left of my marriage worth salvaging. You've just gotta fix this. You feel my pain, Lord . . . fix this . . ."

Tempest

10

I didn't really think Craig would be arrested, especially not so soon. I never admitted he was my rapist, so I couldn't figure out why he'd been picked up by police. The news report said he'd been hauled in for questioning, but I learned by Tuesday afternoon, he still hadn't been released. Craig had no idea what I told the police. His safest bet was to pretend he didn't know what they were talking about, but I had no way of knowing what was going on. The later it got, the more I worried. *Perhaps I can send him a text letting him know not to say anything,* I thought.

I took my cell and went upstairs to my bedroom. I sent Craig a message, stating: CAN YOU CALL ME? I knew it was a long shot, but I thought I'd give it a try anyway. I left the bedroom door cracked so I wouldn't be caught off guard by Ace or Faith. I paced the floor, contemplating my next move and waiting for a return text message of some kind. Less than five minutes later, my phone was ringing. I was glad to see it was Craig.

"Hey, is this you?" I asked upon answering the call.

"Yeah," he said.

"I'm ready to talk to you. Are you alone?"

"Yeah, for now. I got another call this morning. I'm on my way back to interrogation again. Girl, you know you can do some evil shit, right? How anybody put up with your ass, I don't know?"

I ignored the questions. "I saw you on TV. You looked a mess." I giggled. "Why were you in handcuffs?"

"Just to embarrass a brother, I guess. I've spent too much time downtown already, man . . . they've taken blood samples and shit. I don't know what to think. What's up though? What did you do, man?"

"Not much, and I'm not your man. You need to talk to me better than that."

"Word. Whatever, Tempest, man. I ain't in the mood for all this, ya know?"

"Yeah, I can imagine. Anyway, I'm calling to tell you to just deny everything until we can talk. Give me a shout when you leave there."

"Man, this is jacked up. It's gon' take me a long time to get over this one. I don't know what you gon' do, but you need to get me out of this mess."

"Hmph. We'll talk."

"Look, on my way into the building now. I'll get at you if they ever let me leave this place."

Craig hung up on me. He and I were going to have to talk, but I needed to get out of the house in order for that to happen. I paced my bedroom again, trying to come up with an excuse to go out for a while. The house phone rang, and I answered it. It was Lynette.

"Hey girl," she said. "What're you doing?"

"Hey, Lynette. I'm not doing anything right now, but I'm about to go downstairs and try to entertain our new in-house aide, so I can't stay on the phone long."

"Oh, so she's moved on in now?"

"Yeah."

ALISHA YVONNE

Another voice spoke up. "See . . . now everybody ain't
got easy living like that," the woman said.
"Who is this?" I asked.
"Hey Tempest. It's me—Tracey."
"Oh. Hi Tracey. Hadn't spoken to you in a while, huh?
You doing alright?"
"Yeah, I'm cool. What about you?"
"I'm alright. I guess. That depends on whether you two
are about to double team me on something."
"Girl, naw," Lynette answered. "We just called to see if
you saw the news. Your boy, Craig Dennison, got picked up in
Memphis for allegedly raping some woman."
"I saw that, but why he gotta be my boy?"
"Well, you and Ace were cool with him in college, right?"
"Yeah, and he was over here yesterday to see *Ace*, not me.
So, just 'cause I went to school with him doesn't make him my
boy."
"A'ight, well *Ace's* boy is in trouble then," Tracey said.
"What did your husband have to say about the situation?"
I sighed. "He didn't seem happy."
"Aw, poor Ace," Lynette said. "I imagine Lem would be
hurt if he found out one of his friends got into trouble like that."
"Well, ladies, Ace is calling me, so I need to go," I lied.
"I'll probably hit you back on tomorrow."
"Okay," I heard them say before I hung up.
I didn't mean to get off the phone with them so abruptly,
but they were clouding my thoughts. I needed an out to leave the
house and be gone for a while. Then it came to me. I went
downstairs to the den. I stopped just outside the entryway, took a
deep breath then walked in.
"What are you two doing for dinner?" I asked upon enter-
ing the room.
"I was just telling Faith we needed to decide something,"
Ace said. "Why? What do you have in mind?"

79

"Um . . . well, I hate to do this, but something came up and I need to go to Marion."

"Tonight? You're going across the bridge tonight, Tempest?" Ace asked.

"I told you something came up, didn't I? I've been across the bridge at night before. I'm a big girl. I know how to take care of myself—thank you very much."

"I take it that must've been Lynette who called?" he questioned.

"Yes. She and Tracey were on the phone."

Ace sat up on the couch. "Is everything alright?"

"Oh yeah. Everything is fine. I just need to run over there . . . you know . . . for girl talk. I'll try not to be gone too long."

"I'm not use to you going across that bridge at night by yourself. Since you say you've done it before, and you'll be fine, I'll accept that. Just call me at some point, so I won't worry," he said. "Are you sure you don't want Faith to ride with you?"

Now he was starting to piss me off. "Ace, I know anything could happen at night, but the same goes for in the daylight. When have you known me not to be able to handle myself? I've got a cell phone, and I know the number to 9-1-1. C'mon now, and stop acting brand new."

"Nobody's acting brand new, Tempest. You're my wife. I kinda thought I'm supposed to be concerned. G'on. Have fun."

"Thank you," I responded, heading out of the den.

Ace stopped me. "Hey, I was thinking Faith could fix something quick and easy, like opening up a bag of that frozen chicken and penne pasta with alfredo sauce. Do you want us to prepare enough for you?"

"No. I'll grab something while I'm out. There's some garlic bread in the bread box, so enjoy."

I picked up my purse then headed out of the house. As I backed out of the driveway, I dialed Lynette's phone number.

"Hello," she answered.

"Lynette, what's up?"

"Hey Tempest. Is everything alright with Ace?"

"Yeah, he's fine. He didn't want anything. Look . . . I had to step out of the house for a bit. I told Ace I'm heading to Marion, so don't call my house."

"What? C'mon, Tempest. You know I don't like to be in the middle of mess."

"You won't be in the middle of mess if you don't call my house."

"What if Ace calls me?"

"You got caller ID, don't you? Ignore his ass and then call and let me know he's trying to be nosey."

"Hmm, alright," she said in a reluctant tone.

"And call Tracey, too. I know she hardly ever calls my house, but I don't want this to be the one time she does."

"I'll let her know, but Tempest, you need to settle your butt down. I don't know what you're up to, but you're worrying me."

"I'm cool, Mother Hen. I just got some business to take care of. I'll call you once I get home. How about that?"

"I'll be waiting."

I hung up the phone then drove to Popeye's to order three mild wings and a biscuit. It was uncertain when and if Craig would be able to call, so I drove downtown and cruised the area for a while. I operated on wishful thinking. Nearly two hours passed before my patience paid off. Craig called.

"Where are you?" he asked just after I answered.

"On the riverfront. Do you need me to pick you up?"

"No. I'll take a cab over. What are you driving?"

"I'm in my black BMW."

"I'll meet you soon."

I sat in my car, listening to Soul Classics 103.5FM as I awaited Craig's arrival. I wondered what he had to tell me. As soon as I saw the cab pulling up, I got out of my car because I feared Craig trapping me inside and beating the hell out of me. I clinched my cell phone as I watched Craig pay the driver then get out of the car. The cab took off.

He stood about six feet from me, dressed in the same paisley blue shirt I'd seen him in on TV—very unbecoming of him. Craig was a much better dresser. Why he chose to wear the ugliest thing in his wardrobe was a mystery to me. Perhaps he sensed he was going to jail and didn't want to wear his best. The look on his face was strange, as if he couldn't figure out what stood before him.

"Do you really have to gawk me like that?" I asked.

"To be honest—"

"Yeah. Be honest, Craig. I like it when you're honest."

"You disgust me. I love you, but I hate your ass right now, too."

"Hmph, and you're funny right about now." I laughed. "By the way, I like your flattery, too."

"Look. Let's just get to what I'm here for. Are we going to sit in the car? Or go walking?"

"No. I rather talk right here in the light."

"What are you scared of? You know you fucked up, don't you?"

"So did you," I snapped. "We wouldn't be going through this if you hadn't attacked me."

"You weren't attacked."

"The hell I wasn't."

"We had rough sex, that's all."

"Craig, when I told you to stop, you should've stopped. No means no. I'm sure you learned that many years ago. If you did this to me, I'm positive there were others. I'm just the first one to report you."

"I thought you said you didn't report me."

"Well, I didn't. I mean so to speak."

"How'd they get my name Tempest?"

"You happened to call during my questioning. They put two and two together."

"Yeah, and then you told them you were afraid of this guy because of his celebrity status and all that mumbo jumbo. They gave me bits and pieces of the story you reported."

"So how did things turn out?"

"Well, I told you they got DNA. That's the only reason I'm standing in front of you now, Tempest. I need you to tell them you lied about being raped. Once they compare the samples taken from you and the torn panties they found under the bed in my hotel room, I'm up shit creek. They even got staff members at the hotel who witnessed you leaving seemingly upset and in a hurry. This shit ain't looking good."

"You think?"

Craig took one step forward, and I stepped back. "I ain't with this game you're trying to play, Tempest. Now I think I said I'm sorry, but in the event I didn't, I'm saying it now. I'm sorry. Name your price."

"Why do you keep asking me to name a price?"

"Look . . . I talked to Ace for a bit. I didn't tell him anything about us, but I asked about your relationship with him. He admits you wouldn't be with him if it weren't for the money. He says you're money hungry. We both know I've got plenty of money, so just name your price to call off the dogs."

I was fuming. How dare Ace make me seem like a gold digger. His ass didn't have a dime before we launched our business, and we built it together. True enough I wasn't going anywhere. Together we had finances that took us into the bracket of high class. That still didn't give Ace the right to tell someone this made me money hungry.

"I don't give a damn what Ace told you. When you get through talking, you're in this situation because of your own actions. You took advantage of the wrong one this time."

"Then tell me how to make it right? I just want to make it right with you, and then move on. I've got shit to do, a career to think about, and a fiancée waiting on me back home. I can't be tied up in a rape trial."

Fiancée? Oh, no he didn't throw another woman in my face. I rolled my eyes and said, "I want to help you, Craig. Really, I do, but I haven't pressed charges. This is all the State's doing."

"Then will you at least tell them you weren't raped?"

"Heck no. Then I'll go to jail. Can you imagine how much time and money they've spent into this case already?"

"Well then, tell them you weren't raped by me. I'll admit to us being intimate, but only that it was before you were attacked elsewhere."

"Hmm." I stood thinking.

A minute later, Craig spoke. "What in the world do you have to think about, Tempest?" He leaned against my car.

"I'm thinking you haven't suffered enough, and that perhaps I should get some type of monetary gain from this."

"Man, don't stand here and act like you weren't thinking that all along. I don't know why you keep trying to prolong the game. Now how does a million sound?"

"Puhleeze."

"Okay. one-point-five mil."

"Nigga, I net more than that in half a year. You obviously don't know how popular my company is. You can't easily excite me with crumbs."

He jumped from my car. "Okay . . . two mil. C'mon now, Tempest. You can't tell me you feel you deserve more than two million."

"Why can't I?"

"Okay. Alright. Whatever, man. I want this shit over. What's your price?"

I opened my car door. "I don't know yet."

I started to get in, but Craig grabbed my arm. "Hold up. I know you ain't got me out here to leave me hanging and stranded."

I jerked from him. "You've got a cell phone. Call a cab."

"What about the money, Tempest? When will I hear from you? You know the folks gon' be trying to arrest me soon after they get the results from the DNA."

"Then I suggest you go into hiding. Don't use your cell phone though because they'll be able to track you." I laughed as I got in the car and closed the door.

He yelled through the window. "I gotta go through all of that?"

I cranked my car and cracked the window. "I went through something when you banged the hell out of me and again when I had to be tested for HIV and other disorders. Like I said: you ain't suffered enough yet."

"This shit is all a game to you. I should've known better than to fuck around with you, Tempest."

"Bye, Craig. I'll be talking to you."

I drove away, leaving him standing in the night.

Lynette

11

I t was Friday morning—three whole days since I'd last seen Parnell, and three whole days since I'd seen my husband in a time period long enough for more than a glance. This provided me ample opportunity to chat with Parnell all times of the day and night. We conversed on the Internet via instant messaging as well as on the phone. I began to feel things for Parnell that I knew I shouldn't, but I hadn't let him know because I didn't want to scare him off. I needed Parnell. I was going through a rough time in my marriage, and I know he sensed it, but he wouldn't question it.

Lem continued to act as if he hated me. He'd walk in as I'd be on my way out to work in the mornings, and he wouldn't speak unless he was spoken to. He'd head straight to the shower to keep me from trying to hold a full conversation with him. He knew I wouldn't be waiting on him to get out of the shower because working in education, the principal at my school was very strict about the staff being on time. However, on this day, I called ahead to schedule a late attendance.

ALISHA YVONNE

I had just finished making a cup of Folgers Classic Roast with the French Vanilla creamer when I heard Lem enter the door leading from the garage. He walked in and right past me as I tasted my coffee. I was dressed for work, so I'm sure he thought the morning was about to routinely go as it had for the past few mornings. I climbed the stairs with coffee in hand and patiently waited for him to exit the shower. He was stunned to see me sitting on the bed once he stepped out of the bathroom with a towel around his waist. He stood frowning then went into his underwear drawer.

"You can speak to me, Mr. Rapid," I said. He didn't bother turning around. He just continued to fumble through the drawer. "I am still your wife, and I need some answers."

"I need answers, too," he said. "Why aren't you at work?"

"I'm going. Don't worry about that, but right now what I want to know is where have you been all week?"

He began to dress as we chatted. "Working."

"You've been doing more than working, Lem. Don't make me call Tempest and ask her how many hours you've put in at the bonding company. I don't wanna put her in our business, Lem, but trust me. I will do it. Now talk to me."

"Lynette, why are you trippin' like this? You know I play poker with the fellas, too."

"No. You told me you stopped playing poker—after my momma found out about your infidelities, remember?"

"Well, I started back."

"Why? Anything just to keep from spending time with your wife, huh?" I was close to tears. "Has that tramp of yours been there, too?"

He walked around the room, dressing as quickly as he could. "Look. Had I known you were going to be here this morning to argue, I wouldn't have come home."

"Why, Lem?" I screamed. "Does it even matter to you what your daughter thinks about you not coming home?"

87

"Don't you go discussing grown folk business with our child," he fussed.

"Vicki's clueless, and thank God she is because I'd hate to have to explain your mess to her." I stood and went closer to Lem. "What is it that makes you go back to this hussie? So she's younger, but what does she do for you that I can't?" He wouldn't answer me. "Where're you laying your head these days, Lem?"

"Who says I'm laying my head anywhere?"

"Lem, you know I'm no fool. You can't work all day and play cards all night without sleeping at some point."

He had been standing in the mirror, straightening his tie, but then he turned to me and said, "I don't have time for this shit—"

SPLASH. I tossed the remaining half of my hot coffee into his chest, soiling his seventy dollar, white on white, French cuff, Paul Fredrick dress shirt and tie. He hollered as he quickly removed his shirt from his pants and held the steaming fabric away from his chest.

"Still don't have time?" I asked him.

"Lynette, damnit! I'm sick of you testing me. When I lay your ass out, everybody will look at me like the bad guy."

"That's 'cause you are. You're neglecting your family by thinking with the head between your legs."

He removed his wet shirt and pants. "If I had been thinking about staying home, you just messed it up."

"You can buy another Paul Fredrick shirt, Lem—with my money in fact, considering it's all direct deposited into our joint account, which I don't even know how to access."

"Don't worry. I will."

He disappeared into the bathroom and then into his walk-in closet. I retrieved materials to clean the coffee from our camel-colored carpet while Lem redressed for work. Half an hour later, Lem was on his way out the door. I went behind him.

"Lem," I called just before he stepped out into the garage.

"What, Lynette," he answered, turning to me.

"Do you really want out? Are you really going to destroy our family?"

He stared at me for half a minute before answering. "No."

Relieved, I only had one more question. "Will you come home tonight?"

He gave me a stupid look. "On a Friday night, Lynette?" My eyes flooded with tears. One fell before I answered. "Okay. Fine," I said, walking away.

Surprisingly, Lem called to me. "Lynette," he said. I turned to him. "C'mere." He closed the door and hung his jacket on the door knob. More tears fell, but Lem began to wipe them as he spoke. "I just got back into the game of poker. I kind of missed it. I know it's the weekend, but give me one more night with the fellas. I'll do something with you and Vicki during the day tomorrow."

"Lem, you've had all week with the fellas."

"I know, but Lynette, what you don't understand is that much of our bills are paid because of my winnings at the poker table."

"What?"

"Since Ace has been out of the office, I haven't been favored with as many bonds."

"What about Tempest? She doesn't help you?"

"She does when she's there, but Tempest has been out of the office almost as much as Ace."

"Then let me talk to her. I'll tell her to get that woman who's running things down there to call in more bonds to you."

"Lynette, even if I got more bonds, I can't deny I love the game of poker. We'll do something as a family tomorrow, okay?"

"Promise?"

"I promise," he answered then kissed me softly on the lips.

I hugged him tight and told him I loved him before he left. I felt better about going to work, so I refreshed my makeup then headed to the school.

Tracey called to check on me during my lunch break. She sounded as if she was in a good mood when I answered.

"Hey girl," she said. "Did you get to talk to Lem this morning?"

"Yeah. He showed up, and we talked."

"How did it go?"

"It was rough, but we'll survive. He flat out said he wasn't going to throw away our marriage."

"He did?"

"Well, in so many words. He still plans to stay out late, but he says he's only playing cards. I don't know anything else to do except believe him. I know I want my marriage, so I have to trust him."

"Yeah. You'll be fine."

"So what are you in such a good mood about?" I asked her.

"Girl, I just found out one of my favorite authors will be signing in Memphis this evening. You ought to come on and go with me."

"Well, I don't know. I have to see who I can get to baby sit Vicki. You know Lem won't be home tonight either. Who's the author?"

"Zane, and you know I have all of her books."

"Yeah, I know you don't want to miss her. I liked the one you told me to read—*Total Eclipse of the Heart*. I guess I should go and get my copy signed, too, huh?"

"I'm telling you, girl, let's go. Zane doesn't come to Memphis often."

"Okay. I'll go."

After about a six hour day at work, I was feeling great in spite of how my morning started. Tracey had me all excited about going to Zane's book signing in Memphis. I called my momma on my ride home and asked if she'd mind letting Vicki stay over for the weekend.

"That's fine, Lynette, but make sure she has everything she needs for church," she said soon after I asked. "You know I always welcome the company of my grandbaby."

"She enjoys staying with you, too, Momma."

"So how are things going with you?" she asked.

"Fine."

"Are you sure? You weren't quite yourself when you came to pick Vicki up last Sunday. I've been worried about you. Are you sure there isn't anything you need to talk to me about?"

I knew Momma was trying to pick me for what she already knew. I just wasn't ready to talk to my momma about the woes of my marriage. "No, ma'am. Everything is fine."

"Hmm. Fine, huh?"

"Yes, ma'am."

"You're lying, Lynette, and I don't appreciate it. I'm your mother. You should always feel comfortable enough to come to me."

"Alright, Momma. I know what you're getting at, but I really don't feel comfortable talking about my marital problems right now. Lem told me everything last Saturday, but since then we've decided to work on us. You have nothing to be worried about."

"Okay, but promise me if ever you need to talk, you'll call me."

"I will, Momma. Right now, I just want to leave the past in the past."

"Then I'll say no more. Get my grandbaby on over here because she and I are going to bake brownies and then go outside to catch fireflies this evening."

"Oh, Momma, she's going to like that. I'm going to pick her up from school, and then we'll pack her bag and head over."

"See you soon," she said before hanging up.

91

I had Vicki over to my mom's by five and was back to meet Tracey by six. The signing was from six to eight, so we knew we'd be across the bridge and at the bookstore by or before seven P.M. Tracey had all of her books with her, exposing the fact that she was a true Zane fan. She carried them in a tote while my one book fit right into my purse.

Once we got there, the line was still very long. Many of the people had multiple books in hand just as Tracey. Tracey noticed a sign displaying a new book by Zane.

"Lynette, look," she said, pointing. "Zane's got a new book out. You know I have to get that one."

"Hmm. Looks like it's going to be interesting. I guess I should get one, too, but we both can't get out of line. It's still growing."

"Well, give me your money. I'll go buy each of us a copy. Just hold our spot."

I was in line about fifteen minutes before Tracey returned with our books. Just as she handed it to me along with my change, my cell phone began to ring. I retrieved it from my purse then answered it.

"Hello," I said.

"BITCH, come get your husband before I kill his ass," a female voice said.

I was stunned. I held my finger up to Tracey, signaling I would be back then responded to the woman. "Who is this?"

"BITCH, don't worry about who this is. Just come to Earle, Arkansas and get your crazy ass husband. He's over here acting a fool with me because I don't want him anymore."

"Acting a fool with you how? Exactly where is he?"

"We're near the elementary school. He done wrecked both of our cars, ramming his into mine, trying to keep me from leaving. People are out here looking, and I'm sure someone has called the police, so his ass might be going to jail. You better come and get him," she yelled.

The woman hung up on me. I was crushed by all I'd just heard. I feared breaking down and crying, so I sneaked out of the signing and headed to my car. I searched the caller ID to see if the last caller would show up, and it did. The number was eerily familiar. I kept racking my brain for clues of how I knew the phone number, but nothing would come to me. I decided to call Lem. That's when I noticed that the caller's number matched my husband's with the exception of the last digit. Lem answered on the first ring.

"Lem, what's going on?" I asked, trying to remain calm.

"Nothing, Lynette. Nothing."

"Something is going on. Who was that woman who called me?"

"Nobody. It's nothing."

"Stop saying that. She's gotta be somebody. Just tell me."

"I'll tell you when you come home. When will you be home?"

"Are you over in Earle, Lem?"

"No. When will you be home, Lynette?"

"I don't know if I'm coming home, so you might as well tell me now what you plan to tell me later."

"I need you to come home, Lynette. What time will you be here?"

"Why? Lem, please tell me what's going on. Has your car been wrecked?"

"Yes, but I'm fine. Just let me explain everything when you get here, okay?"

"I don't know. I might come home, and I might not. I'm hurting, Lem, and I'm really sick of being hurt."

"I know. Just come home, okay? We'll talk."

I hung up on him. As bad as I wanted to cry, I couldn't. My cell rang again, but it was Tracey.

"Hey, girl, where are you?" she asked after I answered.

"I'm in my car."

"Why? What's wrong?"

"Just come to the car. I'll tell you when you get here."

"I'm on my way, but I know it's that damn Lem, isn't it? He done said or did something to upset you, hasn't he?"

"That damn Lem" was right. The ounce of niceness Lem had shown that morning replaced my joy, but by nightfall he had managed to steal it back. By now, I knew this marriage needed to be over. In fact, it was.

Faith

12

It seemed as though ever since I entered the Bynum home, Tempest had been in and out of the house, and Saturday morning was no different. She was up bright and early, clamoring about the house before I could get out of bed. When I heard her and Ace fussing, I threw on my housecoat then headed to see if I could be of assistance with anything. Ace and Tempest were on their way back up the stairs when I exited my bedroom.

"Is everything alright?" I called out to them once they were halfway up the stairs.

Tempest turned to me. "Faith, I need your help if you don't mind. I'm heading out of town for the weekend, and I need help packing."

I could see Ace fuming. "Tempest, where're you going? You still haven't told me."

"I'm going to spend some time with my mother in Detroit," she answered, turning her back to him, heading up the stairs. "I'll return on Monday."

This was shocking news to me. The way Ace carried on, her decision to leave had to be out of the blue for him, too. Once up the stairs, I noticed her suitcase opened and half packed on the bed. Ace wouldn't let the argument go.

"Excuse me?" He stood with his hands on his hips. "Detroit, huh?"

"Yeah . . . you know . . . as in Michigan . . . where my mother has been living for the past six years with my brother and his wife."

"I know all of that, Tempest. I'm just trying to figure out why I'm just now hearing that you've planned a trip to Detroit for this weekend."

She huffed and began slamming things into her suitcase. "Well, obviously I just decided this last night. You know I haven't seen my mother and brother in almost ten months. If your mother was still living, you'd understand." She looked at me. "Faith, don't just stand there."

"Alright, Tempest," I said. "What do you need me to do?"

"Get my toiletries out of the bathroom," she demanded. "My toothbrush is the one in the purple tube."

I went into the bathroom, but I could still hear everything Ace and Tempest said.

"I'm not trying to minimize how you feel, Tempest. I'd just appreciate if you start letting me in on your plans, especially something major like this. Does everyone at the office know you won't be in town?"

"Not yet. I'm going to call the office by the time I think many of them are in. It's only seven and my flight doesn't leave until ten A.M. Look . . . you were in bed last night by the time it dawned on me that I should go see my momma today. I didn't think you'd mind since Faith will be here."

"Whether I mind is not the point, Tempest. You've always known me to be an understanding guy. The key to us keeping a great marriage is communication—something you seem to refuse to do."

"So what was I supposed to do? Wake you?"

"That would've been a start."

"Ace, please. You just want to argue. You know full well you've just started sleeping through the night without pain. If I had gotten you up, you would've had something to say about that, too."

"I guess we'll never know how I would've reacted, given you didn't wake me."

I stepped out of the bathroom with everything packed into Tempest's toiletry bag. She took the small tote from me then placed it into her suitcase. "Thanks, Faith," she said.

Ace continued his rant. "You've always got an excuse, Tempest."

"Whatever, Ace. I'm going to Detroit. I'm happy about seeing my mother, and I'm not going to let you spoil my mood."

"Be happy, Tempest. I'm happy for you."

She went into the bathroom and began fumbling around. By the time she came out, I was standing without purpose. I really didn't know what I should be doing next. I expected her to be ugly about me being useless, but instead she was kind.

"Faith, I really appreciate you this morning. Will you help me get this suitcase closed?"

"Sure," I answered, heading over to the bed.

Just as the luggage was zipped, Tempest looked over at Ace. He had just sat on the edge of the bed. "What's wrong, Ace? Are you feeling okay? Is there anything Faith can do for you this morning?"

He looked at her as if he didn't know her. I'd be the first to admit I had already summed her up to having two personalities because she'd just finished snapping him up. I tried not to stare at them.

Ace shook his head. "No," he responded, looking away. "I'm fine."

"Are you sure? Ace, I don't mind helping you if you need help."

He turned to her. "No, Tempest. I said I'm fine."

"So you're not experiencing any pain this morning?"

"No. None. I'm actually feeling better than I've ever felt."

"Well, that's good to hear. Perhaps you should get Faith to take you out of the house today."

"And do what?"

"I don't know. I'm sure you can think of something you like to do. I'm glad the two of you are getting along fine." Tempest looked at me, still speaking to Ace and said, "Surely she doesn't have a problem watching after you. That's what we're paying her to do anyway." She walked away and went to primp in the mirror.

"Tempest, you're gonna wear the lady out before she's been here a week though."

"Don't worry about that. Faith, will you please tell him he's no bother to you," she said, touching up her makeup.

"No, Tempest," he answered before I could. "It just seems I'm only a bother to you."

Tempest turned to face him. "You keep trying to get me started, and I've already told you you're not going to spoil my trip."

"The last thing I want to do is get you started. Go on your trip. Fine. Have a good time, Tempest."

"Oh . . . and if you're worried that my plane ticket cost us an arm and a leg, it didn't. I used one of those last minute vacation planning sites to purchase my flight and rental car."

"Okay. Like I said: Have a good time. Make sure Faith knows where to find the keys to my Lexus. She may need to run out for something."

"I will," she responded, heading toward the door. "Faith, grab my luggage, will you? Take it to the front door. I'm going downstairs to make me a little light breakfast before I go."

"What're you having?" Ace asked her.

"I think I'm just going to make some toast and have a glass of orange juice. You're welcomed to have me make you some."

"I'm not in the mood for toast and orange juice. I'll get Faith to make me something a little more filling later—since you don't have time."

Tempest almost sounded like a snake as she hissed before speaking. One hand was on her hip, and she began to roll her neck. "No, I don't have time, and let me tell you something else." She stepped over to him, pointing her finger and talking about me as though I wasn't standing there. Her voice was stern. "You don't ever have to be worried that I'm mad about you putting Faith to work. Make her do as much extra stuff as possible because I, for one, plan to maximize the dollars we're paying her while she's here anyway." Tempest rolled her eyes, and then walked out.

Ace sat on the bed, shaking his head. "Sorry about that, Faith. I wasn't trying to push her to say those things in front of you."

I didn't know what to say. I just waved my hand at him as if to say I was fine. I carried the luggage downstairs as Tempest had asked. I wanted to get along with her, but just about every time she was going out of the house, she had a way of making me glad she was leaving.

Tempest headed for the airport within the hour, without so much as saying goodbye to Ace or me. As I sat on the edge of my bed, thinking about what household chore to start, Ace called me over the intercom to come upstairs.

"Good morning, Ace," I said, entering the room. "Did you need me?"

"Yes." He pointed to the shirt and pants on his bed. "I'm going to get in the shower before breakfast. You mind ironing those clothes for me?"

"Not at all. I'll have them ready by the time you get out."

He looked me up and down, apparently noticing my loose-fitting sundress and sandals. "Damn, girl, how did you get dressed so fast?"

I smiled. "It doesn't take long to throw on a dress, Ace."

"Well, you look nice."

"Thank you."

"You haven't eaten, have you?" he asked.

"Not yet."

"You think you can hold off until after I get out of the shower. I'd like us to have breakfast together."

"Sure. No problem." I gathered his clothes. "I'll be back up with these shortly."

It only took me ten minutes to knock the wrinkles out of Ace's garments. As I headed back upstairs, the smooth sounds of Kemistry flowed from Ace's room. I stepped inside and noticed the armoire doors opened and the CD/DVD player lights on. Kem's words spoke to the inner me as he sung "Find Your Way (Back In My Life)". I placed Ace's clothes on his bed, and then I was frozen. I began to long for what use to be between him and me.

As Kem sang and I stood reminiscing, my body became heated all over. I snapped out of my trance then turned to walk away, but not before noticing Ace standing just outside the bathroom door, watching me with lustful eyes. His body was partially covered with a towel—just from the waist down. My first thought was to walk away as quickly as I could, but my body wouldn't seem to move. My eyes were fixed on the beads of water as they glistened on top of his mahogany skin. I trailed many of them down to the beginning of the towel. That's when an undeniable distraction came. Ace had an erection that not even the thick terry cloth towel could hide.

By this time, Kem's sweet melodic tune, "I Can't Stop Loving You" crooned. I hoped Ace hadn't realized I couldn't stop heaving. When my eyes slowly rose to meet his, he started toward me. I panicked then attempted to walk away. He grabbed my arm, pulling me to him.

He kissed my forehead then turned his lips to my ear. "I know I said I wouldn't do this anymore," he whispered, "but I need you, Faith."

"I can't. We can't—" I panted.

He ran his hand down the small of my back stopping at my butt. "This is the first erection I've had in over half a year. It's not going anywhere." He kissed my earlobe while whispering, "Please help me."

I moaned as he began to kiss my neck. "Don't make me stoop to this, Ace. I love you, but . . . but—"

He began to place soft pecks on my lips and ran his hand under my dress to meet my warm spot. "But what?" He asked between kisses. "But what, Faith? Huh? I need you, baby."

He gave me space to talk, but not before sliding his finger into my canal. I didn't stop him nor could I speak. I moaned instead. I couldn't help myself. It seemed like ages since I'd been touched like that. He began caressing my breast with his mouth. I felt so far gone—far from the woman I knew me to be. He rose then looked me in the eyes and begged some more.

"Will you help me, baby? Faith, I need you."

"Ace, your wife should be the one to help you."

"She's not here, Faith," he answered, still fondling me. "And if she was, baby, I wouldn't want her. You're the one I want to be inside right now."

I couldn't respond immediately. Ace took it upon himself to lead me to the bed. That's when I spoke up. "No, Ace. Not in the bed you share with her."

"I need you now."

"Not in your bed, Ace."

Ace removed his towel then placed it on the floor. He guided my shoulders downward. As soon as I sat on the towel, he lay me back, pulled off my panties, and then climbed on top of me. I arched my back and moaned when he entered me. His strokes were swift and hard, and before I knew it, he erupted prematurely.

"Get up," I screamed, pushing his hips from me.

"Huh?"

"I'm not on the pill. Get up."

He moved as fast as he could, but unfortunately, most of his fluids had already entered me. My mood quickly went from pleasure to panic, and there was nothing he could say to calm me.

"I'm sorry, Faith. Really I am."

"Ace, I could get pregnant." I jumped up. "I need to go douche."

"Please don't be mad at me, Faith."

"I'm not mad at you." I turned and said, "I'm mad at me." I walked out of the room.

I couldn't stand myself at that very moment. Not only had he convinced me to surrender to his needs, but I wasn't even careful enough to be protected. We were both adults. At least one of us should've had the decency to consider condoms, especially since we'd never had a conversation about birth control. I went to my room feeling like a foolish little girl.

After cleaning myself up, I headed upstairs to make sure Ace wasn't beating himself up about his lack of performance. The bedroom door was open, and he was standing stark naked in the middle of the floor, holding his towel. I had to laugh.

"Some things never change," I said, leaning on the door panel.

"What do you mean?" he asked, turning to me.

"I see you still have a nice ass."

Ace looked down and gasped as if he had forgotten he was naked. He immediately covered himself then let out a light chuckle. "Faith, are you okay?"

As I watched him wrap the towel around his waist, I began feeling aroused once again. My eyes immediately fell to his midsection. At that moment, all of my guilt was gone. I realized I still had needs. Remembering he said he'd been having problems getting an erection, I felt a bit naughty. I wondered what I could do to entice him again.

"I'm fine, but I can't help feeling a bit slighted," I answered.

"I'm really sorry about that . . . about everything. I know you really didn't want to, but it was so hard to control myself."

"I should be fine, Ace. I just remembered that I'm not ovulating."

"How do you know that?"

I gawked at him. "Uh . . . I'm a woman . . . hello. Although I haven't been sexually active since I left my husband a year and a half ago, I still monitor my menstrual cycle to make sure it's normal. You know our bodies change with age. That goes for men, too."

He looked down toward his limp manhood. "Tell me about it. I remember the time when I could hang all day and night."

"I'm sure you still could."

"Yeah. Whatever." He smiled.

I started toward him. "You left me hanging, Mr. Bynum."

I gave him a look that let him know I was serious. If I didn't know any better, I would've said at that moment, he became scared of me.

"What?" he said. "Um, yeah. I know I did, Faith, but I really don't think I can do much to help besides fondle you."

"I bet you can." I removed his towel.

This time, I was the aggressor. I began kissing his neck and massaging between his legs. In less time than I had expected it, Ace was fully aroused. I stopped kissing him long enough to place the towel on the floor. I was in total control. Once he lay on the floor, I lifted my dress and straddled him. I thought I had died and gone to heaven. And if not heaven, certainly I was on a plane other than earth. I couldn't remember the last time I was made to feel so good, and I let him know it.

"Oh, Ace," I moaned, grinding my hips. "I'm gonna . . . I'm gonna . . . aaahhh—"

And just like that, I had a climatic moment like no other. My experience wasn't a solo one. Ace lay panting and trembling as well.

"Are you okay?" I asked.

"Better than you know," he answered.

"Good."

"So what now?"

"I say we clean up for breakfast, and then go shopping."

I found the strength to sit up. "Shopping?"

"Yeah. My treat. We can even find a beauty salon to get your hair and nails done if you'd like. Hell, I know I could use a makeover. What do you say?"

I kissed his lips before answering. "Wow. I don't know what to say besides yes."

"Faith, let me say this: I'm offering you this shopping spree and a makeover for other reasons, too."

"I'm listening."

"I love you, Faith. I don't think anything can change that right now. I also know you have self-esteem issues because of the scar on your forehead. I have the means to help you feel good about yourself. I know once you feel better about yourself, the world can see you as I see you—beautiful from the inside out."

I was choked up. I didn't know what to say behind that. I felt closer to Ace after bonding with him as I once had when we were in high school. I wanted to question God on why Ace couldn't have the love he deserved. He had a wonderful heart, and had I been the one bearing his last name, not a day could've gone by without me trying to make his cares light. I was wrong for making love to a married man, but at that instance, Ace made me proud to be the other woman. I made up my mind, what Tempest didn't know couldn't hurt her.

Tempest

13

The DNA results were back, and Craig Dennison was a wanted man. He immediately went into hiding and had been calling me all week from payphones and private numbers. He kept trying to convince me to report I wasn't raped. I knew he was in deep trouble, but that's what I wanted. I decided on Friday night to meet with Craig in Detroit the next day to discuss how to conclude our situation. True, I needed to visit my momma, but that was the perfect excuse to get near Craig. He owed me royally for what he did to me, and it was time to pay.

I visited Momma and my brother most of the day, and then I was off to the Hyatt Regency Dearborn by five o'clock Saturday evening. Craig knew to call me by late evening so I wanted to already be in position when he did. My phone rang from an unavailable number around seven.

"Hello," I answered.

"Where are you?"

"Hello to you, too, Mr. Dennison."

"Don't call my name like that."

"Do you have my check?"

"You'll get paid. Now where are you?"

"I don't like the tone of your voice."

"What?" he yelled.

"On second thought, perhaps I don't need to see you."

"What game are you playing now, Tempest?" he asked, sounding agitated.

"There's no game. I'm just thinking of my own safety here. I'm at the Hyatt Regency Dearborn in a presidential suite. I need you to join me, but in the meantime, I'm going to call my brother and let him know I'm with you—just in case."

"In case what? I've already told you I want this mess over. Now what's the room number? I'm just going to come pay you and be out of there."

Poor Craig. He really thought I planned to let him off easily. I gave him the room number, and then he hung up on me without another word. I wondered when Craig would really learn about me. He should've known that if I flew all the way to Detroit, it was for a reason.

I called my brother and gave him a heads up of whom I'd be spending the rest of my evening with. He wasn't happy because he liked Ace. I assured him the meeting was cordial and platonic, so he calmed down. I also called my mother to let her know I wouldn't be back for the night, but that I'd spend all day Sunday with her. She sounded disappointed, but she seemed content once I told her I was taking care of business. My mother adored what Ace and I had accomplished in Memphis with our bonding company. The thought of us possibly starting a business in Detroit and moving up there excited her. I hated lying to my mother, but I didn't know any other way to make her understand.

There was a knock on my hotel door around eight-thirty. After carefully checking the peephole, I could see Craig standing in the hallway, wearing a baseball cap and sunglasses. I opened the door.

"Is that really you?" I asked.

He was unkind. "Move, Tempest, and let me in."

I stepped out of the way as he'd demanded, motioning for him to come in. I took a peek up and down the hall to see if anyone had noticed him come into my room. I was relieved to see there wasn't anyone out there. Once I closed the door and turned around, I was startled by Craig who stood only two feet from me.

"Whoa! You scared me," I said, holding my heart. "What the hell are you doing, standing so close?"

He looked me up and down as he held out a check. "Here. I told you I just came to pay you so I can be out."

I placed my hands on my hips, pulling back the thin robe which accompanied my sheer teddy. Craig's eyes couldn't seem to stop roaming my nipples and between my legs. I wasn't so sure he really wanted to go at that point. I reached for the check then looked at it.

"What's this?" I asked.

"Two million. We discussed over the phone that would suffice."

"I know. I'm talking about the signer. This check didn't come from you."

"It shouldn't matter. It's made out to you."

"Craig, are you trying to pull some shit?"

"No. I'm just thinking ahead and being careful. That check came from an attorney friend I trust. I can't write a check to you while the authorities are on my ass. We've got to keep this thing looking innocent."

"Yeah, right . . . like me depositing a check from your entertainment lawyer looks innocent."

"He's not my attorney—just a friend but nobody knows that. If you notice, his company is based in Texas. If anyone questions you, just say it was paid to you for some type of work you did for one of his clients—you know, confidential stuff."

"Hmph. You've got it all figured out, huh?"

"Yeah, now let me out of here."

I placed my hand on the door. "Not so fast."

"What? All I had to do was pay you and all of this would be over."

I shook my head. "I didn't say that. You assumed that."

"Come on, Tempest. Don't start . . . please don't start," he said, holding his head. "What is it now?"

"You still owe me a good time, Craig Dennison." His eyebrows rose. "You destroyed what should've been a wonderful time between me and you, and I'm still looking for what should've been."

He huffed. "Hell naw, Tempest, let me out of here."

"It's been a long time, Craig. I'm sure Ace disclosed his illness to you, but what he probably didn't tell you is he's having trouble in the bedroom. You were supposed to satisfy my sexual craving the last time we were in a hotel room together, but that didn't happen. I just want you for one night. That's it."

His eyes roamed the room and even up to the ceiling as if he had to think about it. "One time?"

"Tonight . . . that's it."

"You promise?"

"I promise. Once the check clears, I'm going to authorities and make up the name of a person who raped me."

"How will you explain my DNA, Tempest?"

"I'll tell them you and I had consensual sex earlier—before I was raped."

"Why can't you just tell them you weren't raped?"

"Craig, you know that would land me in jail. Those people are investigating a rape because that's what I told them. I can't take it back all of a sudden."

"Well, you can't lie on an innocent person either. You know you told them the person is famous."

"Leave that up to me. One thing you should know about me by now is how cunning I am. I'll just tell them I made that part up as an excuse because I feared telling them this person's name. I'll tell them he's an illegal alien who's done some work for me before . . . we had an affair, but once I tried to end it, he raped me."

Craig shook his head. "And all of that came easily for you, didn't it?"

"Hey, what can I say?"

"You're sick. I hope you know that. I've never met a woman who could lie as well as you."

"And, you probably won't meet another. We go way back, Craig. Yes, I lie, and I'm cunning, but one thing you can attest to is once I give you my word, I stand by it. One time . . . tonight. That's all I ask."

Craig stared at me for a moment. I dropped my robe so he could get a clear view. He took off his baseball cap, his sunglasses, and then his shirt. I knew it was about to be on. I headed over to the wet bar.

"Would you like something to drink?" I asked.

"No, Tempest. If we're going to do this, let's do it."

Craig walked over to the bed where he removed the remainder of his garments. I stood watching, drooling upon every stitch that was dropped. I couldn't wait to taste his dark skin upon my lips. Once he finished, he lay back and beckoned me to sit on top of him.

"Not so fast, Craig. We've got to take our time. I don't know when I'll be touched so sensually again. I want to take this slow."

I pulled out a box of condoms from my purse and set them on the nightstand. I removed my teddy then climbed into bed. Craig rolled over on top of me and began kissing me like he loved me. I was about to lose all control as I gave him my tongue while caressing his back. Either he was a great actor or he loved the slow, deliberate raking of my nails on his back. He moaned and grinded his pelvis while licking my neck.

"Craig," I whispered.

"What?"

"Will you taste it?"

He looked at me. "Do what?"

"Please. I want all of you tonight. Please let me have all you have to offer."

"Tempest, let's not ruin—"

"Ruin what?"

"I don't go down—"

"When did you stop? You use to back in the day."

"Stop interrupting me. I was trying to say I don't go down on other men's women."

"Oh? You just screw them, huh?" I huffed. "Like I said: When did you stop?"

"After I got engaged."

I was pissed. "Get up," I demanded.

He rolled off me and sat up in bed. "See. I told you let's not ruin things."

I looked over and noticed his erection. "Craig, I just want us to enjoy each other for this one night. It's been more than six months since Ace has been able to touch me, and it could be another half a year or longer. We don't know. I just know I need you right now. Please," I said just before making my way to lay my tongue on his thigh. I slowly began to lick my way between his legs. As soon as my mouth covered his love-tip, he let out a loud sigh. I rose to look at him. "Can we do this or what?"

Craig reached and grabbed my waist, flipping me so that my bottom mounted his face. We were in the sixty-nine, and I could hardly stand it. It was a wonder that Craig could get any enjoyment because the motion of his wet tongue between my legs and on my cheeks nearly drove me out of my mind. I had a tough time focusing on what I should've been doing for him.

For someone who didn't want to lick another man's woman, Craig didn't seem to mind as I had back to back explosions. After the second one, I could no longer perform. My face lay between his legs as he continued to caress me with his tongue. He soon flipped me over, retrieved a condom then placed it on before entering me.

"Thank you, Craig." I was having the sexual experience of a lifetime. "Oh thank you," I moaned.

"You're welcome, Tempest. And I'm sorry," he said as he gave me slow, deep strokes.

I caressed his strong arms and rolled with him while staring into his eyes. He looked down into mine, biting his bottom lip, seemingly holding back. As bad as I wanted to release with him, I also wanted to be fair and let him have a moment. Besides, we had all night, or so I thought.

"G'on get yours, baby," I told him.

"Are you sure?"

"Yes. Let it go."

At that moment, Craig's body stiffened then jerked repeatedly. "Aw, shit," he screamed.

I rubbed his back as he lay on me. "There you go, Ace."

Craig pulled himself up on his arms and looked at me. "What did you call me?"

Immediately I knew what I had done. "I mean, Craig." I laughed but Craig didn't find anything funny.

He rolled off me. "That was low, Tempest."

"What? You know I didn't say his name intentionally."

"You had me making love to you so you could imagine your husband on top of you?"

"No. Please. You know better than that. I love Ace, but he is where he is. I know who's in bed with me."

Craig got up and started to get dressed. "Whatever, Tempest."

"C'mon, Craig. I know you don't think I can't tell the difference between you and my husband. I slipped because Ace was the last man I laid with and been laying with for years. I wouldn't have intentionally did that to you because I wouldn't have wanted you to ruin my moment by calling me your girl's name."

Craig continued dressing. "I hear you, but you should be straight now, right?"

"What do you mean?"

"I gave you multiple orgasms and a check for two million dollars. You gave me your word, Tempest. We're done, right?"

Out of nowhere I began to feel like crap—like I had nobody to care for me. Ace was nearly a bed-ridden loser who probably hated me because of my behavior toward him, and Craig was going to leave me alone—not only just for the night, but for good. I knew nothing I would say could change Craig's mind.

"Yeah. We're done," I reluctantly answered.

"Good," he said, grabbing his keys. "Have a nice life," he said with his back turned, on his way out.

The hotel door closed, and the way I saw things, so had a chapter in my life.

Lynette

14

I tried to stay out as long as I could. Despite Lem's pleas, I didn't go home Friday night. I dropped Tracey at home then went back to Memphis and got a hotel room. I couldn't catch up with Tempest Saturday, so I walked the malls all day. By the time I decided to call her house, Ace said she'd gone to Detroit on the spur of the moment. I didn't want to bother Tracey with my drama again, so I spent much of Saturday alone.

Lem tried on several occasions to reach me. He had even left a voice message, stating my mother was worried about me. My mother knew how to call my cell phone, so I knew his statement was unlikely true. I called my mother just to be on the safe side. She didn't seem bothered at all. I knew he lied. After getting off the phone with my mother, I decided to head home. It was after eight o'clock at night, and I didn't want to rent another hotel room.

I was surprised to see Lem's car in the garage, unharmed, once I arrived. As soon as I opened the door, Lem greeted me with a hug. Any other time, I would have enjoyed it. This time, I wanted his hands off of me.

"Let me go, Lem."

He refused. "Baby, I missed you."

"Let me go. We've gotta talk."

"We're going to talk, baby, but let me hold you first."

I broke away. "No," I said, staring at him. "You've got some explaining to do. Now I've given you all night to think about how you want to break the news to me, so let me hear it."

"What news, baby?"

"Who is the woman that called me, and why does her cell number look similar to ours?"

He released a deep sigh then grabbed my hand. "C'mere, baby."

"Where're we going?"

"I want to sit down and talk."

I snatched away, shaking my head. "Un-un, Lem. Is the news that bad? Please tell me it's not."

"C'mon, baby. Let's just sit down." I allowed him to pull me into the living room. We sat on the couch before he started again. "Babe, the woman who called you is Tekeysia."

"Why, Lem? What were you doing back around her? I thought things between you two were over. Is that who you've been spending your nights with? She said you wrecked your car. It didn't look wrecked to me. Did you wreck your car?"

Lem seemed frustrated, hanging his head and shaking it. He looked back up at me. "Are you going to let me talk?" he asked. I didn't respond. "Huh? I want to answer your questions, but you won't let me get a word in."

"Okay. I'm going to be quiet. Now talk."

He took a deep breath. "I haven't been spending my nights with her. I've been out playing cards like I told you. I only went to Earle last night to meet with her one last time to retrieve that phone. Her number looks similar to ours because I purchased it for her."

"When? You got us these phones about three years ago. How on earth did she get a number like ours if ours were purchased so far back?"

Lem was silent. Silly me. I was still confused, so I waited for him to respond. He looked all around the room then back at me. I should have known the answer was not good when he grabbed my hands.

"Lynette, the affair started a little more than three years ago."

I jumped to my feet. "What? Are you serious?"

Lem stood, too. "Baby, calm down."

"Three years ago, Lem? So you mean to tell me I was the last to know?"

"Baby, please sit down. We're not finished talking."

"There's more?" I asked. He dropped his head. "Un-un," I said, walking away.

Lem was right behind me. "Hold on, baby."

"No, Lem," I said, climbing the stairs without looking back. "You've been making me feel like crap, not coming home, and telling me you might want out of this marriage, but now all of a sudden you want to make things work." I busted into our bedroom. "I'm not feeling you right now."

He grabbed my arm just as I stopped in front of our bed. "I do want to make things work. That affair is over. I'm done. She and no other woman is worth losing my family."

"Oh yeah? And how'd you decide that all of a sudden?"

Lem stared at me, but he didn't seem to have an answer. After a moment of silence, I let him off the hook by entering the bathroom and closing the door behind me. I stood in the mirror, saying to myself, *Three years, Lynette. You big dummy. For three years, your man carried on an affair, and you thought he wasn't capable of loving another.* I really wanted to cry, but still, I couldn't.

Once I exited the bathroom, Lem was sitting on the bed. He addressed me once again. "Lynette," he said.

"What?" I answered in short.

"I really want to finish this conversation."

"Why? All the times I wanted to talk, you acted like you couldn't stand me. Something's not right about you suddenly wanting to be close to me. I haven't figured it out, but I'm sure I will."

"Well, will you just let me explain one last thing to you? I'll leave you alone. Just let me tell you one more thing."

"What is it, Lem?"

"Tekeysia has a two-year-old son," he said as he took note of my mouth dropping to the floor, "BUT, it's not mine."

I couldn't speak. I was literally speechless. As I lifted my eyes to the heavens, I told myself, *he didn't just say what I thought he said.* I could hear Lem ranting over and over how the child wasn't his, but my shock wouldn't let me respond. I didn't believe him. I already had a sixteen-year-old stepson due to his infidelities, so there was nothing he could say to make me believe Tekeysia's child wasn't his. Once I gathered the strength to say something, I let him have it.

"Lem, you've got me so messed up right now . . . you just don't even know. Do I look like a newborn fool?"

"I didn't say you were, but that child ain't mine, Lynette."

"You've carried on a three year affair with that slut . . . and now there is a two-year-old in the picture that you don't want me to think is yours?"

"Well, Lynette, the affair was off and on. Plus, she had a boyfriend."

I balled up my fists. I wanted to beat him down. "Now I've got to take an AIDS test, too."

"What do you mean?"

"You dumb ASS. Every time you stuck your thang into her, you were sleeping with her man, too."

Lem's face housed surprise. He slowly spoke. "We used condoms."

"You are a liar, Lem," I yelled.

"I'm not lying."

"Well, then you're telling me partial truths—which means you're still lying. You haven't carried on a three year affair with that girl, using condoms the whole time. I may have been fool enough to think you wouldn't mess around on me, but now that I know you have, I'm being smart about everything else. Not only have you deceived me, but you've put my life in danger, too."

He sat on the bed looking stupid. He seemed at a loss for words, but that was okay because I didn't want him to talk. I was so angry, I could spit on him. God, I wanted to cry, but the tears wouldn't come. I didn't understand it. I thought if I could just cry I'd feel a whole lot better. But as hard as I tried, my eyes wouldn't produce water to save my life. I went and sat on the opposite side of the bed. We were both silent until I remembered the car.

"Why did she say your car was wrecked? It looked fine when I pulled into the garage."

"Not that one," he said softly. "It was my '64 Chevy Impala."

I did a double take. "You've got to be kidding me," I responded. I hadn't thought of the Chevy because I had thought it was still parked behind the house. "Lem," I called.

He turned to me. "Yes."

"You're kidding, right? Not the car you told me you spent all of our vacation money on, repairing and fixing it up. You're just joking, right?"

He shook his head. "I wish I was."

I fell back on the bed with my hands on my head. "Where is it?"

"I went ahead and had it towed to a shop."

"So lay it on me. How did it get wrecked? She said you rammed into her."

"Listen. Don't believe anything you hear from her, alright? If she calls you again, just hang up on her. I've told her it's over, so she's gonna have to move on. I only went to her

117

town trying to retrieve that phone. That was my bad, and I'm paying for it."

"Your story is not adding up, Lem. This is it. I can't trust you. I really don't know what to think. I just know I'm tired of being hurt. I want out."

"You don't mean that, Lynette."

"Oh yes the hell I do."

He seemed stunned. He was silent several minutes before responding. "So now you're the one who wants out, huh?"

"Yes. You better get a paternity test done and show me that child is not yours. In the meantime, I'm going to find a lawyer on Monday 'cause I'm filing for a divorce."

Lem got up and left the room. I went to the stairs to see if I could hear what he was doing downstairs. I heard him pick up his keys, and then I heard the door open and close. I went downstairs, double checking to see if he was gone, and he was.

Parnell, please be online, I said to myself as I entered the office. Ever since Parnell and I had become close friends, he would minister to me and read scripture with me. I loved getting his encouraging email and chatting with him in our Instant Messenger. I turned on the computer and discovered Parnell was indeed online. He spoke to me as soon as he noticed my availability.

HOW ARE YOU TODAY, MRS. RAPID? he typed.

NOT SO GOOD.

WHAT'S WRONG? ANYTHING I CAN DO TO HELP?

I DON'T THINK SO.

WELL, MAY I TRY?

THERE'S NOTHING YOU CAN DO, I answered, feeling sorry for myself.

HOLD ON. I'M CALLING YOU.

Within a minute, my cell was ringing. It was Parnell calling, just as he'd stated. I answered after about three rings.

"Hi Parnell."

"Lynette, are you alright?"

"No."

"Talk to me. What's going on?"

"You sure you've got time? This could take a while."

"Well, just let me log everything off of my computer, and then I'm all yours."

"Okay."

Parnell put me on hold for a minute and then returned to the phone. I gave him the whole synopsis of everything that happened between the day before and that day. I even admitted to him that I was considering a divorce. Parnell began to pray with me, and then we read scripture together before he began to minister to me. An hour passed by then Parnell asked to put me on hold again.

"Lynette, I'm so sorry to have to do this to you again, but it's my daughter's bed time, so I need to place you on hold one more time."

"Oh, it's fine. I know the routine by now. I think it's awfully sweet of you to tuck your nine-year-old in bed and say prayers with her."

"Thanks. I try my best to be the greatest father I can be. That's why it's hurting me so not to have my sixteen-year-old daughter, Anisa, in the house with me."

"I can tell. You talk about Anisa each time we speak."

"She lived with us for years, and there were some problems between her and my wife."

"Yes, but Parnell, your daughter was much younger then. She's grown up now."

"That's true, but my wife is having a fit every day because of the subject of Anisa returning. She says she'll move out and let us have this house before that happens."

"I'm so sorry to hear that, Parnell. That must be a crushing thing to hear."

"It is." He sighed. "Just do me a favor and hold on, okay? I'll be back shortly."

"I'll be here."

Parnell placed me on hold for nearly ten minutes. I had time to reflect on some of the things he'd shared with me, and how wonderful our prayer time had been. I wondered why he couldn't have been the one I ended up married to. My husband was not praying with me or our daughter. Parnell seemed like everything I had ever wanted in a husband—everything Lem was not. I was happy to hear his smooth, deep voice return to the phone.

"Sorry about that, Lynette. I'm back."

"Parnell, I can't help but admire your love and dedication to your family. By the way, where is the Mrs?"

"Upstairs in her office doing her usual—on the computer."

"Really? She's there every night while we talk."

"She's a bit of a workaholic, so most nights I'm in bed before her. If you ask me, she's trying to avoid further argument about Anisa possibly coming back."

"Parnell, I don't mean any harm, but sounds like your issues at home are just as serious as mine."

"I find it interesting you'd say that. We should be okay."

"I was just thinking. You probably won't admit it, but anytime your wife rather be on the computer all times of the night than to lay next to her husband, something is dreadfully wrong."

He huffed. "Because I feel we need each other's friendship and honesty right now, I'll tell you you're right. I wouldn't have ever admitted it because I love my wife and our family. I still think she equals the greatest gift God has given me—love. It's just that right now, we need to rediscover ways to be into each other. Our careers are so very different, and we're each trying to take them to the next level, but I can see our separate interests are driving us apart, not to mention the issue of me wanting Anisa back in the house with us."

"Wow. I don't know what to say. For all these days, I've been thinking you have the model household that I've been longing for."

"Not so," he replied, sounding sad. "Enough about me. This call was made so I could be your shoulder, my friend."

"Parnell, you're special to me. I need you to make me a promise."

"What's that?"

"Let's change the topic from me to the Fender household. It's my turn to be of support. Promise you'll let me be a friend to you tonight."

"Lynette, you're special to me, too. I'm a minister—"

"You're a man first, Parnell. I can tell you're hurting. It's okay to be strong for me, but when the time comes, who will be strong for you? I can understand your reluctance if you feel your wife will hear the discussion."

"That's not it. I'm downstairs in my office, and trust me. She's locked up in her office for most of the night."

"Then you have no excuse. Now do you promise to let me be a friend?"

Parnell let out a slight giggle. "I promise."

And with that said, I not only gave him my ear, but as I listened intently, I gave him my heart. By the end of our call, we'd made plans to meet each other the next weekend in Birmingham, Alabama for a change of scenery and a little fresh company.

Ace

15

F aith and I stopped off at a number of shops on Saturday. I nearly spent six thousand dollars on new clothes, shoes, her hair and makeup, massages and other pampering for both of us. Tempest had no idea what a favor she'd done me by leaving me alone with Faith. We laughed and made love all weekend, and not once did I feel guilty for betraying Tempest. I hadn't felt so wanted and so necessary in a long time. Faith did that for me.

Faith's new hairdo was gorgeous. Although I had no problem with her short, curly natural, I knew she'd feel more comfortable with a style that covered her scar. After checking into several salons, we finally found one with a beautician who could take a walk-in for a sew-in weave. The stylist even took Faith and I to the beauty supply store to choose the hair. She picked out something called European deep wave. It felt really soft, and Faith seemed to like the hair so we purchased it and headed back to the salon.

I fell asleep while Faith was getting pampered. I woke up when I heard her calling my name. She stood over me looking like a million bucks. The hairdresser had cut bangs over Faith's scar, and wavy hair flowed past her shoulders. She looked too good to just take home, so we went to Texas de Brazil for dinner then to see a movie.

Monday afternoon, Faith and I lay cuddled in her bed after a hot and heavy round of sex. I was starting to scare myself with this newfound sex drive. I couldn't get enough of Faith. She lay in my arms, extremely quiet. I wondered what was on her mind.

"Is everything okay, Faith?"

"Um-hmm. Why do you ask?"

"You haven't talked very much since we woke up this morning. I'm just concerned."

"I'm okay."

"Is that it? Just okay."

She nodded then got out of bed and retrieved her robe. "It's one o'clock, Ace. Don't you think you should head upstairs to shower before your wife comes home?"

I sat up. "Yeah, you're right. She called and said she wouldn't be in until five, but I still better get up."

Faith tied up her robe then left the room. As I walked down the hallway, I heard her throwing things around in the laundry room. I started to go talk to her, but decided I could wait until after I'd showered.

It only took me half an hour to shower and dress. Once I came back downstairs, I found Faith still in her bathrobe, making up her bed. She turned to see me in the doorway, but she didn't say anything. She kept pulling on the sheets and pillows. I offered to help.

"May I give you a hand?" I asked.

"No, I got it. You sure did what you had to do quickly. I haven't even showered yet."

"I heard you in the laundry room. Anything I can do to help you? Well, I guess if you put that load of clothes in the dryer once they finish, that would help me. I'd like very much to have had my shower and be dressed when your *wife* comes."

"I huffed. "Why do you keep saying it like that?"

"Saying what?"

"You keep stressing the *wife* part."

"Well, that's what she is."

"Yeah, but you keep making it sound so . . . so—"

"So what, Ace?"

"I don't know. I just don't like how you keep saying it."

We heard a buzz. "Oh, I forgot I left the door open to the laundry room," she said, walking past me. "The clothes are done. I'll put them in the dryer myself." Her voice faded down the hall.

I decided to go behind her. Faith began tossing the clothes into the dryer. She moved so fast, I didn't have a chance to offer assistance. She slammed the dryer shut then turned to walk past me. I caught her in the hallway.

"Faith, wait a minute," I said, pulling her arm.

"What?" She frowned.

"Talk to me. Please don't treat me like this. We've got to be able to communicate." I pulled her into the den with me where we sat on the couch. "What is it? What's bothering you?"

"It's just . . . just—"

"Just what? C'mon. You can tell me," I said, stroking her hair.

"The weekend has been great, Ace."

"No. It's been fantastic."

"Right. But Tempest will be home shortly, and I don't know how I'm going to face her. At first I thought I could be okay with being the other woman, but now I'm feeling pretty low. All weekend while she wasn't here, it was easy for me to pretend she didn't exist. While she was away, I borrowed her world so to speak—you know . . . filled her shoes. Once she returns, I've got to retreat to reality. You're not mine, Ace."

"I hear what you're saying, babe, but in my heart you're mine and I'm yours."

Faith stood then walked to the other side of the room. "That doesn't count, Ace. Not in God's eyes. What we did this weekend was wrong." She turned her back on me.

"Faith, please don't start with another guilt trip. I can appreciate you having a conscience and all, but I don't think your being here is by coincidence or accident. Do you?"

She turned to look at me. "No."

"Alright then. Yes, we were immoral, and I'll pray about that. In the meantime, try not to be too hard on yourself. The time we shared over the weekend was wrong, but you have to admit it happened because we both had a need to fill voids in our lives."

"We can't make excuses, Ace."

"True. There is no acceptable excuse, but if you have to ask yourself how and why, then the void was our motivation."

"But, your wife . . . how do I look at this woman every day and pretend to be innocent? I love you, Ace, and I don't know how to change that."

"C'mere," I said, patting the couch. "Come sit down next to me."

Faith walked over and took a seat. "Ace, you've made me feel like I'm wanted—"

"You've done the same for me, Faith."

"And like a princess—"

"Baby, you're a queen."

Her eyes became glassy. "I don't wanna step back."

"You don't have to."

"Ace, yes I do. Tempest may be rude and mean as all get out, but you married her. She's your wife. Although I stepped over the boundaries this weekend, I do understand I have to respect your union." She looked down, and that's when a tear fell. "I should leave this job."

"What?" I yelled. "No . . . no . . . no . . . Faith, listen." I lifted her chin. "Listen to me, baby. There's no way I'm letting you walk out on me." She didn't say anything. "Baby, please. I know I turned my back on you years ago, but please don't give me the same payback. I need you. What do I have to do to keep you here?"

She began to cry uncontrollably. "I don't know, Ace. This is so hard for me. This cheating and sneaking around stuff ain't me."

"So let's work on just being friends. The weekend is gone. We'll move forward from here as friends."

"Ace, you said something similar before, but look what happened."

I slid to the floor, kneeling before her with my head in her lap. "You can't leave me, Faith. I just found happiness again. Don't destroy me by walking out." She began rubbing my hair. "Please . . . this is hurting me so bad . . . you can't even imagine. I love you, too, babe. If you leave, I don't know what I'm going to do—"

"I won't leave," she interrupted. I looked up at her. "At least not yet. But, we can't go on like this, Ace."

"Okay," I whispered, dropping my head in her lap.

"I'm mad at you, and I'm even madder at me for letting you wake up in my bed two mornings in a row. Now I have to find a way to act like that never happened. Do you have any idea how hard that's gonna be?"

"I do. It's gonna be hard for me, too, Faith, but you're saying this is what you want. I'm going to respect that because I don't want you to leave me." She continued to sob. I reached up and wiped her tears. "You don't have to cry. We love each other. The greatest of all emotions is love—something Tempest and I struggle to share. It feels one-sided in our marriage. I know love will eventually bring you and me together. In the meantime, we'll have to be patient, learn how to be friends above anything else, and just wait—"

We heard two quick beeps, signaling someone had just opened the front door. Faith gasped then sprinted out of the den and down the hall to her bedroom. I jumped up from the sofa, drying my face with my hands, and then headed to the foyer. Tempest had a strange look on her face as she walked toward me, dragging her bag behind her. I put a huge grin on my face and pretended to be excited she was back.

"Hi, honey. I thought you said you wouldn't be in until five." I reached to hug her. She stood motionless while I wrapped my arms around her. "What's wrong," I asked when I pulled away.

She looked me up and down before responding. "Where's Faith?"

"Um . . . she's in her room, I think."

Tempest started down the hallway. "Was that her I saw running?" she asked, walking very fast.

"No," I answered, going behind her. "No, honey. What are you talking about?"

Tempest stopped in front of Faith's bedroom door then placed her ear on the door. My heart was about to jump out of my chest.

"Tempest, what're you doing?"

She didn't answer. She knocked on Faith's door. After two knocks, she decided to twist the knob. The door was unlocked so Tempest opened it then walked in. I couldn't stop my heart from pounding so loudly, so I decided to talk over it.

"Tempest, please tell me what you are doing."

She looked over at the bathroom door, which was closed, but we could hear water running in the shower. Tempest looked at me then turned up her lip.

"I know I saw that bitch running from the den when I came in."

I tried to play things off as best as I could. "Are you out of your mind? Did you have a bad trip or something?"

Tempest walked out of the room, so I followed her, closing Faith's door behind me. She returned to the foyer to retrieve her bag then headed upstairs. I continued to trail her like a lost puppy. She tossed her luggage on the bed then began to unpack. I went over to help, but once I picked up a garment, she snapped at me.

"I don't need your help," she said.

"Okay." I went to the chair beside the bed then sat down. "So tell me about your trip."

"There's nothing to tell."

"Nothing? I know there has to be something you liked about Detroit."

"Yeah. I was glad to be away from Memphis for a change. You know, you and me use to fly away often . . . remember . . . Puerto Rico, Hawaii, Aruba, London, Switzerland, Paris . . . remember, Ace? Huh? Do you?"

Yep. Tempest was back. I tried to remain cordial though. It took everything in me not to cuss at her. I was already shaken by the thought of Faith leaving me. I certainly didn't need the Wicked Witch of the West to return and taunt me about my illness and how it was holding her back. I pretended she hadn't even tried to take the argument there. My response came out of left field.

"So, I take it your momma and brother are doing well. What about your sister-in-law Karen? How are things going with her and the new job?"

Tempest looked at me as though she was throwing a thousand daggers at me with her eyes. Surprisingly, she answered without malice. "They're fine." She marched an arm load of clothes to the hamper.

I spoke loud enough so she'd hear me in the bathroom. "I thought you said your flight didn't get in until five."

She stepped out of the bathroom with a sour face. "I said if I missed my eleven A.M. flight, the next one wouldn't have me home until five. Why? Did I interrupt something?" she asked with her hand on her hip.

"Say what? Naw. Something like what?"

"I don't, Ace. You tell me."

128

"Tempest, please don't get started. You just got home. Can't we be amiable to each other for once? I really want to get along with my wife, but I need my wife to want the same thing. You think she can play along—at least for today?"

She rolled her eyes—her favorite thing to do—then closed the empty suitcase. She walked over to the closet, and then placed it in the corner. Once she stepped out, she was nice all over again.

"How was your weekend, Ace?"

"It was fine. I took Faith shopping. She and I both got makeovers."

"What?" she yelled.

"Yeah. I spent just about six thousand dollars—"

Tempest quickly walked up and stood over me with her hands on her hips. "Do what? Please tell me you're lying."

"Huh? Aren't you the one who said I should get Faith to take me out of the house?"

"I didn't tell you to go on shopping sprees." She felt my forehead.

"What? I'm not sick. I haven't been all weekend."

"Then you should've had your ass at work, not spending up all our money."

"Oh, Tempest, please. We're not going to miss that little change. That little outing did me some good, and Faith, too. She has a whole new confidence about herself."

Tempest yelled with all her might, pounding into her fist as she fussed. "I didn't hire that bitch to spend my money."

"You know what. You're going to have to learn how not to be so evil. I'm your husband. If it made me feel good to boost somebody else's confidence, then you shouldn't be mad about that. I'm not a big spender. The one time I decided to go on a shopping spree with a friend—"

"Oh now she's your friend, huh?"

"That's right. I consider her a friend, and I managed to spend less on the two of us than you do just on yourself every other month."

"The difference is I work and make the money I spend. You've been laid up for awhile, Ace."

"Regardless, you can't deny Bynum Bail Bonding is still my company."

"Our company."

I stood to leave. "Whatever, Tempest. I'm going back downstairs. Join me when your cool personality returns."

I walked out on her without looking back. When I got to the kitchen, Faith was in there, preparing for dinner. She turned to look at me. Her face had worry on it. I shook my head then took a seat at the table. Faith walked over and began whispering.

"Is everything okay? I heard you arguing."

I shook my head again. "She may come down in a minute, but try not to give her your energy. Let her be mad all by herself, okay?"

Faith nodded. I quickly changed the subject to the Jamie Foxx movie we went to see over the weekend. Faith and I began to laugh and communicate as if Tempest hadn't returned home. I was glad to see Faith relax. She brought a bowl of potatoes over to the table and began peeling them as we chatted. I went and got a knife to help.

When Tempest walked in, Faith and I were cracking our sides with laughter. Faith spoke, but Tempest didn't respond. She went into the refrigerator, got an apple then rinsed it off. I winked at Faith then continued our conversation. Tempest interrupted.

"What are you two talking about?" she asked.

"Oh we went to see that new movie this weekend," I responded. "You know the one with Jamie Foxx and—"

"To the movies?" she snapped.

"Yeah," I answered.

"You went shopping and to the movies—what else did you do?" She looked at Faith. "By the way, bitch, your hair looks nice—very similar to mine minus the bangs, but don't worry. I'll be changing my hairstyle in the morning."

"Tempest," I yelled.

"What?" she screamed back.

Faith couldn't mask being hurt. She had stopped peeling the potatoes, and she stared at Tempest with drooping eyes. I noticed her bottom lip trembling, and I prayed she could keep her composure. I tried to put Tempest in check, but the matter only got worse.

"You're wrong for calling this woman out of her name, Tempest. You hired her to tend to me, and now you want to be mad at her."

"Yeah, but becoming overfriendly with my husband was nowhere to be found on the application. Shopping sprees, make-overs, movies—that's way too much for me to ignore." She turned to address Faith again. "Are you fucking my husband, too?" Faith's eyes grew large, and so did mine. "Huh? I want to know because that's what's left."

"Tempest," I yelled. "That's enough." I turned to Faith whose eyes were so welled with tears the next blink would surely bring about a waterfall. "Faith, will you excuse us?"

She nodded. I got up from the table and asked Tempest to join me upstairs. She chunked her half-eaten apple in the garbage then brushed past me. It was hard for me to look at Faith again because I knew she was hurting, and I couldn't do anything about it at the moment.

When I got upstairs to our bedroom, Tempest was pacing in front of the mirror. She ripped into me as soon as I closed the door.

"You let her get my hairstyle, Ace?"

"Is it? The two of you look different to me." She plopped down on the bed. "Tempest, what's going on with you? I'm use to you being mean, but something is telling me your blow up isn't about the money I spent this weekend—not even the issue with the hair. Something else is bothering you."

"I think we should let her go, Ace."

My heart dropped. "Excuse me?"

"You keep saying you feel better. I don't think we'll be needing her services as much as I originally thought."

"Tempest, I'm in one of my good spells. You know how this disorder is. We can't let Faith go. What happens when I go back into one of my long periods of illness?"

"We'll cross that bridge when it comes, but as for now, she has to go."

I couldn't believe my ears. I sat down on the bed. "No," I answered, shaking my head. "Un-un. We've upset that woman's life. She gave up her apartment to move here with us."

Tempest slid closer to me. "Then why can't we just help her find another place to live. I want her gone, Ace."

I stared into Tempest's eyes and found something I hadn't seen in a long time—concern. "Why are you so adamant about her leaving? If I didn't know any better, I'd say you've become jealous of Faith."

Tempest was silent for a moment then she spoke. "I feel like I'm losing you."

I wondered if I had heard her correctly. "What'd you say?"

"I know I haven't been the best wife lately, and I'm sorry. You're right. I am jealous. Looking at you and Faith laughing and having a good time reminds me of how we use to be. I want that back. I don't want another woman to take my place."

I started to pinch myself to see if I was dreaming. I figured the words I'd just heard couldn't have come out of Tempest's mouth. I didn't even know how to respond to her. Tempest's personality had switched from mean to evil and then to nice many times before, so I was afraid to take her seriously.

"How do I know you're not going to flip on me the moment I go back into a sick spell?"

She shrugged. "I can only tell you I won't. I'm asking you to forgive me for the past and begin trusting me from this point on."

I looked into Tempest's eyes again. This time, I found sincerity and compassion. At this moment, I understood what Faith meant when she mention having to step back. As bad as I wanted to forget I ever married Tempest, I couldn't. Regardless to how I felt, Tempest was still my wife. I decided to give her a chance.

"Okay, Tempest. I hear you, but we're not firing Faith, moving her out, or cutting her hours. I refuse to strain her anymore than we already have."

Tempest looked at me, and then slowly nodded. "Okay. I understand."

I was dumbfounded. I thought we'd have to argue about the situation some more. I didn't expect Tempest to agree so easily, nor did I expect what happened next. She collapsed into my arms and cried like a baby.

Tempest

16

D etroit felt like a wasted trip for me. Although I got my groove on and my pockets were two million dollars richer, I couldn't shake the feeling of rejection. I only wanted to teach Craig a lesson for what he did to me. We were supposed to still be friends once we came away from the drama. If only he hadn't been so selfish in the beginning, we'd still be kicking it. I knew I had to accept that our fling was over before it could ever really begin.

Coming home to see Ace so happy sent up a red flag. Something wasn't right about him and Faith being close like that. I tried to tell myself that perhaps Ace was just finally excited to have company. After all, I hadn't been there for him like a spouse should. I had no one to blame but myself. Still, I didn't like him throwing that in my face. I knew my behavior had caused Ace to feel as though I didn't love him. Despite my telling him that I did, he stressed over and over that my actions said otherwise. We'd shared too many years for me not to love him, but I couldn't be sure of how he felt about me. After Craig's rejection and getting a sense that Faith was trying to step in, I was ready to do more than just love my husband. I wanted to be *in* love with him.

By Wednesday, I still hadn't apologized to Faith, and she and I said as little as possible to each other. I stayed late at the office the night before so I wouldn't have to face her once I got in. I had planned to do the same thing again. I called Lynette to see if we could hook up and talk. I had a lot on my mind—things I couldn't share with my momma nor with Ace. I caught Lynette on her lunch break.

"So we flying out of town on the spur of the moment now, huh?" she said to me upon answering the phone.

"What's up, girl? How's life treating you?"

"Hmph. Do you really wanna know?"

"Lynette, is Lemont still cutting up?"

"Him and me both."

"Say what?"

"You heard me."

"Girl, what does that mean?"

"My lunch break isn't long enough for me to even begin explaining."

"Wow."

"Yeah. That's right, but what about you? Mom, brother, sister-in-law, and everybody else okay?"

"They're fine."

"What about, Ace? How'd he get along with the hired help while you were out?"

"A little too well if you ask me."

Lynette gasped. "Huh? Ace? Are you serious?"

"Very. Look. Let's meet up when you get off. I need to exhale."

"Oh, I can't. Today is Wednesday. You know I have Bible study. Come on over and go to church with me. Pastor will be glad to see you."

"Un-un. Naw. I'll pass."

"Come on, Tempest. Now I know it's been at least a year since you visited my church. In fact, when is the last time you went to anybody's church?"

"I can't think back that far."

"Ooo, now see. You wrong for that. Tempest, God has been good to you. You need to invest some time with Him."

"Maybe so, but it won't be tonight. Just call me when you leave church. I'll try to be in the area so we can meet up as soon as you leave."

"Okay. Talk with you later."

Just as I hung up with Lynette, her husband stepped up to my office door, knocking on the panel. "Hi Lemont. Come on in."

"What's going on, Tempest? How are things with you?"

"I'm alright. I'll do."

"You'll do? I heard that. Is Ace getting any better? I need to go over and see him."

"Ace is doing fine believe it or not. He says he has his ups and downs, but I can say he's been more up lately."

"Good. Maybe he'll come back to work soon."

"Hmph. That's what I said. We'll see."

"Tempest, you think you can get me in a few extra bonds. Not a lot more—just a few more. Lynette and I gotta catch up on some bills."

"I'll see what I can do. I try to be fair to everybody around here, you know."

"I know."

"What about bounty hunting? Mr. Cooper over there at Bester Bonding asked me yesterday if I had someone who wouldn't mind making some extra money bounty hunting for him."

"I know Mr. Cooper. That dude's getting old."

"Yeah, and he hates bounty hunting, too."

"He's too old," Lemont said, laughing.

136

"He says he'll write bonds 24/7, but it's the bounty hunting he can't stand. Oh, and he says he'll pay ten percent of the bond."

"Well, I'm his man. You know I never have problems tracking folks down."

"Here's his card. I told him I'd find somebody for him."

"Cool. Thanks, Tempest," Lemont said, leaving the office.

"No problem," I yelled to him.

I stayed at the office until six-thirty then headed across the bridge. By the time Lynette called me, I had just walked into the I-Hop in her area. She agreed to meet me there. I took a seat and ordered some coffee, awaiting her arrival. She showed up in a very good mood.

"Hey girl," she said, sliding into the booth.

"Hey yourself."

"What's up? Have you ordered something to eat?"

"Not yet. I was waiting on you."

Lynette picked up a menu. "Well, I can't have very much. I over did it at lunch."

"You're just not going to give up on that damn Weight Watchers stuff are you?"

She shook her head. "Nope, and it's going to work for me. You'll see. I weighed in when I got off work today."

"And? How did you do?"

"Very well. I'm not going to go into numbers until you all can see a significant difference. I'll make you guess then." She smiled.

"Oh great. Guessing games. I really love it when you play those with us," I said, rolling my eyes.

Lynette laughed. The waitress came over and took our orders. As soon as she left, Lynette and I spilled everything that had been going on with us. I told her everything—from the very beginning of what went down with Craig Dennison to the blow up at home when I got back from Detroit. Lynette seemed to be taken aback by all she'd heard.

"Girl, I'm still trying to absorb all of this," she said as the waitress set our plates down. "Why on earth did that man take advantage of you like that?"

I thanked the waitress and waited until she was a great distance away. "Pride I guess. The same thing that made me go a fool on him."

"But you are going to get him off the hook with the police, aren't you? He made a mistake, Tempest. I'm sure he learned his lesson."

"I shouldn't let him off, but I am. After all, I've got his two million."

"Ooo, Lawd, what I wouldn't do for that kind of money right about now."

"Speaking of which . . . what is your price?"

"What're you talking about?"

"You said you're going to Birmingham to meet with this Parnell guy. I can't imagine the Lynette Rapid I know, stepping out on her husband."

"I don't know that I'll sleep with him. I really don't want any more intimacy than just plain ole cuddling."

I laughed, almost choking on my food. "Girl, if he's any kind of man, especially a real one, he's not driving miles away from home to go lay up and hold some woman who's not his wife." Lynette and I laughed. "Why Birmingham, Alabama?"

"I don't know. I think he just wants to get away from Texas and get me away from Arkansas, so we can be alone in an altogether different environment."

"See . . . that doesn't sound good to me, Lynette. I think you better stay your inexperienced ass at home," I told her.

She shook her head. "I hear you, but when I think about how much control over my life Lem has, I just want to act like a runaway child—show him I'm my own person."

"Yeah, but in most cases, a runaway child is a disobedient kid. The fact that you'd use that terminology tells me Lemont has even affected what you think of yourself. The Weight Watchers. . . that's him, too, right?"

"Well, he says my weight doesn't matter, but I know it does."

"You say that plan is going to work for you, but I don't believe it will until it's something you truly want for yourself."

"I do. Maybe not at first, but now I want to lose weight for me. I know I can look and feel better. Besides, by the time I get back from Birmingham, Lemont may be out of the picture anyway."

"Okay. Yeah right. Whatever, Lynette. Eat your kibbles. That's about all you ordered."

"I know you don't believe me, but you'll see. Anyway, what about Ace and his new woman?" She laughed. "I'm sorry. I was just joking, and that wasn't very nice of me. I just don't see Ace messing around on you. I don't care what kind of makeover he bought this woman. Even with your hairstyle, she can't be half as beautiful as you."

"Not to sound conceited, but she doesn't even come close. It just pissed me off so bad that he'd even take her to a shop and have them do that. I couldn't get down to Tia's fast enough yesterday."

"Maybe he didn't realize how similar her hair was to yours. You were gone all weekend."

"Girl, how many times have I worn Remi European deep wave?"

"Plenty."

"Thank you. Once they got the weave in that woman's head, he should've notice the extreme likeness. He didn't care."

"Men don't understand how we are about stuff like that. A hairdo is a hairdo to them."

I shook my head then called the waitress over for a refill of coffee. My nerves were on edge. My house wasn't in order, and I desperately needed to figure out a way to tighten it back up.

"Lynette, what do I do? This woman has only been around a matter of days, just over a week and she's already taking over my home."

"She can't if you don't let her. I know Ace doesn't want to fire her right now, but one thing I know about your husband is he loves attention. Make sure you're the one giving it to him. Things have run smoothly down at that office ever since Ace laid himself off. Business has kept up just as Mr. and Mrs. Bynum would have it, without them hanging out there every day—at least that's what Lem has said about you two. Until Ace is ready to go back to work, you need to be there for him."

"Yeah, but that kills my hopes of having space again. Remember it's been a while since I haven't been cooped up, taking care of Ace."

"You asked me for a suggestion, and I just gave you one. If I had gotten myself in a predicament like yours . . . a woman staying at my house with my husband, and I suspect something is going on, some things would change with the quickness. She'd barely have room to breathe by the time I got through with her, and she'd make the decision on her own to leave."

A light bulb went off in my head. I smiled and nodded. "Aahh . . . I hear you. You know I do know how to make people's lives miserable. Just ask Craig Dennison."

"Now hold on, Tempest. I didn't say be evil."

"You and Ace know y'all love that word. I'm not evil—conniving—but not evil."

"Look. Go to God about it. You can't go wrong with prayer."

"I know you're not talking, Ms.-I'm-going-to-Birmingham. Did God tell you to do that?" She dropped her head. "Huh? I can't hear you?" She still didn't respond. "I didn't think so. And it's funny how even now I can't embarrass you into not going."

She began to stumble over her words. "I-I-I just . . . I just feel like it's something I have to do. I can't explain it."

"I want you to be careful, girl. I love you. I'd be sick if something were to happen to you."

"Aw, Tempest, you haven't said anything that sweet to me in a long time."

"Shut up. You say that every time I say something sweet." We laughed. "Look. Eat those crumbs so I can go. I'm taking your advice. I'm going home to spend some quality time with my husband."

"Aw shucks now. That's what I'm talking about. Ace is going to be so surprised."

"You ain't lying. He's going to claim it's one of my multiple personalities—one of the nicer ones." We laughed. "I bet he thinks I need medication for real."

"Girl, stop. You're so silly."

We got the waitress to give us our ticket. Lynette reached to hug me before she left. It had been a while since we embraced, and it felt nice. I knew if no one was my friend, Lynette certainly was. I'd given her a hard time over the years, cussing and fussing over the simplest of things, but she'd take my tantrums like a charm every time. She'd call me the next day like nothing happened. Tracey was a friend, too, but she and her husband were introduced to Ace and I by Lynette some years after our company was started. Lynette and I had more years of friendship, so I felt closer to her by default. Truth be told, Tracey didn't tolerate me as much as Lynette either.

Shortly after pulling up to my house, I began to feel nervous. It was a quarter till nine. Unlike the night before, I was home before anyone's bedtime. I had a flashback of what happened when I returned home on Monday. In spite of Ace swearing I didn't see anything, I knew I caught a glimpse of a darting shadow as it whisked out of the den. I feared walking in on something that would bring out the absolute worst in me, and that could mean somebody would get hurt.

I took a deep breath, got out of the car then entered my house. I hurriedly walked toward the den, but slowed when I saw there were no lights on in there. I turned to face the kitchen. The light was on, and I heard the clinging sound of dishes and cabinet doors shutting. I walked toward the noise and was surprised to see only Faith in the kitchen. She didn't notice me, so I made my presence known.

"Good evening," I said.

Faith turned to me, seemingly surprised to hear my voice. "Good evening," she responded. "I didn't know if you'd be home in time for dinner, but I cooked enough just in case."

"That was nice."

"Would you like me to fix you a plate?"

"No, thank you. I appreciate you thinking of me though." I looked around and noticed the kitchen was spotless. "You know, Faith, you really do great work around here. I need to apologize for the way I treated you Monday. I was way out of line, and I'm sorry. Your new look is really pretty, and I'm glad Ace was so generous to you."

Faith stood staring. She seemed at a loss for words. I hated to lie to her like that, but if I was going to get her off my husband, I couldn't keep being the enemy in the situation. Ace might've thought Faith's new look was pretty, and perhaps she even thought she was gorgeous, but I didn't. She looked better, not beautiful.

She finally thought of something to say. "Thanks for all the kind words, Tempest."

"You're welcomed. So, where is the love of my life?" I asked, looking toward the kitchen door.

I could've sworn I saw Faith do a double-take in my peripheral vision. I turned to look at her. She opened her mouth to speak, but nothing came out at first. She turned her back to continue putting up the dishes.

"Um, he's um, Ace is um," she stumbled. I could tell she was caught off guard by my comment of Ace being the love of my life. "He should be upstairs."

"Really? You think he's sleeping? I hope not because I really want to just cuddle up with my husband and watch a movie tonight."

Her rapid movements suddenly came to a halt. She turned to me. "That sounds nice, Tempest. I'm sure Ace would like that." She began to walk away. "I hope you'll excuse me. I'm pretty tired, so I'm going to bed now."

"Sure. Have a good night." I caught her before she exited. "Oh, and by the way. You can sleep in late. I'm going to get up and fix Ace's breakfast in the morning."

Her face turned solemn. "Great. Well, good night."

I couldn't help smiling inside as she walked away. I turned out the lights then headed upstairs. Ace was sitting up in bed, reading a magazine. He looked surprised to see me.

"Hey, honey," I said. "Whatcha reading?"

He slowly closed the magazine then removed his reading glasses. "Hi. I didn't think you'd be home this early. Is everything alright at the office?"

I sat on the edge of the bed next to him then leaned in and gave him a kiss. "Oh, everything is fine. I made sure to get out of there before you went to bed so we could have some quality time."

"Quality time?" He turned to look at the digital clock on the nightstand. "I was just going to read this magazine then turn in to bed early."

"Aw, c'mon, Ace. You can stay up and watch a movie with me. It's not like you're going to work in the morning, and neither am I."

"You're not going to work?"

"No. I told you I'm trying to be a better wife, so I'm giving Faith a break tomorrow."

Ace didn't say a word. He stared at me like he didn't know who I was. I began to undress in front of him—something I hadn't done in months. He pretended to be into his magazine, but I caught him glimpsing every time I took off another piece of garment. I bent over and picked up all of my clothes then started toward the bathroom.

"I'm going to shower, but I won't be long, honey."

I turned to look at him before closing the door. He seemed to be in deep thought, and that look was priceless. I did what I had to do in the bathroom, and was out of there in twenty minutes. I sprayed on a dash of Very Sexy just before reentering the bedroom. Ace lay asleep with the magazine opened face down on his chest and wearing his reading glasses. I went into my panty drawer and put on a cute, lace top and boy-shorts set then walked around to his side of the bed. I eased the magazine off him then removed his glasses. He woke up and stared at me.

"Are you okay, honey?" I asked.

He nodded then stretched. "I'm fine. Just tired." I climbed on top of him. "What're you doing," he asked.

"Ace, it's been a long time since we even tried," I said, grinding on him. "You seemed to be feeling pretty well. Can't we at least try?" I leaned over and began tonguing him. He didn't kiss me back. I was hurt. "What's wrong?"

"Nothing," he answered.

"Then why aren't you kissing me?"

"I told you I'm tired. I'm just not in the mood."

I began to grind rigorously. "Oh really? I wonder if there is anything I can do about that."

Ace became aroused. I was so happy I could've jumped up and clicked my heels. I kissed his neck as I began to remove my boy-shorts. That's when he began to sound like a little bitch.

"Tempest, stop."

"Huh?" I grabbed his hand and place it between my legs but he withdrew.

"Stop it, Tempest."

"Why, honey? You've got an erection. Why are we stopping? I'll do all the work."

"Tempest, I don't want this?"

I rolled off of him, staring like he was crazy. "Say what?"

"My erection probably won't last long because I don't want this," he said. "Go to sleep. We'll talk tomorrow."

He turned out the lamp then rolled his back to me. I was speechless. *How could he not want me,* I thought. Then it dawned on me. *Faith!* He'd begun to take a liking to Faith in my absence. I had no way of determining if they'd been intimate or not, but I knew she had to get out of there. By hook or crook, walking or limping—it didn't matter. She was getting out of my house.

Lynette

17

I left for Birmingham only an hour after I got off work. Vicki was out of school for some type of teacher in-service day, so I took her over to my mom's and pre-packed the night before. This kept me from having to get on the road at night. I decided the best time to tell Lem would be while I was on the highway. We hadn't said much to each other all week, which kept me fueled about leaving town. I called his cell phone to break the news to him.

"What's up," he answered.

"Oh nothing. Are you home yet?"

"Naw. Why?"

I began to play with him to see what he'd say. "I was trying to see if you had anything planned for us tonight."

He huffed. "We gotta go through this again?"

"What do you mean?"

"Lynette, what do I do on Friday nights?"

"So you're going to play cards, huh?" He didn't answer. "Well, what about tomorrow night?"

"I'm working."

"Working?"

"Yeah. I told you I was going to ask Tempest for some extra work. She referred me to another bonding company to do some of their bounty hunting. I gotta be in Chicago in the morning. You wanna go?"

"Bounty hunting, huh? Take your wife bounty hunting .. . that's your idea of quality time, huh?" He didn't say anything. "I realize I've let you brainwash me into believing and doing a lot of things other women wouldn't have, but it's a new day, Lem."

"What are you talking about, Lynette?"

"You really want me to think you're going out to play cards all night, and then leave early to drive ten hours to Chicago in the morning?"

He was silent for a moment. "I'm not going by myself. I asked Rick if he'd ride with me."

"Really? Don't make me call Tracey on three-way to verify her husband is going out of town with you."

"Why you gotta call Tracey? Why can't you call Rick? He may not have told his wife we're leaving in the morning yet."

"You're full of it, Lem. I'm not going to even bother Tracey or worry myself with this. G'on and sleep with your slut tonight. In fact, take her out of town with you. Perhaps she'd like bounty hunting. I'm on my way out of town, too, except I'm doing some other kind of hunting."

"What? Where are you?"

"I'm heading down Highway 78, and I'll see you Sunday. How about that?"

"Lynette, don't make me call your momma and ask her where you are."

"My momma doesn't know where I'm going. Besides, you wouldn't dare call her. You know my momma can't stand you right about now."

"Lynette, you shouldn't be going out of town and not telling somebody where you'll be."

"I'll be in the company of another, Lem. I'm playing one of your games."

"I don't believe you."

"Whatever. Let me get off of this airtime. Didn't you tell me not to talk on my cell too much in the daytime?"

"Our minutes to each other are free."

"Oh. Well, it still doesn't matter. I need to go so I can be sure I know what hotel I'm checking into. Buh-bye now."

I heard Lem calling to me before I hung up, but I ignored him. He kept calling back so I turned the ringer on vibrate then put in my favorite gospel CD, "This Is Who I Am" by Kelly Price. Kelly ministered to my spirit so much that by the time I was half an hour outside of Birmingham, I wanted to turn around and go home. I began to have second thoughts about keeping company with another man. Just as I turned down the radio, I heard my phone vibrating. I had come upon a red light, so I picked up the cell to see if it was Lem again. It wasn't him. It was Parnell.

I flipped open the phone and answered. "I'm almost there," I told him.

"Great. I can't wait to see you. Now as I told you, we're staying at the Embassy Suites in downtown Birmingham. You're going to love it here. If you need directions once you get downtown, call me back."

"So we actually have one bedroom?"

"Well, yeah. Lynette, you said that would be fine."

"Oh, I know. I was just asking."

"I just checked in. I haven't even unpacked, so if it's going to be a problem, just let me know. I can go back to the front desk and make new arrangements."

I wanted to scream YES. "No. I'm not going to put you through that. Where you are is fine. I'll see you in a little bit."

"Okay. See you soon," he said before hanging up.

What am I doing? I asked myself. I know I can't lay with another man, let alone someone else's husband. I further told myself to just push on since I had come so far. Besides, going home to an empty house wasn't going to make me feel any better either.

Parnell met me downstairs in the lobby. He looked scrumptious in a pair of dark jeans and a short-sleeved Polo shirt. I still had on my work attire, so I felt a little overdressed. Parnell assured me I was fine.

"Lynette, you look wonderful. In fact, I'm going to call a bellman over here to take your luggage to the room, while I take you out to eat. You look much too splendid to just order room service."

"Wow. That's nice of you, Parnell. Where're we going?"

"Anywhere you'd like. This weekend is on me."

"Well, I see they have a Ruth's Chris Steak House onsite. What do you think?"

"Sounds fine to me."

We got over to the restaurant and were seated in great timing. Parnell couldn't seem to stop staring at me. I blushed every time I noticed him staring. I decided to call him on it before our food made it to the table.

"You've been staring since we sat down, Parnell."

"I'm sorry. I can't help it. I just can't believe you're here."

"Well, that makes two of us." We laughed. "Parnell, why do you think I'm here?"

He raised his eyebrows. "Well, um . . . you're here because um . . . we're friends, and we need each other."

"True, but what happened to lead us here? What did we say or do that led to an attraction for one another. Be honest."

"Okay, Lynette. I'll be honest. I was happy to see you at the class reunion. I was even more happy that we would keep in touch because I love making new friends. Once I discovered you had marital problems, I figured as a minister and your friend, the least I could do was counsel you in your time of need. It was a pleasure to talk with you, pray with you, and comfort you with whatever encouragement I could. As we continued to talk, we grew attracted to each other on a different level.

"I was fully aware this could happen, but as strong as I've been in my ministry, I felt confident I could avoid feeling this way. What we've done is become emotionally seduced by each other. I can tell you I know you're attracted to the care and attention I've given you. And more recently, I became attracted to the sensitivity you displayed toward my issues. Bottom line.. . we're here to fulfill a need for each other."

He made perfect sense. I did have a need I wanted met. I was confident Parnell was just the man to caress me the way I needed and to make me feel loved. The only problem was I didn't feel any more comfortable about being there with him than I did before arriving.

We finished dinner then headed to the room. After settling down in the chair next to the bed, my cell began to vibrate on the nightstand. Parnell and I looked at each other. I sat, ignoring the rattling of the phone against the wood. Parnell seemed concerned.

"Don't you think you should get that?" he asked.

I shook my head then stared at the phone. "No."

"No?"

"No."

"Why?"

"It's probably just Lem."

"Lynette, that's all the more reason you should answer it. You didn't tell him where you are and who you're with, did you?"

Shaking my head again, I answered, "No."

"Then, why won't you answer."

I looked up at Parnell. "Because he's where he wants to be, and so am I."

I meant what I said, but that didn't mean my courage had built up. I was where I wanted to be. I just wasn't so sure I was where God wanted me to be. I began to feel a heavy sense of betrayal on my part—not toward Lem, but toward God. *How do I get out of this?* I asked myself. Parnell pulled out a pair of pajamas then addressed me.

"Well, should I go shower or would you like to go first? I always say ladies first, but it's up to you."

My stomach turned then I sighed. "Wow. Are we hitting the sack already?" My nerves were a wreck. "Isn't it too early for bed?"

Parnell looked at his watch. "Lynette, it's ten till ten. I figured by the time we've had our showers, we can just lie in bed and watch TV or whatever you'd like to do."

I swallowed hard. "Oh. Well, usually on Friday's I don't go to sleep until much later because I don't have to be at work the next morning. But, I get your point." I wondered if he'd noticed my nervous twitches and the rocking of my knee. "I'll let you shower first. I need to make a goodnight call to my mother and daughter. I should be done once you get out."

"Okay."

Parnell grabbed his pajamas and toiletries then went into the bathroom. As soon as he closed the bathroom door, I jumped up from the chair and began pacing the room, talking to myself. I knew the inner voice was God speaking to my conscience, but silly me couldn't hear clearly what I was supposed to do. I finally fell to my knees and did what I do best—prayed.

After an extensive prayer, I calmed down then called my child. I spoke to my mother as well. Thank goodness neither of them asked me where I was or what I was doing. Our conversations were brief, and I was off the phone only a minute before Parnell stepped out of the bathroom.

He picked up his watch. "Ten-fifteen. That didn't take me long at all, huh?" He smiled.

"No. That was great timing. I just hung up with my child. Perhaps you want to give your family a call while I'm in the shower."

"I will. It's a bit steamy in there right now, so you might want to let things air out before getting in there," he said.

"I will," I answered, not knowing what else to say.

He walked over to his overnight bag and fumbled around in there. I got up to retrieve my night clothes and toiletries. The room was silent—dead silent. Parnell was the first to talk.

"It sure is quiet in here," he said.

"You're right. It is. Let's turn on the TV. Do you watch CNN? My husband watches CNN."

Parnell looked at me funny as though I'd committed a crime by mentioning my husband. "Sometimes I do. I work so much I hardly have time for television. But, if that's what you want to watch, we can."

"Oh, no. I was just asking."

The look he gave me before responding made me feel stupid. This was my first encounter with planning infidelity. I didn't realize I should be cautious of mentioning my husband. I went over to sit back down in the chair. Parnell walked into the bathroom then returned with a prognosis.

"It's all clear. You can take your shower now," he said.

I gathered my things. "Great. I'll try not to be too long." I closed the door behind me.

Considering the extreme condition of my nerves, perhaps there is no need to say I took the longest shower in history. I've taken long, hot baths before—to the point that when I got out of the tub, the palms of my hands and the bottom of feet where drawn up and wrinkled. Well, any time that can happen after a shower, the shower was way too lengthy.

I didn't realize how long I had been in there because I was too busy playing with my cuticles. They looked good by the time I decided I should bathe, but then I realized I didn't trust the hotel towels. I hopped out of the shower and turned off the cold water, making sure heavy steam flowed from the shower head. I repeatedly scalded the hotel washcloth with soap and the hot water, perhaps a dozen times before using it. It took me a while because the water was actually too hot for my hands. Once I decided the towel was okay, I added some cold water to the hot, creating just the right temperature for a soothing shower. But, I didn't bathe right away because I felt the need to have more conversation with God.

If all of that wasn't enough to get a sense of how much time went by, let me add that I couldn't dry off with the hotel towel either. I examined the dry towel thoroughly. It seemed clean, but I just wasn't use to the idea of other people using the towel. Unlike the washcloth, I couldn't scald it and still be able to dry off. Parnell just had to wait. I had to let my skin air dry enough to put on my lotion and then my nightgown. I brushed my teeth and took my time, wrapping my hair.

When I stepped out of the bathroom, Parnell was sitting up in bed. He wouldn't even look at me. He stared straight ahead at the TV. I got a glimpse of the clock on the nightstand and saw that it was twelve-thirty. *No wonder he won't look at me,* I thought. I almost felt bad. I was comfortable walking around in my gown because it was long and loose, showing no curves and only the skin on my arms. I put away my things then slid into bed. Parnell still wouldn't look at me or speak. I figured I better break the ice.

"So, did you get to speak to your family?" I asked.

Staring straight ahead he answered, "Umhmm."

"Good. That's good." Things went silent between us again, so I tried to open up more dialogue. "Was everybody okay?"

"Yeah. They're fine," he answered, still looking at TV.

I glanced at the screen then at him. "So what's on?"

He took a few moments before responding. "I'm not sure what this is."

"I mean, is it a movie or—"

"I don't know," he said, cutting me off.

I wanted him to make eye contact with me at least once. "Parnell, will you look at me?"

He did. "What's up, Lynette?"

I stared for a moment then answered. "Are you not ashamed?"

Parnell picked up the remote, turned down the volume on the television then looked at me. "Shame is what kept you in the bathroom all that time, didn't it?"

"I know we talked about it, but I'm still not sure why we're here. We both know right from wrong."

"We both know right from wrong, and we understand what God loves. So, why are we here, you ask?"

I nodded. "Yes. We both know better, and if God is in control, why are we here?"

"We're here because God has given us free will. I'll be honest, and tell you it's not His Will that we share each other's bed tonight. This is a test. We're either going to decide we want to make our situations right and good for us the best we know how then pray about it later, or we're going to choose to not to turn a death ear on God." He paused. "Judging by the time you spent in the bathroom, I take it you choose to hear God."

I looked away then back at him. "Are you mad at me?"

He didn't answer right away. He looked down at the comforter and responded. "I'll be okay."

"I have to leave in the morning. If you'll give me your receipts, I'll be happy to reimburse you for whatever you've spent."

He looked at me. "No. That won't be necessary." Parnell slid out of bed, heading for the living room. "I'm sure you'll be more comfortable without me in the bed, so I'll be on the couch. Sleep tight," he said then exited.

I wanted to feel bad, but truth is, I was relieved. As messed up as my home life was, I still couldn't cheat on Lem. Even the sense of betrayal had shifted, and I had begun to feel sorry for doing Lem this way. I reached to the nightstand and picked up my cell phone. He hadn't tried to call me since just before ten. It was a quarter to one in the morning, but knowing my husband, he was still out playing cards. My conscience wouldn't let me sleep until I had attempted to apologize. I decided to see if he'd answer me. After three rings, I was starting to think, he wouldn't pick up, but then I heard a soft sigh in the phone.

"Hello," the feminine voice answered.

I couldn't speak. I was frozen solid. I held on to the phone, and then I heard Lem's groggy voice in the background. "Are you on my phone?" he asked.

"No, this is my phone," the woman said.

"No, it's not. That's my phone. Why are you on my phone?" he questioned.

"It was ringing. I thought it was my phone," she answered.

He apparently snatched the phone from her quickly. "Hello," he said. I didn't say anything at first. "Hello," he said again.

"I hate you, Lem. I really hate you," I said calmly before hanging up.

I began to cry, but in the midst of my tears, I went into the living room and stood over Parnell. He opened his eyes, and then rose with confusion on his face.

"Lynette, are you okay?"

"Parnell, will you still have me?" More tears dropped. "I'm all yours if you want me."

He looked intensely into my eyes then reached for my hand. He pulled me down to the couch where I knew an unthinkable act against God would occur.

Ace

18

My wife was acting really, really odd—nice, but for Tempest, that was strange behavior. At one point, she didn't care if I touched her or not. But shortly after she moved another woman into our house, she suddenly needed love and attention. Tempest tried five days, unsuccessfully, to get me to make love to her. I couldn't do it. Sure, I got a rise, but mentally and emotionally, I couldn't go there with her. Sunday night must've been her limit because by Monday morning, she got up in one of her funks and went back to work.

Although I'd promised to trust her kindness, I didn't. Tempest had been mean for so long, it was tough letting my guard down. Had she changed before bringing Faith into the picture, things might've been a little easier for me to accept. I was in trouble because I loved Faith, and I knew she loved me. We were doing well with being friends without benefits—not what my heart wanted, but I aimed to be selfless and respect what Faith wanted. I met her downstairs for breakfast.

"So what time did she leave?" Faith asked, pouring me a cup of coffee.

I shrugged. "Long before the office opened, and she wasn't happy when she left."

"Why? Did you tell her to go to work?"

"No. I believe that besides her being displeased with me not touching her, she was quite ready to turn back into the old Tempest anyway. Trust me. Being nice was killing her."

"You really believe that about your wife."

"I've had too many years with the woman not to know her."

Faith pulled out a chair and sat down. "You'd be surprised, Ace. I've learned first hand that people can change. Tempest could very well have a conscience about some things now."

I shook my head. "Then we must be talking about some other Tempest, not the one I married."

"And not to be too personal, but why won't you touch her?"

I looked down into my coffee then sighed. I took two sips before replying. "I can't do it."

"She's beautiful, and she's your wife."

"I know, but I'm not emotionally attached to her. When I make love, I want it to be more than just sex. I haven't been getting many erections as it is. I don't want to waste my energy only to be left feeling empty afterwards."

"Oh, Ace, you sound like a woman. Men usually don't care about anything but getting off."

"That can't be true because I'm a man. And that's how I feel." We stared at each other for a minute. "I'm suffering, Faith. I'm doing my best to respect your wishes, but I have to let you know that I'm worn down each day that goes by and I haven't at least kissed you."

She sighed. "You think perhaps you're in lust?"

I shook my head. "Definitely not lust. Just a need to be affectionate with the woman who shows me consistent care. Yes, you get a paycheck, but look at me and tell me you wouldn't care for me if you weren't being paid." She remained silent. "That's what I thought. You love me, Faith, and I love you. It's not fair that we can't have each other."

Faith got up from the table. I tried to look into her eyes, but she wouldn't look at me. Her voice let me know she was masking tears. "I've got work to do, Ace. I'll see you at lunchtime." She excused herself from the kitchen.

Faith might not have understood it, but Tempest had caused me to fall out of love with her soon after Fibromyalgia invaded my body. I could appreciate her wanting and trying to do better, but falling back in love with her wasn't going to be an easy task, considering the amount of time she'd spent dishonoring me—not to mention she unknowingly moved in my first love.

I went upstairs to my bedroom to think. It was obvious Faith wasn't going to give in to me. I told myself, the best thing I should do was figure out a way to want my wife. I looked over at my cell on the nightstand and decided that after having not been so attentive to her, the least I could do was give her an unexpected call at work. I hoped that she'd view that as a gesture of kindness, and maybe once she got home, we could start things over. I sat in my favorite chair to place the call.

I was shocked to catch her in her office. "Hello, Bynum Bail Bonding," she answered.

"Hi there." I didn't state who I was because I knew she'd seen the caller ID.

"What do you want?"

"To check in with my wife." Tempest was extremely quiet. I imagined she was speechless. "Hello," I said.

"I'm here . . . I'm . . . I'm sorry. I just thought I heard you said you had called to check in with your wife."

I smiled. "Well, you are my wife, aren't you?"

Her tone was pleasant as if she was smiling back. "Yes. Yes. You know I am."

"So tell me. How's your morning going so far?"

"Well, all I can say is good thing I came to work this morning because we're minus some people."

"Really? Who's out?"

"Milton's not here, and from my understanding it's because his wife just found out she has terminal cancer."

"What? Are you serious? I've got to call him."

"I haven't spoken with him, so you might want to call. I'm just going on what the receptionist told me."

"Okay. I'll call him, but who else is out?"

"Lemont is on bounty hunting again for Bester, and he took Rick with him."

"What do you mean again? He recently asked me for some extra assignments, so I suggested he help Bester, but I meant in his spare time. I didn't know he'd neglect what needed to be done around here."

"I'll talk to him. Leave that up to me. I appreciate you holding things down at the office. I'm going to start making myself go in at least twice a week until I feel I can do more. It's not fair that I've put so much responsibility on you."

"Oh . . . well, um . . . get well first, honey. I rather you be in great health than to push yourself too hard."

"Alright."

"Hey," she called, "how would you like me to wrap up a little early so we can watch a DVD movie tonight?"

"That'll be nice, Tempest."

"Really?" I could hear more surprise in her voice.

"I'll get Faith to put dinner on early for us."

"Okay. Thanks, honey. I can't wait to see you."

"See you soon."

After hanging up, I realized being nice to her didn't hurt at all. I was glad I made the call. I set the phone back on the nightstand and picked up my television remote, clicking to the TV Guide station. The house phone began to ring. It was on the other side of the bed, so I didn't budge. Faith knew to take care of answering it. Several minutes went by without her alerting me, so I figured the caller must've been a salesperson.

Hmm, *Cops* is on, I said to myself as I glanced at the guide. *I haven't watched that in a while.* Before I could click a button, my cell rang. It was odd for my cell to ring during the morning because most of the bondsmen at my company were either at court or the jailhouse until late afternoon. I thought perhaps Tempest was calling me back. I glanced at the caller ID. I didn't recognize the number, but I answered it anyway.

"This is Bynum," I stated, assuming it was a business call.

"Ace, man, what's up?" the voice said.

"Not much. Who's this?"

"This is Craig Dennison. I called your house phone, but the aide suggested I try reaching you on your cell."

"Craig, man, what's going on? I've been worried about you since that stuff was reported on the news. Are you okay?"

"I'm cool, man. I don't want to go into details about the situation, but I'm still trying to get everything straightened out right now."

"I sure hate this happened with you. You've got to be careful about these women you're letting into your life, man."

"When I tell you I've learned my lesson, believe I have."

"Good . . . good. I wish you nothing but the best, man. It's nice to have you call me, but I have to admit I'm surprised to be hearing from you so soon. Is there something I can do for you?"

"Um, yeah. Well, kind of. If you don't mind, would you have Tempest give me a shout?"

Tempest? I pondered. "Oh . . . um, you want me to give her your number?"

"To tell you the truth, man, she has it."

"Really?" Now I was really confused.

"Yeah. I've asked her to do something for me, but it doesn't seem she's gotten it done . . . so, I'm basically double-checking up on the job. She won't answer any of her phones, and when I just called your house, the hired help said she should be at the office."

"Wow. I don't know what's going on, Craig. I can't imagine why she'd be dodging your calls."

"She's already been paid. Let her know I've discovered the check has cleared. I just want the job done, so I can continue to take care of my business."

"Craig, man, I have to tell you that first, I'm shocked that you'd have business with my wife and I'm the last to know. Second, I've come to the realization that her little trip to Detroit wasn't about seeing her family at all. I'm not gonna lie to you. What you're telling me, worries me."

"Don't worry, Ace. I hate to say it like this, but the business I have with your wife is private. If she wants to tell you about it, which I doubt, then that's on her. Sorry, man. I just need you to tell her I know the task hasn't been completed, and I'm not happy. Take care, man."

Craig hung up on me without another word. My heart sank. I didn't know what to think or feel. The house phone rang again, but since I doubted it was Tempest calling, I remained seated. A minute later, Faith came upstairs and knocked on my door.

"Come in," I told her. "Sorry to disturb you, Ace, but there's a Detective Williams on the phone for you."

"For me?" I asked. She nodded. "He asked to speak to me?" She nodded again. "Will you get me that cordless phone over there, Faith," I asked, pointing.

"Sure."

Things were getting stranger by the minute. I thanked Faith as she left the room. I tried to remain calm when I answered the phone.

"This is Ace Bynum."

"Mr. Bynum, I'm Detective Williams. How are you today?"

"That depends on the nature of this call, Detective."

161

"I understand. I'm not calling to alarm you of anything. I just need your assistance with getting a hold of your wife. I have some questions for her about a case."

"You tell me you need my wife for questioning, yet you say you're not trying to alarm me."

"Mr. Bynum, your wife is not in any trouble. I just need to speak with her."

I reached for the pen and paper on the nightstand. "Give me your number, Detective Williams. I'll make sure she returns your call."

When we hung up, my stomach was in knots. I went downstairs to confide in Faith about the odd phone calls. Neither of us could make sense of things. I wanted to call Tempest immediately, but decided I'd wait until she got home so we could talk face to face.

By four o'clock, I sat at the kitchen table, keeping Faith company as she prepared dinner. I expected Tempest to arrive at any minute. When I heard the chime on the door, my heart began to pound. I told myself to remain calm. She walked into the kitchen without a clue of what I was about to hit her with.

"Hello," she sang as she headed over to kiss my cheek.

I sat silent, but Faith spoke back. "Good afternoon, Tempest. Ace asked me to prepare something light, so I'm making chicken wraps for the two of you. They're almost ready."

"Sounds great. I'm starving. I skipped lunch so I could finish up at the office and get home to my husband." She went over to the sink and washed her hands. As she dried them, she turned to me and said, "How's the love of my life doing this afternoon?"

"The love of who's life?" I answered, unable to mask my anger. My tone was harsh, and the frown on my face seemed to have her taken aback.

She walked over to the table and sat down across from me. "Something wrong, honey?"

"You tell me, Tempest. You're the one getting all the mysterious phone calls today—people with big names looking for you. Why are you dodging calls, Tempest?"

"Who? Nobody's called me today besides you, honey. I don't have the faintest what you're talking about."

"Really? Okay. Tell me this? What business does Craig Dennison have with you?"

She frowned and shrugged. "Craig—"

"Don't lie, Tempest. He's already called and talked to me. I don't appreciate the two of you making business behind my back."

"I didn't—"

"STOP lying to me, woman. Something is terribly wrong, Tempest. How is it that my wife can do business with Craig Dennison, a man who is in trouble, without me knowing about it? On top of that, both Craig and a local detective called me, looking for you today." She dropped her head. "Un-un . . . I need eye contact. Talk to me, Tempest. What check is Craig talking about that's already cleared, and how much was it for?"

"Honey, Craig hired me to do something for him in regard to that rape case, but he didn't want anyone else to know about it."

"I'm not just 'anyone else.' I'm your husband. I called the bank. There's nothing abnormal in our account. That could mean one of two things: this thing you're doing for Craig is personal and not business at all, or you're stealing from me because Bynum Bonding belongs to both of us. Explain. I'm listening."

Tempest looked at Faith, who was pouring ice tea into glasses. "Faith, would you mind excusing us," she asked.

I slammed my fist on the table. "Faith doesn't have to go anywhere. You're going to answer my questions, and I mean now," I yelled.

"No," she screamed back. "This matter is between you and me. I don't care to discuss anything in front of her."

"I don't give a damn about you being uncomfortable right now. I've been uncomfortable ever since I got those calls this morning."

"You should've called me."

"No. I did right. I wanted to study your eyes and body language. It's clear to me you're lying and withholding information, Tempest. Just when I thought we could start over, this mess pops up with you. I can't trust you worth a damn."

I got up from the table. "I suggest you go upstairs to my nightstand and retrieve Detective Williams's number."

"I will, but I wanted to sit and have a nice meal with you first, honey. Please don't walk away."

I turned to her, making sure she understood the look on my face to be that of disgust. "I would, but now that you're here, I've suddenly lost my appetite." I turned to Faith. "If you don't mind, Faith, wrap my dinner up. Hopefully I'll feel like eating it later."

I went upstairs to our bedroom and lay across the bed. All sorts of thoughts went through my mind. *What if Tempest is the woman Craig is accused of raping?* I also thought about how dumbfounded Tempest seemed when Craig came to visit. She wasn't interested in sticking around at all. I needed to get to the bottom of things. My wife was being sneakier than usual, and it had to be for devious reasons.

Despite having said she wanted to watch a DVD movie with me, Tempest made certain not to set foot into our bedroom until she was sure I had gone to bed. Her entrance woke me. I peeked at the clock. It was eleven-thirty. She got out of her clothes, showered then joined me in bed. Although the room was dark, she must've sensed I wasn't asleep because she whispered my name.

"Ace," she said softly.

I answered with my back to her. "What?"

She no longer whispered. "I love you, honey." Her comment was sweet, but I wasn't feeling it. I remained silent as she continued. "I really have changed. Please don't let what happened today determine the future of our marriage."

I flipped on my back and stared at the ceiling. "What happened today, Tempest? I still don't know anything."

"Honey, I told you. Craig paid me to do some investigative type work for him. I deposited the money in my personal account because Bynum Bonding doesn't do private investigations."

"And neither do you, Tempest."

"I told him that, but he insisted. The price was right, so I took him up on his offer. You're right. I'm not a private investigator, so it took me much longer than Craig had anticipated."

"Fourteen years, and you've still got a lot to learn about being my wife."

"I'm never too old to learn, honey."

"Yeah, and neither am I. It took you all day to come up with excuses, huh?"

"Please, honey, stop fussing. I knew you were angry. I just wanted to give you some space. That's all."

She placed her arm across me and began rubbing my stomach. Her hand slowly made its way to my midsection. I didn't tell her to stop right away because her touch actually felt nice. As soon as she got the rise out of me she wanted, she proceeded to straddle me. I didn't want her, so I broke the silence.

"No, Tempest," I said, pushing her off me.

"No?"

"My mind ain't right for that."

"You know . . . you've been saying that a lot lately, but at least one of your heads is thinking about it—the one that counts, might I add."

"Just leave me alone," I said, turning my back on her.

She huffed and turned over, pulling most of the cover with her. "I'm getting really sick of this, Ace. Real tired."

I gave her no response. I lay there for a little over an hour, thinking about our marriage—what it use to be, and what no longer was. Tempest wasn't going to change her lying, conniving ways. I didn't love her like I use to, so I really needed to decide what I wanted to do.

I began to think about Faith and the last time I made love to her. It was magical. I became aroused just thinking about her. I slinked out of bed and tiptoed to the bedroom door, making sure not to wake Tempest. I managed to open and close the door behind with ease. Once downstairs, I headed to Faith's bedroom. Her door was closed, and I prayed it wasn't locked. I turned the knob and discovered it wasn't.

Faith didn't hear me enter. She lay asleep in one of the Victoria's Secret nightgowns I'd bought her. When I climbed into bed with her, she was startled.

"Ace," she whispered loudly. "What are you doing?"

"Sshh," I told her. I grabbed her hand and placed it between my legs. "Sshh," I said again.

I raised her gown and caressed her thigh, making my way between her legs. She let out a soft moan then spread her legs wide. I pulled down my pajama pants then climbed on top of her. She let out more sensual sighs.

"Oh Ace," she said. "Where's Tempest?"

"Asleep," I answered, kissing her ear.

"Please stop. You're going to get us in so much trouble," she whispered.

"Grind with me," I said, stroking her.

"Oooo, Ace. You've gotta stop."

"Grind with me, baby. Release with me, and then I'll stop."

"Okaaaayyy," she moaned.

Less than a minute later, we made harmonious cries of pleasure simultaneously. I didn't want to leave her bed. In fact, I made up my mind that I wouldn't until I got good and ready.

Faith

19

There were many times in my life when I had to wonder if I was just plum crazy, including the times I'd gone back to my ex-husband after he'd beat me half to death. The night I made love to Ace after he sneaked into my room while his wife was lying upstairs asleep was another time I could add to my insanity list. I felt I really loved Ace—that or either I was just mentally unstable.

I wanted Ace to leave my bed because I knew we were wrong. But when he refused, I didn't immediately argue because another part of me wanted him there. I loved holding him after sex. He knew how to make me feel wanted. We were in straight violation. Tempest had every right to wake up and bash both our heads in if we were caught. However, I didn't fear her wrath—not then. Ace's warm body next to mine felt so surreal. My mouth eventually said leave my room, but my heart longed for him to stay forever. We had a make-believe argument about the fact he needed to leave.

"Ace, I've enjoyed you, but you know you've got to get back into bed with Tempest before she wakes up," I whispered.

"She's not going to wake up."

"How do you know?"

"I just know. Even if she did, she couldn't care less about me missing from our bed."

"Ace, I hope you're right, but I still say we've got to do better. I love having you next to me, but doing this while Tempest is in the house isn't safe."

"I know, but I just had to have you. I got an arousal, and I wanted to share it with you."

I sighed. "Ace, you've got to give her a little more respect than this. So do I. I'm being just as disrespectful as you, but I'm not the one sneaking into your bed at night to entice you. Please . . . we've got to do better than this."

"I know. And you're right. I've lost respect for her. I'm not proud of how I feel, but she's got to know she has contributed to my feelings."

"Let's not make excuses. Let's just make an effort to do better. Okay?"

"Okay."

Five more minutes went by and Ace still hadn't left my bed. He kept saying he was going, but I couldn't get him to budge. He actually lay there snoring for a minute. I shook him, waking him.

"Oh, no, Ace. This is insane. You've got to get out of here."

"Alright, alright," he said, rising then sitting on the side of the bed. "You sure you don't want to try one more quickie?"

I had to giggle. He was being funny. "Ace, quit trippin' and get out of here."

He giggled too. "A'ight . . . it's your loss."

"I rather accept a loss than to be found dead by daylight. You know Tempest would kill us, don't you?"

"Well, she'd be angry—that's for sure, but I've never known her to be violent."

"I think finding her husband in my bed would take her over the edge, don't you think?"

He shrugged. "Maybe. I get your point. I'm leaving."

Then, the worse thing that could happen that night happened. Tempest called out to Ace from down the hall.

"Ace," she called. "Ace, where are you?"

Both our eyes looked like flashlights in the dark. If Ace felt anything like me, he was sick. I wished I could be like Jeannie from I Dream of Jeannie and just blink myself into another day and time. Judging by Tempest's voice, she was just down the hall and rapidly coming near. There was no escaping for Ace. He jumped off the bed then grabbed his pajamas.

"Where're you going?" I asked.

He shrugged, throwing on his PJ's. "I can't go any-where."

I'd never seen Ace do anything so fast. He was dressed in no time. He stood behind the door then reached to lock it, but just then, Tempest opened my door. I imagined Ace was pressed against the door and the wall. I sat halfway up in bed. She stood, staring with a strange, twisted face. I tried to make my voice sound as if I'd just woken up as I address her.

"What's going on, Tempest?"

She didn't answer right away. When she did she said, "Is Ace in here?"

"Excuse me?" I asked, sounding confused.

"You heard me. Ace left our bed about two hours ago. I've checked the kitchen and the other bedrooms. I don't see him anywhere. How about you? Have you seen him?" She had one hand on the door knob and the other on her hip.

I knew I couldn't answer her question with a straight yes or no without sounding shaky, so I took the easiest route around her question. "Tempest, do you realize it's almost two o'clock in the morning?"

"I know exactly what time it is, but how would you know? Didn't I just wake you?"

I was stomped. I couldn't answer her. Instead of Tempest coming back with another response, she made her way into my room. I was half naked under my covers, and I began shaking like a leaf on a tree. She walked around to the other side of my bed then fell to her knees to look under the bed. I pretended to be dumbfounded.

"Tempest, have you lost your mind? How dare you barge in here and look under my bed. What are you thinking?"

She rose and pounded her fist on my mattress. "I'm thinking you're a sneaky bitch—that's what I'm thinking. You and Ace both are playing me for a fool, but I know better."

"Tempest, you're going way too far."

She stood then headed toward my bathroom. "Oh yeah. Well, I'll see about that. I haven't found Ace anywhere else in this house. He has to be in here."

I did my best to alert Ace of her movements. "Tempest, please come out of my bathroom, and don't go into the closet in there. I haven't cleaned it up yet."

Ace flew from behind the bedroom door then out of my room. I heard the rings on my shower curtain slide back, and then I could hear Tempest opening the bathroom closet door. My heart raced like it was on a mission to win a blood pumping marathon.

Tempest turned off the light in my bathroom before exiting. She stood at the foot of my bed with a look of repulsion. I couldn't say anything. I knew she sensed something—probably the guilt that reeked from my pores. I made up my mind to remain silent for as long as she would.

After about a minute, we heard two beeps, signaling someone had opened a door to the house. Tempest darted into the hall. I jumped up and grabbed my robe off the chair. I could hear yelling and screaming in the hallway. By the time I made it out there, Ace and Tempest had made it to the foot of the stairs and stopped. Their voices traveled down the hall to where I stood just outside my room, listening.

"I'm not stupid, Ace," she screamed.

"Tempest, get out of my way. I told you I was sitting on the back patio. You might've looked everywhere, but you didn't come out there, did you?"

"It's two in the morning," she ranted. "Why on earth would I think to look for you on the patio? And look how long you've been gone from our bed."

"And? What? We got rules now that say I have to stay in bed once I get in?" It was quiet for a minute. "Tempest, you're being pathetic. I hope you know that. Now, let's take this upstairs before we wake up Faith."

"I'm gon' let you keep thinking I'm stupid, Ace. You and that thing down the hall."

"What did you say?"

"You heard me. That *thing* . . . that *it* . . . down that hall there just tried to make me believe I'm a dimwit and out of my mind, but y'all ain't seen crazy yet. Keep doing me like this, Ace, and I'm gon' show you just how extreme I can be."

They were silent for a few moments. I didn't hear any movements so I knew they hadn't gone upstairs. Then I heard sniffling. Ace confirmed what I had figured.

"Are you crying?" he asked.

"Yeah," she snapped.

"Why? What's wrong with you, Tempest?"

"I don't deserve this, Ace. I haven't been the best wife in the world, but still, I don't deserve this."

"Deserve what? I told you—"

"Stop," she interrupted. "Just stop. Nothing you can say will make me believe differently. You want Faith, and I don't have the slightest idea why."

"Faith and I are friends. Tempest you made it possible."

"I know. You don't have to rub it in my face. I regret the day I ever let her step foot in here. I did this to us. You happy now? I admit it: I brought another woman into my home so she could have her way with my husband."

Ace's voice had become meek. "Tempest, we can't get back what we had overnight. Things between us didn't become messed up that quickly, so why do you expect a turnaround already. It's obvious you can't trust me, nor can I trust you."

"But I can't even trust you in our own home," she yelled.

"That's because you choose not to. You're making assumptions. You haven't seen me doing anything."

"And you've assumed because I didn't tell you about my work with Craig that I'm sleeping with him."

"Then what do we do now? We can file for divorce and move on."

"You'd like that, wouldn't you? You'd love to take what we built and share it with that mud duck, but that'll happen over my dead body . . . and I mean that."

I heard them stomping up the stairs, still arguing. Tempest made the comment 'over her dead body.' Well, I knew she really meant over *my* dead body. I knew if I didn't get out of that woman's house, I would be in grave danger. Her tone and her body language while she was in my room made me well aware of that. I didn't want to break Ace's heart, much less my own, but it was time for me to leave. End of discussion.

Tempest

20

A ce didn't know I felt him get out of bed. I pretended to be asleep because I really didn't have anything to say to him. I was taken totally by surprise when he left our bedroom. I dreaded another argument, so I didn't go behind him right away. He had gone to bed without eating, so I figured he'd probably gone downstairs to get the plate Faith left for him. When Ace didn't return to bed until nearly two hours later, I got a sick sense he did a little more than feed his stomach. I couldn't keep my cool. When I got downstairs and went to the refrigerator, I noticed the plate still there, covered up. I was pissed. I didn't catch Faith and Ace red-handed, but my instincts told me they were being closer than close and in my own home.

I didn't sleep well after having to look for Ace in the middle of the night. I got out of bed at five A.M. My mind was all over the place. I couldn't prove Ace and Faith were having an affair, but I knew I couldn't make it easy for them just in case. I raked my brain for things I could do to get her out of my house.

The longer I stayed at home, the angrier I became. I decided to leave for work early. Faith came into the kitchen just as I was about to leave.

"Good morning, Tempest," she said.

I turned and looked her up and down. I shook my head. "You know . . . you've got to be stuck on stupid not to understand I don't like you, Faith."

"I realize that, Tempest, but what am I supposed to do? Not speak?"

"No, leave," I yelled. "You ever thought about that? I wouldn't want to live around someone who doesn't like me."

"I tried to leave, but Ace asked me to stay."

"Listen. Ace isn't the only one who runs things around here. I'm the woman of the house, and I'm saying you've got to go. Now, I realize most landlords give people a thirty-day eviction notice before throwing their things out, so I'm willing to do that. One month is ample time for you to find another job assignment and be out of my house. Otherwise, you'll find your shit on the curb, minus the things my husband paid for. Do I make myself clear?"

I didn't know Faith could make an evil face until then. "Crystal clear," she answered.

"Good. I'm going to pour myself a cup of coffee. Would you like one?"

Rather than answer me, she just gawked. Ace came into the kitchen to find us having a staring match. "What's going on?" he asked.

"Nothing, honey," I stated. "Faith and I were just discussing that she will be moving out soon."

He gave Faith a perplexed look. She responded before he could say anything. "It's for the best, Ace. Tempest is not happy with me here, and I don't want to be the cause of friction in your marriage."

He answered her. "If you're leaving because Tempest said you've got to go, there's going to be more than just friction in our marriage." He turned to me. "What did you say to her, Tempest?"

I was infuriated. "Hell yeah . . . I told her to leave. She's no longer welcomed in this house by me. I hired her, and now I'm firing her."

Ace was enraged as well. "Damnit, if Faith goes, I go. Now if you don't believe me, try me."

I decided not to have that cup of coffee after all. I grabbed my things then headed for the door. "Whatever, Ace."

I left them, standing to wonder what else was on my mind. I couldn't leave the house fast enough. I still had to deal with Craig, and he was about to get a piece of my mind like never before. Had it not been for him calling Ace, my husband and I would be on the path of recovery. About halfway to my place of business, I called Craig.

"It's about damn time you dialed my number," Craig said upon answering the phone.

"You know what. You're testing me right now," I said to him. "I keep trying to be a better person, but you and Ace won't let me."

"I ain't got shit to do with what Ace won't let you do."

"Oh, but you do. See when you called him, you knew Ace would wonder why you and I had dealings. You wanted to cause hostility in my home."

"And? Look at all the trouble you've caused in my life. I done paid your ass, so why the hell you ain't covered your end of the bargain?"

"Trick, if you had waited until I could call you back, you would've known that it's all been taken care of."

"Then why are these people still harassing me? I'm still being questioned and investigated."

"Because this stupid Detective Williams guy in Memphis doesn't want me to drop everything. He's case happy—talking about he's convinced I'm covering for you."

"If you told him I didn't rape you that's all should matter."

"I've told him and so many others the same thing. They have no case."

"Then my worries are over, huh?"

"With the authorities, yes."

"What's that supposed to mean?"

"Because of your idiocy with calling my husband, my house isn't happy. I'll be damned if all will be gleeful on your end while my home is a wreck."

He began to yell. "Tempest, don't start your little petty games."

"This ain't games, baby. It's war," I said before hanging up on him.

I turned the ringer off because I was sure he'd try calling me back. I made it to the office before any of the guys. My desk phone was ringing the minute I stepped foot into the door. I noticed it was Lynette calling, so I answered.

"Hey, girl. If you're tryna catch your man, he's not here yet," I said just after picking up.

"Hey Tempest. I'm not looking for Lem. I tried calling your cell, but you didn't answer."

"Girl, I had to turn the ringer off. You're not going to believe what that Craig Dennison did."

"What'd he do?"

"Can you believe he called Ace?"

She gasped. "Please tell me he didn't spill the beans."

"No. At least I don't think so. Ace would've kicked my ass out of the house if he had."

"So what did Craig call to tell him?"

"It's a long story. We'll have to be sitting over drinks to talk about this one."

"I'm game. I've got more drama of my own. I could use a drink."

"You wanna meet me after you get off work?"

"I'm not at work today. I'm stressed. I just couldn't make it."

"I'm sorry to hear that. Well, as soon as the receptionist and a couple of the guys show up, I can come to you if you'd like."

"Let me ask you something, Tempest."

"Go ahead."

"Did you know Lem has an office outside of the one at your company?"

"Say what? He has his own company?"

"No. He's still operating under your company, but apparently he's rented an office space separate from Bynum."

"Of course I didn't know that. How'd you find this out?"

"Well, I went snooping around our house after locking him out upon my return from Birmingham."

"Oh Birmingham. That's something else you've got to share with me. Go on."

"There's nothing to tell except that I thought I couldn't lay with Parnell, but then I called Lem and his slut answered the phone, so I tried to make Parnell take me, but he wouldn't."

"Wait a minute. You said that kind of fast. Parnell changed his mind?"

"Yes. He sat me down and explained why he couldn't take advantage of me. He told me he loved me, and he'd be my friend as long as I needed him, but we didn't have sex one time. I drove back to Memphis on Saturday."

"Damn. Sorry to hear that." I chuckled. "Now get back to this office thing."

"Anyway, I went snooping and found paperwork—a lease of some kind for office space. I want to go there today and see what's there."

"Do you have keys?"

"Lem keeps spare keys all on one key holder here at the house. I'll play around with them until I come up with the right one."

"Hold on, girl. I'll go with you. Where's the place located?"

"Apparently it's in West Memphis. I know Lem called and told you he was bounty hunting yesterday. Well, he was, but that's because he didn't have work attire once I locked him out. I balled up most of his stuff into garbage bags on yesterday and set them outside, so he may be in this morning. Call me if he shows up, and then you can meet me."

"Okay. I can't wait to see this place."

"You and me both. I'm going to let you go for now. I've got some more rummaging to do. I'm snooping because I'm trying to build a case for my divorce. It's over, Tempest. I'm past tired."

"Hey. You know I've got your back on whatever you decide. See you soon, girl."

When we hung up, I called Detective Williams to reiterate I was no longer interested in talking with him, and that the guy who raped me was not Craig Dennison. He had a tough time accepting my response, speaking on the DNA evidence. I wasn't giving in to what he wanted me to say. I confessed to an affair with Craig, but again stated he was not the man who had raped me. I determined by his tone that Detective Williams was not happy with me. I didn't care. I had other ways I planned to make Craig suffer. I chastised the detective for calling my home when I had given him distinct instructions not to. He reluctantly agreed to drop the case and not to bother me again.

Lemont and Rick walked in the door shortly after I got off the phone. "What's up guys?" I asked.

"Not much," Lemont said. "Getting ready to get some paperwork done and get over here to this jailhouse."

"Besides going to the jailhouse, will you guys be around here pretty much today? I need to run out for a while."

"I know I will," Lemont said.

"Me, too," Rick answered. "I've gotta take care of some things for Milton. He won't be in again today."

"How's his wife doing? Have you heard anything," I asked.

"Yeah, we went over to his place last night," Lemont answered. "He's not expecting her to make it through the month."

"Oh no. This was so sudden, too," I said.

"Milton says she's been sick a year, but kept it from him," Rick stated.

I shook my head. "My heart goes out to them both." I picked up my purse and keys. "I'm going to go ahead and get out of here so I can come on back. You guys hold the fort down, a'ight?"

"We've got it," Lemont said.

I jumped in my car then called Lynette once I was out of viewing distance of the office. She gave me directions to Lemont's other office, and I met her there. She was sitting in her car, waiting for me once I pulled up. The office space was located in a small business strip. We got out of our cars simultaneously.

"Hey girl," I said. "Are you nervous?"

She shook her head as she began trying keys. "Not nervous—anxious."

"I just hope he doesn't have an alarm on this place."

"Shoot. I hadn't thought about that," she said, pausing with a key in the door.

"Well, I don't see any security warning signs or stickers, so keep going. Try another key."

The very next key Lynette tried was the correct one. She looked at me with wide eyes. "It's on now," she said. She began to push the door open.

"Wait. Open it slowly."

"Why? If there's an alarm, it's gonna go off whether I open the door fast or slow."

She had a point. "You're right. Let's go in."

179

After stepping inside, we discovered there wasn't an alarm. Lynette found the light switch. The office space appeared to be sixteen by eighteen with a small storage closet and one bathroom. Lemont hadn't done much decorating and not many files were present. Lynette sat at the desk then turned on the computer while I opened a desk drawer and began searching it. I stumbled across something I never would have thought in a million years to find.

"Lynette," I said, holding a piece of paper before my eyes.

"Huh?" she answered. I looked up and noticed she was clicking through his document files on the computer.

"Lynette, sweetie, you might want to postpone looking at that, and view what I have in my hands."

She looked at me as though she was afraid. "What is it?"

"Who is Tekeysia Houston?" I asked.

"Tekeysia is the name of Lem's girlfriend."

"Well, apparently she left something here for you to find or else Lem forgot he left this here."

She snatched the paper from my hands and read it. "Oh no . . . oh my God . . . oh no," she cried. "See . . . see this is the reason I told him I needed to be tested. I knew she was nasty. Syphilis," she screamed. "That's the closest thing out there to HIV and AIDS."

Tears came from each corner of Lynette's eyes. "Calm down, Lynette. I think you're okay. You would've known if you were infected with Syphilis."

"I can't stand him, Tempest. I really can't stand him."

She placed her head down on the desk and continued to cry. I told her to take her time while I finished searching the office for her. I made copies of everything and packed the originals, too. By the time we left there, we'd confiscated pictures of Lem and his mistress along with her child at Chuck E. Cheese's, the park, and the zoo. We also found a video tape in which we were certain contained more incriminating evidence of

Lemont's infidelity, so we took it to Tracey's house for viewing. Tracey tried to talk us out of it.

"Just put the damn video in, Tracey," I fussed. "Ain't nobody asked for your opinion."

"Well, I'm at my house where I know my opinion counts," she responded. She turned to Lynette. "Girl, you're already broken. You say you've made up your mind you're going to leave no matter what. Why pour salt on an open wound?"

"I want to know, Tracey," Lynette responded. "I just gotta see how little this man respected me."

"I don't agree with what you're doing, but if you want me to put it on, I will," Tracey said.

"I do," Lynette answered.

Lynette saw what she already knew only three seconds after the video began to play. The video was so awful, I had to jump on Tracey's side and demand to turn it off. I couldn't believe Lemont would film such lewd sexual acts with his hussie. Lynette balled up on Tracey's couch and cried like a baby. I hated to see my friend so hurt. I wanted to go back to my office and slap the taste out Lemont's mouth.

We stayed over to Tracey's house for a few hours, having a girlfriends chat. Lynette finally stopped crying, but her hurt had turned to anger. Tracey spent the better part of our time together trying to convince Lynette to forget about what she wanted to do to Lemont and put more focus on her health. She needed to be tested immediately.

Lynette's situation made me wonder what was going on at my home. I figured I better do a drop by at my house, just to check in.

"Ladies, I need to go," I told them.

"You've got to get back to the office, right?" Tracey asked.

"No. Both of your husbands are there taking care of things. I need to get to my own home to see what's going on."

"What do you mean?"

I picked up my purse and all of the originals for Lynette's case. "Lynette, I have the original paperwork and the video with me for safe keeping. Bring Tracey up to speed for me. I've got to go. I just really feel like I need to go home right now."

"Be careful, Tempest," Tracey said.

"I will."

Before heading home, I called the house. No one answered. I dialed once I was on the road, and no one answered again. My heart began to pound. I tried listening to the radio, but that didn't distract me. All I could think about was Faith and my husband in some compromising position, which made my foot heavy on the gas pedal. Thank goodness I wasn't spotted by police.

As I pulled up to my house, I notice Ace's Lexus wasn't in the garage. I went inside the house and called out to Ace as I searched for him. He nor Faith were there. I called his cell.

"Hello," he answered.

"Honey, where are you?" I asked.

"Why?"

I bit my bottom lip then took a deep breath before answering. "Because I'm concerned, honey. I came home to see you, but you aren't here."

"I'm in good hands."

"Ace, your sarcasm is unwarranted. I'm genuinely concerned, and you want to—"

"Who's being sarcastic? You? Sorry you feel that way."

"Yeah. Okay. Well, will you be home soon?"

"I doubt it. Why?"

"'Cause we need to talk."

"Tempest, I have nothing else to say about you and Craig and Detective Williams. You're not going to be truthful with me anyway, so I'm not going to press you."

"Well we don't have to talk about that. Just come home."

"I'll be there when I get there. Right now, Faith and I are just out enjoying the sunshine. See you later."

He hung up on me, pissing me off beyond belief. Ace wanted to play hard with me. He should've known no one is better at playing around than me. My gut told me he was banging that ugly duckling, and it was time to set out to get my proof. If he thought he was going to divorce me and have his way, he had another thing coming.

Lynette

21

dirty dog—that's what Lemont Rapid equaled to me. I left Tracey's house on a mission. I made an emergency appointment with my doctor, and then I pulled over to Sonic's and made a much needed phone call, blocking my number so there would be no hesitation for the other party.

"Tekeysia, this is Lynette Rapid—Lemont's wife. We need to talk. Is this a good time for you?"

She wasn't saying anything, but I knew she was there. I could hear a small child singing and the television playing in the background. I gave her a moment to think about it. She finally responded.

"Well, I was about to feed my child, but I have a few minutes," she answered.

"Okay. This will only take a few minutes. I just want to ask if you truly love my husband."

Tekeysia seemed reluctant to answer. She sighed heavily then said, "I do. He's been good to me and my son."

"Your son is only a year old. Am I correct?"

"Lynette, I know what you're thinking, but he's not Lemont's child."

"Then you two will have no trouble submitting to a DNA test, correct?"

She sighed again. "I will, but you're wasting your money and your time. This is not his child."

"Well, from my understanding, you've been sleeping with Lemont for well over two years. I've found paperwork proving he's included you and your son on our medical insurance, pretending you're employed by him. He's paying for your car and the insurance, your cell phone bill, the two of you have a bank account together in Forrest City, and those are just all the things I can prove. God only knows what else he's spending our income on to support you."

"I can't deny he's very good to me."

"But are you good to him? I also found papers proving you've been tested for Syphilis."

She gasped. "Where did you find that? I gave that to Lemont to prove I'm negative. Didn't you read the results?"

"I read them, but the fact that you even had to be tested tells me that you were unsure."

"No. Lemont was unsure. He saw a hair bump on me and made me get tested."

"Well, Tekeysia, if your son is not my husband's, then you have slept with at least one other man."

She was silent for a moment. "True." We both held the phone briefly then Tekeysia said, "I've got to feed my son. What can I do for you, Lynette?"

"Why don't you leave my husband alone? If your son is not his, you shouldn't have any problem letting him go on with his family."

I heard many sighs from Tekeysia before she finally responded. "I'll try, but I can't promise you anything. I'm sorry, Lynette, but I love Lemont, and I know he loves me."

"Hmm. Is that right? Then you leave me no other choice. He's all yours now. I'm on my way to my attorney's office with this video tape and other evidence."

"Lynette, don't do that. You've got Lemont's heart, too. You don't have to destroy your family."

"My family's already destroyed, but I didn't do it. You and Lemont did. When I married him, it was because I thought I'd only have to share his heart with God. I'll never knowingly share his heart with you and no other woman. I have more self-respect than that."

"Don't hurt him like that, Lynette?"

"Tekeysia, you're young, and you have a lot to learn. I just hope you don't get to be as old as me, and be as dumb as I have. Take care of your child. Bye."

I hung up on her then drove home. I called Lem on the way and asked him to meet me there. He agreed. When I got home I went to our bedroom and spread all the evidence I had on him across the bed. The only thing that was missing was the video tape. I knew he thought he was coming home to mediate, but he was in for a rude awakening. I went downstairs when I heard the doorbell.

I opened the door to let him in. "Hi," I said, studying his face to see if his mistress had called him. I couldn't tell.

"Hi," he answered. "Thanks for inviting me home."

I closed the door behind him. "This isn't home for you anymore. However, I do have a surprise for you upstairs on the bed."

He gave me a strange look. "Do I need to go up there now?"

"You do if you want to see the surprise." I smiled.

He led the way. He slowly pushed the bedroom door open, seemingly afraid of what he'd find. I had to shove him into the bedroom. He walked over to the bed and stared at the paperwork. I picked up a piece and handed it to him.

"Don't be scared," I told him. "All of this belongs to you."

He stared at the sheet I'd given him then looked at me. "Lynette—"

"Oh, before you say anything, just let me say that I have the originals in safe keeping. Everything you see here will be in my attorney's office by morning, including one very sexually incriminating video tape of you and your whore."

I'd never seen Lemont so speechless. He sat on the bed then cried. I was unmoved. I stood over him with my arms folded, waiting for him to speak. I knew he couldn't shed such massive amount of tears without submitting a plea for mercy. It didn't take him long either.

"I'm sorry, Lynette. I can let her go. My family is too important to me."

"Is that right? Hmm. Three years too late, Lem."

"Lynette, please don't be so cold. You know a divorce would hurt Vicki. Don't do this to our family."

"You sound like your little girlfriend," I fussed. He looked at me as if he didn't know what I was talking about. "Oh, she didn't call you yet? I spoke with her today. Although she says she can't let you go, she also says there's no need for me to ruin my family. Y'all sound like some simple-minded fools. According to the Word, I don't have to accept your infidelity."

"I'm going to stop. Can't you just forgive me?"

"Forgive?" I placed my finger on my temple and looked up at the ceiling. "Hmm . . . let me see." I looked back at him. "Yes. I can forgive you, but that doesn't mean I have to remain married to you. Sorry."

"What can I do? You want me to take the blood test for that baby? He's not mine, Lynette."

"I'm sure my attorneys and divorce court will order a paternity test. I'm not worried about that. I'll find out if the kid is yours one way or another."

"Lynette, please," he cried.

His cell phone began to ring. "It's her, isn't it?" I asked as he glanced at the caller ID.

He looked at me with wet, sad eyes. "I'm not going to answer. I'm done with her."

"When? As of this minute? Puhleeze, Lem. Answer her. There's nothing else to hide, right?" He shook his head. "Then answer the girl."

He opened the flip. "Hello," he said. I couldn't hear what Tekeysia was saying, but Lem began to plead with her. "Tekeysia, Lynette is talking divorce. We've got to get that paternity test done."

I spoke over him. "Paternity test or not, I'm out, Lem. I've already told her. The two of you can have each other. I'm making sure of it, but not before I take you to the cleaners."

More tears fell, and then he removed the phone from his ear. I heard Tekeysia rambling something, but I couldn't determine what she was saying before he closed the flip on the phone.

"Why'd you hang up on her?" I asked.

"She isn't talking about anything."

"Why not? She told me she loved you. I'm sure she's hurting, too. I suggest you go to her because I'm fine. I don't need you in my face right now."

Lem kept crying. He slid off the bed to the floor. I never thought I wouldn't be able to stand the sight of him. I picked up my cell phone and texted Tekeysia. IF U REALLY LUV HIM AS MUCH AS U SAY, THEN COME CONSOLE HIM. HE'S GETTING ON MY NERVES WIT ALL HIS WHINING! I found it funny that she didn't respond.

"I texted the little girl and told her to come console you, but she didn't respond." He remained silent. "I'm ready to be alone now, Lem. Would you please leave?"

"I can't," he answered.

"Sure you can. All I have to do is call Tempest and ask her if she's got a bond for you to do. You'll run out of here then. History has proven that. Job, mistress, friends and everything else has always come before Vicki and me." He still didn't budge. "Lem, get up. Go . . . I need some time to myself."

He picked himself up then walked out peacefully. It felt great having the upper hand for once. My life was about to change drastically, but with the kind of God I served, I knew I could begin to celebrate a new beginning.

Ace

22

ilton Greene, one of the bonding company's associates, lost his wife only two weeks after learning she was terminally ill with cancer. She'd been sick a long time, but kept it from him until nearly the end. Her funeral was on a Tuesday during the middle of the day, so Tempest and I made the decision to close the bonding company so everyone could attend. Although both Lemont and I were having marital problems, we both attended the service with our wives. Tracey and Rick were there, also.

The funeral was sad. Milton cried the whole time. His three children were all over eighteen and seemed to be taking their mother's death well. I imagined she must've told her children early on but sensed Milton would have a tougher time accepting her illness. Seeing him so broken affected everyone around. Tempest clang to me, laying her head on my shoulder for most of the funeral. She kept whispering, "Poor Milton." Any other time I might've felt awkward with her choosing to be so close to me, but truth be told, everyone attending needed someone to lean on.

Thank goodness the funeral wasn't a long one. It began at noon, but we were all heading out of the church half an hour later. I prayed the burial ceremony would be just as brief if not shorter. Tempest and I held a bit of a conversation on the ride to the burial.

"I feel so sorry for Milton and those kids," Tempest said. "Ace, I can't imagine life without you."

I glanced over at her as she continued to drive. "Tempest, I think you may be more so in love with the years we've shared than anything."

"How can you say that?"

"Because it's true."

"That's not true. I found out that you're always telling people I don't care for you and that I'm money hungry. You need to check yourself. I'm still with you because I love you."

I shook my head. "Then perhaps you should redefine the meaning. True love keeps a marriage sacred."

"Say what? Come on out with it, Ace. What are you saying? That I've messed around on you?"

"You said it. I didn't."

"I'm not saying a damn thing," she fussed. "I just asked a question."

"Yeah. I think you have."

"Oh, you're incredible."

"No, you are, Tempest. When I really think about it, I realize you've been fooling me for years—as far back as college even."

"So, now we're going to dig up the past. Okay. What about the past?"

"People use to try to tell me you and Craig Dennison were cheating behind my back, but I wouldn't listen. I kept saying, 'not my girl. She wouldn't do that to me.' I wasn't so sure about Craig, but I just knew you wouldn't deceive me."

191

"Ace, you knew everyone who came to you with mess like that were jealous of our relationship. You should know where my heart was then and now. Who did I marry?"

"Something just tells me the recent incident with Craig Dennison wasn't happenstance. There's more the two of you aren't sharing with me."

"Here we go again. I thought we could leave Craig's name out of our mouths. I see you can't."

"I never told you I would."

"Okay, so since you really want to take this conversation there, let me express that I think you're the one who's been unfaithful."

She kept driving as I stared at her. "It doesn't surprise me you'd think that."

"Oh yeah? Why?"

"Besides the fact that I haven't touched you in forever, I know many times the cheater in the marriage does accuse the other."

"So, I'm just making accusations?"

"Yeah. What proof do you have that I've messed around?"

"I don't have proof, and neither do you," she said, pulling into the cemetery. "In fact, this is a sad day for us as well as for some people very close to us. Let's not make things worse with this argument. Let's just bring the discussion to a close right now."

I turned my head then got out of the car. I had a good mind to walk off and leave her, but instead, I held up my arm for her cup it. We walked arm in arm to the burial site.

After the burial, Tempest and I headed to the repast, where we handed Milton and his children a hefty check from our company. Lynette had disappeared from Lemont, but Tracey and Rick were there. We had only been there half an hour when I began to have some small aches, so I walked around the room, looking for Tempest. I spotted her chatting with one of Milton's children.

"Hey, are you okay," she asked just as I walked up holding my arm.

"No. I'm experiencing some discomfort in my arm and lower back. Do you mind if we go now?"

"Of course not. Let's get you home."

We said our goodbyes then went straight to the house. Faith was washing clothes. She stepped out of the laundry room when she heard us enter. Tempest immediately got on her.

"Faith, make a small sandwich for Ace, and bring him a glass of water upstairs. He needs to take his medicine," Tempest said.

"I don't need a sandwich, Faith," I told her. "Just a glass of water will do."

"Honey, you didn't eat much at the repast," Tempest interjected. "You can't take those pills on such a light stomach."

"Then why don't you make me a sandwich? Don't you hear the washing machine in there," I said, pointing. "Faith is busy."

"No, I hadn't paid attention. I'm only concerned with you, honey. I want you well." She turned to Faith. "Never mind the sandwich. I'll fix it."

"Sure," Faith responded then looked at me. "Are you going to be okay, Ace?"

"He's going to be fine," Tempest snapped. "You can go back to doing the laundry." Faith turned to leave, but Tempest had more to say. "And you better not have touched my things. I told you the other day not to bother my clothes."

Faith snapped back. "You couldn't pay me enough to touch your dirty drawers again."

Tempest's blood must've been boiling because I'd never seen her so red. "You wanna-be-good-looking bitch," she screamed. "How dare you be smart with me in my own house? Why don't you just quit? I'll give you the remaining month's salary. Just go, so I won't have to look at your made-for-Halloween face."

"No problem. Pay me today, and I'll go—"

"Ladies, please," I yelled, stopping the madness. "I'm not feeling well. Forget the sandwich, Tempest, and just help me up the stairs." She grabbed my arm. "Faith, will you bring me a glass of water, please?"

"I sure will, Ace," she answered. "I'm getting it now."

My back pained with every lift of my legs to climb the stairs. It took us a good while to get to the top. I went into the room and sat on the bed. Tempest went searching for my medicine in the bathroom.

"Ace, I don't see your prescription," she called from the bathroom. Just as she walked out, she found Faith handing my pills to me with a glass of water. "Oh, so you had his medicine, huh?" Tempest asked.

"We keep them in his nightstand," Faith answered. "Easy access when he's in pain."

Tempest folded her arms and rolled her eyes. "Well, thanks, but I need you to leave so I can undress my husband and get him into bed."

Faith turned to me. "Call me if you need me, Ace."

"He most certainly will NOT," Tempest said.

Faith rolled her eyes then walked out, closing the door behind her. I was much too weak to argue. Tempest peeled off my suit and undershirt then retrieved my pajamas. After helping me put them on, she began to get comfortable.

"I hope you don't mind, Ace, but I think I'm going to join you in bed."

"Tempest, I'm hurting. I don't feel like cuddling and nothing else."

"I won't touch you. I just want to be next to you, honey." I didn't respond. She seemed offended. "You know what. You just saw your friend broken over having lost his wife. If nothing else, you should've learned life is too short. You should at least try to be a little nicer to me. It makes no sense for me to have to keep begging you."

"Lay down, Tempest. I don't care."

Shortly after I slid under the covers, Tempest slid in bed, too. She turned on the television and handed me the remote. I remember watching a few highlights on CNN, and then apparently I drifted because I don't recall much else until Tempest pulled the cover, waking me.

I turned to look at her. She seemed to be sleeping like a baby. Her face was soft and illuminated with beauty. I had to ask myself if she was really my wife laying there. This was the first time in a while that I'd seen suppleness in her face. I began to think perhaps I hadn't been trying hard enough to get over Tempest's old ways. She did seem to want to be a better person. I rolled over then tried to ease out of bed to use the bathroom. Tempest felt me move.

"How're you feeling, honey?" she asked with her eyes closed.

"Great. I feel like that painful episode didn't happen a couple of hours ago."

"That's good." She began kicking the covers off her. "Man, it's hot, isn't it?" She tossed about.

"I'll have Faith adjust the temperature when I get out of the bathroom."

The clock in the bathroom displayed it was only five o'clock in the evening. We hadn't discussed dinner with Faith, so I imagined she was downstairs waiting for instructions. Tempest must've been on the same wavelength because she mentioned dinner as soon as I got out of the bathroom.

She lay on her back with her eyes closed and one arm above her head. "Honey, do you have any idea what you want for dinner?" she asked in a lazy tone.

I couldn't answer her immediately because I was smitten by how sexy she looked as she lay with her gown raised just above her mound. "Um . . . no. I hadn't thought about it," I said, standing with a hard on.

Tempest opened her eyes. I was caught staring. Her eyes served me up. I thought she'd get excited and beg me to make love to her, but she didn't. Instead, her face became long and sad just before she turned her back to me. I went over and slid in bed, facing her. She lay motionless with her eyes closed. I imagined her reluctance to say anything was because she feared rejection. Even with her eyes closed, she looked sad. I slid close and placed my arm around her.

"Tempest, look at me for a minute."

"Yes?" she asked, gazing.

"I'm not going to lie to you. We've grown apart, and the only thing that has kept me from running down to a divorce attorney is our years. We've built some things, including our business, but I've come to realize that one of them isn't love like I had thought."

"So you don't love me, Ace?" she asked. I was silent. "I know you haven't told me in a very long time, but I always tell you."

"I hear you when you say you love me, Tempest, but I've been made to feel it's all conditional. Like the only time you can love me is when I'm doing well, in good strength and health, and when it doesn't appear that someone else might care something for me."

She placed her hand across my waist. "I don't mean to take my frustrations out on you. Two years ago, I understood fine that your disorder wasn't your fault. It's become very difficult for me to cope with because all I can think about is how much of a good time we use to have. We use to travel and shop and do things that kept us longing for each other. When you're not happy, it's hard for me to be happy. I just want you restored to the health you once had."

"You ever thought that perhaps God sees a lesson fit for you in all of this? I may not be delivered until you get the understanding in the situation that's designed for you. I'm thinking the drama that happened with Craig and the detective was for a reason. I know you're saying your involvement with Craig was strictly business and platonic, but you can't exclude me on important decisions or keep secrets and think our marriage will withstand."

She squeezed me then nodded. "Okay. Can we forget about a certain NFL player and move on with our lives. I just want to work on us from this point on."

This was the second time I'd seen sincerity in her eyes—very becoming. I still had a hard on, and her sexiness called me. I placed my hand on her butt and began to massage it. Her eyes widened at first, and then she closed them and began kissing me. I had forgotten what it felt like to kiss my wife and love it. When we'd make love in previous months, Tempest would climb on top to spare my energy because of my illness. When she attempted to climb on top this day, I stopped her. She looked concerned.

"Are we stopping?" she asked.

I lay her on her back. "Not at all," I said, spreading her legs. "I owe you."

She moaned and thanked me as I entered her tunnel. She felt wonderful—no amazing—no, in all honesty, it was indescribable. I missed her. God, I really missed her.

Tempest

23

little more than three weeks after I'd told Faith she needed to get out, she was still there. Her excuse was she didn't want to crowd out her parents' home, so she was waiting for her new apartment to be ready. Although Ace regularly pleaded with her not to leave, Faith wasn't the fool I thought she was. She insisted she was leaving. Perhaps she knew I wasn't playing games with her and feared what would come to her if she didn't.

It was Saturday and many of our clothes needed to be taken to the cleaners. I invited Ace to ride with me, but he refused.

"Faith would be happy to handle the dry cleaning," he said, sitting up in bed. "I'm not feeling well."

I put my hand on my hip. "How many times do I have to tell you I don't want that lady doing anything for me?"

"Well, it won't be much longer before you won't have to worry about her period. She'll be moving soon."

"Not soon enough," I replied, rolling my eyes. I grabbed the laundry then headed for the door. "I'll be back as quick as I can. I'm ready to pick out our new bedroom furniture from that catalog on the dresser."

"I'll be here. Judging by the way I'm feeling, I doubt if I even get out of bed before you get back."

"Okay. See you soon."

Just as I got downstairs, I met Faith in the hallway. She saw me with the bundle of clothes and looked as if she wanted to ask a question but didn't. I had a notion that she was excited to see me going somewhere, so I thought of a way to burst her bubble before leaving.

"Oh, Faith," I called.

"Yes," she said as she turned to me.

"I'm heading to the dry cleaners. I'll be back very soon. I've asked Ace if he needs you for anything until I return, but he says he doesn't want to be bothered."

She tried to mask being crushed, but she couldn't hide it. "Oh, well, that's fine. I won't bother him unless he calls."

"Great. Now listen. This is what you can do while I'm gone. The kitchen floor could really stand a thorough cleaning and wax job. I purchased a new wax product. It's under the sink. Start in the far left corner so you won't be in my way once I return to cook breakfast for my husband." I smiled.

"No problem." Faith returned a fake smile, and it was certainly brief.

I left the house and jumped into my car. I had just backed out of the driveway when my cell rang. When I noticed the Detroit area code, I knew exactly who it was. Craig was calling to confront me about my latest antic against him. I answered the phone with a huge smile on my face.

"Helloooooo," I sang.

"You're a dirty bitch, you know that?" Craig fussed.

"So I've been told, but you really didn't have to remind me. What's wrong with you now?" I asked, pretending to be unaware of why he was calling.

"You know damn well what you did. When is it going to stop, Tempest?"

"When is what going to stop? I haven't the faintest idea what you're talking about?" I could tell my sweet and innocent tone got on Craig's nerves.

"Well, you got the reaction out of my fiancée you were looking for with that false VD paper. I don't know how much you paid that Tekeysia Houston person for that information, or does she even know you have it?"

"Wait . . . wait . . . wait. I'm confused. Craig, you mean to tell me you caught a venereal disease? Do I need to be concerned about my health? You know you did rape me without a condom once. I guess I need to follow up with the Rape Crisis Center to make sure I'm okay, huh?"

"Bitch, you know what you did. Now stop acting dumb. Who is this Tekeysia Houston? If you don't tell me, I swear I'll hire a private investigator to find out."

"I wouldn't care. Spend your money on a private investigator. Wouldn't bother me one bit, Craig." I laughed.

"Okay. You know what? Game over. I need you to figure out a way to ease my fiancée's mind. She needs to know I've never slept with this Tekeysia Houston lady, and that I don't know her. My wedding has been postponed because of your mess, so you're going to fix this, and I mean TODAY."

I laughed so hard, I'm sure I hurt Craig's ear drums. "Stop . . . stop, Craig. You're killing me. I'm trying to drive here."

"Tempest, my life has been nothing but havoc since I decided to hook up with you in Memphis. I regret the day you walked into the Madison and said hello. I've paid you to get out of life, and you're still here."

"You brought me back in," I yelled. "Remember the call you placed to my husband. I told you if there couldn't be harmony in my house, yours would suffer, too."

"I ain't tryna hear any of that right now. Like I said: Game over. Fix this today or else."

"Or else what, Craig? I ain't scared of you getting a private investigator. All I have to do is contact Ms. Houston and convince her she did sleep with you—that in fact it was rape just like you did with me. After all, the situation does pay well. I'm sure once she finds out you'd pay two million dollars, convincing her to go along wouldn't be hard at all."

Craig began to mumble something I couldn't hear. I laughed some more then he responded. "Alright. You can't say I didn't warn you. Be safe, Tempest," he said then hung up.

Be safe, I thought. *What the hell is he talking about? Did he just threaten me?* I started to pull over so I could call him back, but I was so close to the cleaners I decided against it. Faith was still home with my husband, so I tried to avoid giving her and Ace any unnecessary time alone. I pulled into the parking lot at the cleaners then grabbed my clothes and went in. Tara, the regular attendant, was at the counter wearing that God-awful, yellow uniform shirt. She spoke as I struggled with the arm load of clothes.

"How's it going, Mrs. Bynum?"

"Oh, everything is fine, Tara," I said, dumping my load. "I know you haven't seen me in a while, and this big bundle proves it, huh?"

"You're right," she answered, sorting the pieces. "I have to tell you, you might not like the final bill. Mr. Turner went up on the prices since you were last here."

I shrugged. "I'm not worried about price. Besides, it is his place, isn't it? That's what happens when you own something. You operate it like you think it needs to be done. I tried convincing him his staff need better looking uniforms, but he wouldn't listen. Perhaps now that his prices have gone up, he won't mind paying the price to upgrade you all."

Tara laughed. "Maybe, but I doubt it. One of my shirts has a hole in it. I asked Mr. Turner for another one. He offered

201

to have the seamstress sew it up rather than order me a new one."
Tara laughed and shook her head. "Anyway, I just try to give all
our customers a fair warning about the increase."

"Oh well. It is what it is, I guess. I appreciate you letting
me know," I said as I turned to leave. "Everything should be
ready by Monday, right?"

"Yes, ma'am, and you know how I do. If I don't see you
in a week, I'll call to remind you."

"Great. Have a nice weekend, Tara."

I walked out of the cleaners then headed to my BMW,
which was parked only ten feet from the cleaner's door. Two
very large, butch-looking women stood beside the driver door. I
didn't know if they were going to rob me or what. They made me
nervous, but I also knew it was broad daylight and tons of people
were around. I even looked back and saw that Tara was still
standing at the counter. I figured surely the women wouldn't rob
me with a risk of getting caught. Once I reached my car, I begged
their pardon.

"Excuse me, but this is my car, and you're blocking my
entrance," I said as nice as I could.

The women looked at each other then nodded. Before I
knew it, they attacked me. I was literally thrown into my car like
a rag doll. The back of my head hit the car door window,
cracking the glass. The pain was excruciating and everything
became a blur. All I could see was fuzzy images of the ladies
drawing back their fists to persecute me. For the first minute and
a half, my attackers said nothing as they pounded my body,
slapped my face, and kicked me in the stomach and ribs. I
struggled to breathe, and I felt like my life was about to end. My
wind felt like it was just about gone. One of them grabbed my
hair then lifted my head off the ground and whispered in my ear,
"Still don't wanna fix that situation with Craig and his fiancée?"
I couldn't answer if I had wanted to. I was losing consciousness.
I wanted to pass out. I knew more pain was to come, and I didn't

think I could handle any more. I was saved when I heard Tara's voice.

"Let her go," she screamed. "I've called the cops, so just let her go."

"This shit ain't over, bitch," the one gripping my hair said. "Not until you right your wrong." She slammed my head against the concrete.

I heard them running then I heard a car screeching away. I lay helplessly in pain. I felt someone next to me. I could barely open my eyes. Had it not been for that God-awful, yellow shirt of Tara's, I wouldn't have been able to make out who she was. Her voice was tender and concerned.

"Mrs. Bynum, are you okay?" she asked. I couldn't respond. I just wanted to breathe, which it felt like I wasn't. "Mrs. Bynum," she called.

Her voice began to fade. I was losing consciousness, and no matter how I tried, I couldn't fight it. I could only hope I wasn't dying.

Several hours later, I regained consciousness in the hospital. My room seemed to be lined with people. Both Ace and Faith were there, and so were Lynette and Tracey. A doctor and a nurse walked up to me as soon as they noticed I was awake.

"Mrs. Bynum, can you see us?" the doctor asked. I ached so bad, I was afraid to try to talk. "Can you speak, Mrs. Bynum?"

I decided it might hurt less to talk than it would to nod or shake my head. "I think so," I answered with a dry mouth.

"Great," he said. "What about your vision? Any impairment?"

"No. I can see fine."

"Glad to hear it. We've run some tests, including a CAT Scan to make sure everything is okay, but in the meantime, do you feel you need some pain medicine?"

My head was throbbing. "My head hurts," I said.

"Okay. As soon as some of the lab results come back, I'm going to get the nurse to administer some type of pain relief.

There are a couple of detectives who asked me to give them a call as soon as you woke up, so I'm going to get them back out here, if you don't mind."

"Detectives?"

"Yes, a Detective Williams and one other guy were here around the same time you were brought in."

I looked at Ace. My poor husband looked worried and confused. "I don't need to talk to any detectives."

"Mrs. Bynum, I think they only want to get descriptions and such of your attackers," the doctor said. "The attendant at the cleaners and other witnesses say they can't give thorough descriptions. All anyone knows is they were masculine-looking females."

Ace interrupted. "I think my wife might need some time. She just woke up, so let's discuss this later."

The doctor agreed then left. The nurse followed behind. Ace walked over and stood next to me. "Tempest, I don't have a clue who those women were, and I doubt very seriously you're familiar with them. But given they only attacked you rather than rob you, I believe somehow they think they know you."

Before I could say anything, Lynette stepped closer and said, "That's what I was thinking, too. Tempest, I'm thinking we might need to put you in hiding until these people are found."

Tracey didn't let me respond either. "Yeah, Tempest. Did they say anything before they attacked you?"

I thought about my answer for a second then said, "No. They don't know me. They were just a couple of thugged-out women who got mad because I asked them to move out of my way. They were blocking my car door when I went to get in."

Ace huffed. "So you got smart with them rather than asking them politely to move, right?"

"Well, you know how I am," I said.

"Just what I thought," Ace stated. "Tempest, you've really got to learn how to keep your mouth shut sometimes." He positioned himself on the very edge of the bed, facing me. "We don't have the best marriage in the world, but who does? You're still my wife, and I don't like seeing you like this, baby."

Baby? I thought. *He ain't called me baby or any other pet name in months. Maybe something good has come out of me getting my ass kicked after all.* I reached to stroke his face. He took my hand and kissed it. This moment felt as special to me as my wedding day. My husband was there expressing concern, and so were my friends. Oh, and Faith was there, sitting with her arms folded, looking like a sick puppy. I began to wonder if she'd had my husband. Ace recovered my attention when he kissed my hand again. I looked into his eyes and thought, *Who cares if they did? I've done my dirt, too. If they had been intimate, it's over now because I can see it in my man's eyes. Nobody matters more than me right now.*

The doctor returned with a clipboard in his hand. Lynette spoke to him first. "Do you have the pain medicine, doctor?"

"No," he answered shortly. He glanced around the room then spoke to my visitors. "I'm afraid I'm going to have to ask all of you to step out of the room while I speak with Mrs. Bynum."

Ace didn't want to leave. "No, doc," he said. "If you're going to discuss my wife's health, I need to be here."

Nothing about the doctor's face was eased, so I grew alarmed. I wondered if they had found some type of dangerous blood clot or cancer. Milton's wife had just died from cancer, so I began to think the worse. I was going to need my friends' support, so I demanded they stay.

"We're all family," I said to the doctor. "I'd like them to stay. I got the feeling I'm going to need their support."

He looked at the clipboard then nodded. "Okay," he answered. He flipped a few pages then went back to the first page before continuing. "Mrs. Bynum, for the most part you've come out of this ordeal okay—a few cuts, bumps and bruises here and there, but no broken bones so you can be thankful for that."

205

"Yes, that is good news, but don't beat around the bush, doctor. If there's something on those papers I should be concerned about, go ahead and lay it on me. You've got me extremely anxious."

"Alright, Mrs. Bynum. I'm concerned about the kick you received to the stomach."

"What?" I panicked. "Is there a blood clot in my stomach?"

"No, Mrs. Bynum," he answered. "We've discovered something a lot larger than a blood clot." He paused then looked at Ace before returning his attention to me. "There's a baby in that region."

The whole room went silent. My husband jumped from the side of my bed and stood back, staring at me with wide eyes. Lynette broke the silence.

"Oh my goodness," she said. "Doctor, a baby is great news, but will the baby be okay?"

"I don't know," he answered. "I'm going to have to get Mrs. Bynum to ultrasound and determine how far along she is. Judging by the fact that we were able to determine positive results from the urine we got out of the catheter, I'd say she's approximately seven weeks along. Ultrasound is just down the hall. As soon as my staff's loads lighten, I'll get a couple of nurses to roll her down there." He turned to Ace then patted him on his back. "I'll just say congratulations for now, Mr. Bynum."

Ace didn't move. His eyes ripped me to shreds. Tracey tried to walk over to him and congratulate him as well.

"Congratu—" she started.

Ace darted out of the room, and Faith went behind him. Every time I thought our happiness was about to begin, a taste of reality would kick us in the ass. Lynette and Tracey were real confused.

"What's up with that?" Tracey asked, pointing toward the door. "Why the hell did he run out of here like that?"

I sighed heavily. "Because he's no fool, Tracey."

"What does that mean?" she asked, looking back and forth between Lynette and me.

Knowing Tracey would only ridicule me, I reluctantly answered. "He knows the math doesn't add up." Tracey still looked confused. "Seven weeks pregnant . . . umph."

"I've got that part . . . so what?" Tracey asked.

"The one time Ace and I had sex was only three weeks ago."

Tracey yelled. "Get the HELL out of here. Tempest, what the? I mean, who the? I mean . . . tell me you're lying."

I closed my eyes in shame. "I wish I was, Tracey. I swear I wish I was."

Why didn't I take that damn Morning After pill? I thought. All the years of having unconfined sex with my husband, I never got pregnant. One night of meaningless, unprotected and non-consensual sex with a man who cared absolutely nothing for me then I end up pregnant. I lay in that hospital bed and asked God if He hated me or what, and if not me, then what was it about my husband He couldn't stand?

I had no clue where Ace ran off to or if he would be back. Even if he had returned, I had no words for him. I was fresh out of lies. My closest friends stood staring as if they were trying to figure me out. Ever so often, Tracey would shake her head, and Lynette would raise her hands to the ceiling, mumbling something to God. I started to tell her to save her breath because turning me a favor seemed to be the last thing He wanted to do.

So, Craig made good on his threat, unknowingly causing the turnout to go one step further with destroying me and my husband's lives. However, given I was pregnant with Craig's baby, him having the last say would be impossible, and I couldn't wait to inform him.

Lynette

24

Nearly a month after Lem was served divorce papers, he was still popping up outside the house every morning, hoping I'd talk to him before going to work. I'd make him drive the hour to Forest City just to have visitation with Vicki. She was torn about her father and I being separated, but besides talking with her, there wasn't much I could do to help her understand. I didn't share with her how nasty her father was. Lucky for him my health results were all negative. I still loved Lemont. After twenty-two years, I couldn't help it. I had made up my mind that I loved God more. I loved me more. I loved our little girl more.

Our period of separation was the most I'd seen Lemont at church. Before, he'd claim he had to make bonds, especially during Wednesday night Bible Study. It was good he started attending church more, but too bad he wasn't fooling me. I still wanted the divorce.

Parnell and I had been keeping in touch. He texted me regularly during my work day, emailed often, and called to check on me nightly. It was strange wanting and needing someone else's husband so much. My heart softened toward Lem's mistress for that very reason. She was young, and if she was as needy as I was for attention, I understood the power Lem had over her. Lem was attractive, mature and well off. I could imagine he fed her every emotion and gave her all the stability she needed, just as Parnell did for me. I longed to hear from Parnell. I had come to expect to hear from him each day.

Tempest got out of the hospital the day after her attack. I spent half days at work so I could visit her every day. She needed me. Ace took off to Chicago to visit his brother, leaving her alone with Faith, whom she couldn't stand. Tempest was around there limping and in pain. I just couldn't leave my friend hanging like that. Out of the blue she asked me to go to Cancun, Mexico with her for the weekend at her expense. I agreed but reminded her Tracey would want to go, too. The fact that Tempest agreed easily and didn't put up an argument let me know she needed both of us. Tracey was extremely excited when I informed her. She and I put in a vacation day for the upcoming Monday because our last-minute trip wasn't scheduled to return until then.

Around six A.M. that Saturday morning, I was up going over some paperwork I had taken home from my job. I packed some of it with me. I figured since Tempest was pregnant, she might get tired and need a day of rest, so at least I'll have the work on my job to catch up on.

I sat at the desk in my home office with Parnell heavy on my mind. I had just finished composing a reading exercise for one of the third grade classrooms when a surprising text came through. It read: I LOVE YOU, LYNETTE. It was from Parnell. I looked at the time. It was six-twenty in the morning. Even with the hour time difference between our states, it was still very early for him, especially on a Saturday morning.

Parnell's message stunned me. I knew responding could lead to trouble, but I cared as much for him as he did for me, and I wanted him to know it. I texted him back. I LOVE YOU, 2, PARNELL, BUT YOU SHOULDN'T SEND ME SUCH MESSAGES. He responded: WHY NOT? I answered: IT'S NOT SAFE. I'M STILL MARRIED AND SO ARE YOU. He responded: NOT FOR LONG. I sent him a final message for the day: DON'T YOU HAVE YOUR FAMILY TO TEND TO? I'LL CALL YOU BEFORE I LEAVE. Despite what I said, Parnell sent me another message: I'LL BE IN MARION NEXT WEEKEND. LET'S PLAN TO SEE EACH OTHER. I didn't respond. I figured we'd have that argument once we talked later.

I knew even if Parnell divorced his wife, he and I wouldn't be together. At least not right away. I'd been with Lem too many years to just rush into something serious with another man. I was still in the process of rediscovering myself. I loved Parnell because he was like my sun after the rain. I could always count on him to place a smile on my face.

I went back to work, drawing to a close about an hour later. I headed upstairs to finish packing. I was interrupted by my ringing house phone. I answered it. "Hello," I said.

"Lynette, it's Lemont."

"Yes, Lem. How may I help you?"

"I know you don't want to see me, but I'm hurting. I just want to sit down with you and talk one more time."

"You can't possibly be hurting that bad, Lem. You've got somebody's little girl comforting you."

"Lynette, let's talk. I need to come over and get a few things anyway."

I looked at my watch. "Alright, Lem. I'll give you half an hour, and that includes the time it takes you to get here."

"What?"

"You heard me. I'm on my way out, and I can't let you hold me up."

"Stay there. I'm on my way."

He wasn't kidding. Lem got to the house in fifteen minutes flat. He looked the same, but he took time to admire my slimmer frame. It was true that I had accomplished losing twenty-pounds on my Weight Watcher's Program, but I questioned Lem's sincerity about how beautiful I was. He might've

210

meant all the kind words he used, but my guess was that he was reaching for something that would melt the ice around my heart. He followed me upstairs, flapping his chops.

"So, I'm thinking about another month of separation would do us some good," he said. "By then, you should realize we need each other and be ready for me to come home. Just get your attorney to stop all of the proceedings because my attorney says he can do that."

I turned and fanned at him like a fly. "Lem, you don't get it."

"Get what? That it's over? Lynette, baby, it can't be over." He pulled out a piece of paper and handed it to me. "Here. I did what you told me."

I read the letter, stating he wasn't the father of Tekeysia's son. Though shocked, I was unmoved. I passed the paper back to him. "And . . . so?"

"So, did you read it?"

"Yes, I read it. I think you got very lucky on that one, but my mind hasn't changed."

"Lynette, I only held on for so long because I believed that boy was mine."

"You told me you knew he wasn't. Get your lies straight, Lem."

"Listen. I've lied in the past, but today, I'm telling you the truth." Tears came to Lem's eyes. "I really thought her son was mine, but I wasn't going to tell you that. I begged her to lie to you also. We had no intentions on doing a paternity test. I had hoped you'd forget about everything soon and be ready to move on with our lives. Once things came to a head, I decided to take a paternity test on a hunch and a hope to save my marriage. The child isn't mine, and I had really thought he was." Lem wiped a lone tear from his cheek. "I'm hurt because I grew to love the boy. But, can't you see this is God giving us a chance to go forward with our lives. We can't let one infidelity come between us. Baby, we're made of more substance than that."

"Really? One very long infidelity, I might add. Would you say the same, Lem, if I had cheated on you?"

"Well, you did, didn't you?"

"No," I yelled. "I tried. God knows I tried on that weekend I told you I was spending the night with another man, but I couldn't do it. I guess I'm not made of the stuff you're made of." He sat on the bed, looking at the floor. "But know this: I can't promise I won't go all the way if given another opportunity."

I walked away to retrieve my new swimsuit from the drawer. The surprise on Lem's face when he saw it said he wondered if I was crazy. I could tell he was holding back, so I freed him to say something.

"Yes, this is a swimsuit, darling," I told him as I put it in my suitcase.

"Lynette, are you going somewhere?" he asked.

"How'd you guess?" I closed my luggage and zipped it. "Did this big ole suitcase give it away?"

"Yeah. Where're you going?"

I smiled. "To Cancun, Mexico. Can you believe it? I've been begging you for years to take me, and now we're not together, the chance for me to go is here. Imagine that."

"Who're you going with?"

I smiled again. "You're funny."

"Seriously, Lynette. Who're you going with?"

I didn't answer him. I went into the bathroom to retrieve my toiletries. I was in there for a good while, and when I returned, I discovered Lem going through my cell phone.

"Lem, what're you doing?" I yelled.

He gave me a dazed look before responding. "You really are cheating, aren't you?"

"What are you talking about? I just told you I haven't."

He produced the text where I had told Parnell I loved him, too, and that we shouldn't send such messages. I didn't know what to say. I just stared at him.

"This is the man you spent the night with, isn't it?"

212

"Lem, he slept on the couch. Nothing happened."

"If nothing happened, how is it the two of you love each other so much?"

"He's been a friend to me, alright? And, I've been there for him also. Just as a friend." I reached for my cell. "Give me that. You shouldn't have been going through my personal stuff anyway."

He wouldn't hand over the phone. He pulled it around his back. "Lynette, I still pay the bill for this phone. I'm not going to give you easy access to chat with another man. Are you getting ready to go to Cancun with this man?"

"No. Now give me my phone. I'm going to need it."

"How do I know you're not going to Cancun with him?"

"Because I'm not. Call Tempest. She'll tell you Tracey and I are going with her."

"I thought Tempest was hurt. That's what Ace told me before he went out of town."

"She did get hurt, and I don't have time to go into all of that. She offered Tracey and me an all expense paid trip to Cancun to keep her company, so we're going. She says she just needs to get away. Quite frankly, so do I. I'm going to need that phone, Lem."

"This one won't do you any good then." He pulled off one of the two cell phones on his hip then handed it to me. "Here," he said. "This is the only phone on our plan that has international calling. Take this one."

"Lem, I don't even know the number to this phone."

"I'll give it to you, and I'll make sure Vicki has it so she can reach you."

I stood staring at him. Despite how much he'd hurt me, I didn't want to see him so sad. "You believe me when I say I'm going to Cancun with Tempest, right?"

"Yeah. I believe you. That's the least of my worries right now. I'm just trying to figure out how to get you to at least think about giving our family another chance." We were silent for a moment. "Lynette, please."

"I'll think about it, Lem, but can you do something for me?"

He seemed to have perked up. "What is it, baby?"

"Go get Vicki and stay here with her while I'm away. Don't give time to your mistress this weekend. Can you do that?"

"Lynette—"

"No, Lem. I don't want to hear any lies. I've come to realize that given the years you've had with that young lady, there's an emotional attachment between the two of you, making it hard for either of you to let go. If you could have your cake and eat it, too, you would. In order for me to give *us* some thought, I need to know you can give an honest effort to stay away from her. Prove it to me this weekend."

He grabbed me around the waist. "I can do it, babe. You'll see. I've told you, I've already let go."

And with that said, he helped me finish packing and even drove Tracey and me to Memphis International Airport. Tempest was already at our gate waiting for us. We almost didn't recognize her in such heavy make-up and big sunglasses. I had to step to her to get a closer look, making sure it was her. She almost cussed me out.

"It's me damnit," she said, pulling her sunglasses to her forehead and back over her eyes swiftly. Tracey and I chuckled. "I'm glad the two of you can find some humor in this."

I felt bad. "I'm sorry, Tempest. We didn't mean to laugh. You really don't look so terrible though."

"Yeah, thanks to all the makeup," she answered.

"Anyway," I said, "aren't you excited? I know I am."

"Me, too," Tracey said. "My husband is so jealous."

"Girl mine is, too," I seconded.

Tempest's neck must've been feeling a whole lot better because she didn't seem to have any problems snapping it around to look at me. "Who's husband?" she asked.

"Mine," I reiterated.

"I'm confused," Tempest said. "When did you see him?"

"He came by this morning. I finally gave in to his plea to talk. We may work things out. I don't know. He's got a lot to prove first."

"I'd say," Tracey said.

I continued. "Anyway, Tempest, he drove Tracey and me to the airport. He's going to pick up Vicki from my mom's and spend time with her at our house over the weekend."

"Really," Tempest questioned. "So, no mistress this weekend, huh?"

"I told you I'm making him prove something. We called Vicki to let her know he's on his way to pick her up. They're going to the movies tonight."

"Vicki will like that," Tempest said solemnly.

I reached over and rubbed her shoulder. "Hey, are you okay?"

"I'm fine. Just thinking about what I'm going to do with this baby."

Tracey spoke up. "What do you mean? Tempest, if you're considering not keeping this baby, you better be talking adoption."

A tear rolled from under Tempest's sunglasses. I went into my purse and got her a tissue. She dabbed her eyes then quickly replaced the shades. I had to second Tracey's statement.

"Tempest, you know we're your girls, right? We're here for you no matter what, but I truly hope you'll listen to me if you're considering abortion. God knows I don't want you to do that."

"I don't want to either," Tempest said. "For a long time I've pictured myself with child. I just never thought that when the day would come, the child wouldn't be that of my husband." We were all silent for a moment. I rubbed her shoulder until she spoke again. "Ace is never going to accept another man's child."

Tracey offered consolation. "It's too early to tell, Tempest. Wait until Ace return and the two of you talk before making that assessment."

"She's right, Tempest. He probably just needed time away to think."

Tempest nodded. We heard the announcement that it was time to board our flight. "Listen, ladies," Tempest said, standing with her purse and carry-on bag on her shoulder. "The reason I asked you along on this trip is so I can get away and clear my head. I'm leaving my troubles with Ace, Craig, Faith and all other drama back here in the States. I'm asking the two of you to do the same." We nodded. She turned to me. "Lynette, I'm glad to hear things are looking up for you and Lemont, but I'm asking that if you must call back to the States to only speak with your child. The last thing I want to deal with is Lemont upsetting you somehow."

"We're on good terms now, Tempest. That's not going to happen, but I understand where you're coming from."

"Good. Of course you ladies know I can't drink, but I still plan to have a good time being sober."

Tracey high-fived her. "Then it's on," she said.

Just a little over two hours later, we landed in Cancun, Mexico. We could hardly make it to our hotel room in peace because tour agents bombarded us from the airport all the way to the lobby of our hotel, the beautiful Cancun Melia. Tempest kept turning them all down. While she stood in line to check us in our room, we listened to one of the agents spiel about what we should do that night. He offered a pirate cruise that sounded like a whole lot of fun for a very good rate. Given Tempest was paying for everything, Tracey and I had to wait until she finished checking in. I let Tracey do all the talking because I knew she was more likely to convince Tempest than I would.

Tempest gave in. She bought the three cruise tickets then we hurried off to our two bedroom suite to get ready. We only had three hours until cruise time. We were all excited, including Tempest. I was glad to see she had perked up.

Tracey had just come out of the bathroom, and she looked beautiful. I hadn't seen her in a sundress and sandals in a while. I still hadn't decided what I wanted to wear so I let Tempest go into the bathroom next. Tracey went through my luggage to help me.

"Girl, your problem is you have too many choices," she said. "Here." She handed me one of my dresses. "Put an iron to this one before Tempest comes out of the bathroom, cussing."

I laughed. "I know that's right." I held the dress to me in the mirror. "Okay. I'll wear this one. I still can't believe I'm here. Tracey, do you see how beautiful this place is?"

"Yes . . . I can't stop soaking it up."

The cell Lem let me borrow began to ring. I looked at Tracey then went to retrieve the phone. I knew it was either Lem or my child because Lem had said he would transfer all calls until he or Vicki wanted to reach me. "Hello," I answered. It was Vicki. She stated she still hadn't seen her father. I assured her I would call him then get back to her. "Can you believe that?" I said to Tracey.

"What?"

"That was Vicki. She hasn't heard a thing from Lem."

I dialed his other cell number. He didn't answer. I dialed several more times, but he still didn't answer. After about fifteen minutes, the phone rang again. I answered it quickly, thinking Lem was returning my call, but it wasn't him. It was one of his clients. Lem had neglected to transfer the phone line. I became very irritated as I began to think he was spending some last-minute time with his mistress before picking up Vicki. I decided to give his phone one more try. He didn't answer. I was sick. Just when I had thought we could possibly put our family back together, Lem went and failed my test. I sat at the table and put my head down.

Tempest came out of the bathroom and noticed I wasn't preparing to go in behind her. "Lynette, what're you doing? Don't get sleepy on me now. We've got a cruise to catch."

I couldn't respond to her. I kept my head down while Tracey tried to explain what was going on. "Tempest, Vicki hadn't heard from Lemont."

"Okay . . . and?" I heard her say.

"Well, Lynette is a bit torn."

"About what?" Tempest asked in a harsh tone. "Vicki's at her mom's, right? She's fine, right?"

Tracey attempted to defend me. "Yes, but can't you understand, Tempest? Lynette had gotten her hopes up that Lemont was gonna pass her test."

"So, what're you telling me? She's not going on the cruise? I've already spent my money for her to go, so I suggest she pick herself up from that table and get ready."

I couldn't take any more. "I'll give your money back, Tempest. I really can't help the way I'm feeling right now."

"Yes, you can," she fussed. "How did you end up on the phone anyway? We ain't been here half a day yet, and you're already making calls to the States?"

"I didn't make any calls, Tempest. Vicki called me. That's my child. I was supposed to answer her." I began to cry.

"So now you're just going to sit here and cry over him?" she asked.

I had become angry. "I was doing fine until he stepped in and built up my hopes this morning," I screamed at her. "He could've just told me the truth—that he couldn't let go of his tramp. I didn't ask for false promises. I didn't need to be pacified."

I picked up the cell and began dialing. Tracey walked over to me. "What're you doing, Lynette? Don't make yourself feel any worse than you already do."

"I'm calling that bimbo. I know he's with her," I said.

Tempest plopped down on the couch. "I don't believe this shit."

"Tempest," Tracey called. "Chill out now. Lynette's going to be fine. Just give her a minute."

"A minute to do what?" Tempest asked, mean-mugging us.

Lemont's floozy answered the phone. "Hello," she said. "Tekeysia, this is Lynette," I said, fully composed. "Are you with my husband?"

She paused before she answered. "Lynette, you really shouldn't call and ask me anything like that."

She was just as collected as I had been, but I lost my cool. "Bitch, are you still screwing my husband?" I screamed to the top of my lungs.

I heard Lemont's voice in the background. He had apparently been in another room and was surprised to see her on the phone. "Who're you talking to?" Lemont asked her. "You begged me to stay, and now you're on the phone. I'm supposed to be with my kid right now. Are we gonna watch this movie or what?"

"Put him on the phone," I said returning back to my calm. "You sure you want to talk to him?"

I bit my bottom lip and hit the table because I almost called her out of her name again. "I've never been more positive."

There was a pause then he answered. "Hello," he said. "No, trick . . . it's goodbye," I said then hung up.

I turned to Tempest who stared at me with a seriously bruised and yet disgusted look on her face. She was so angry, her breathing seem labored. Her arms were folded across her chest and they rose and fell just as her chest did. I really didn't care.

"Be mad, Tempest Bynum. I don't care. I'm not going on that cruise so call me whatever makes you feel good. I'll pay your money back when we get home."

She looked at Tracey. "I guess you're not going either, huh?"

Tracey hesitated then answered. "No. Lynette is hurting, Tempest. I can't leave her."

Tempest went a fool crazy as she stormed off to her bedroom. "I'da done better bringing two bitches I didn't know with me. I should've known better than to waste my money on you two." She slammed her bedroom door.

Tracey came closer and rubbed my back. "This ain't the first time Tempest has been mad at us, and it damn sure ain't the last," she said.

I put my head down and continued to sulk. I told myself to try to let it all go. Tempest was right. My issues with Lem needed to stay where I left them. When I stopped crying, I made a conscious decision to take back my joy by morning.

Ace

25

Finding out my wife was pregnant with another man's baby was my final straw. I thought I was willing to deal with Tempest, but she'd stooped lower than I thought she ever could. Although I wasn't feeling well, I had to get out of town before I did something I would later regret. I went to Chicago on the first flight smoking—immediately after leaving the hospital. I hardly had time to pack. I apologized profusely to Faith for not taking her with me, but I just needed space. My life was about to be impacted one way or another, and I didn't need any more outside influence clouding my thoughts of what to do.

I didn't return to Memphis until that following Monday afternoon. I called Faith to pick me up from the airport. I asked her to have my meds with her because I didn't take enough with me to Chicago, and I was in pain. She was waiting outside the terminal for me when I stepped out the door. She handed me the pills and a bottle of water as soon as I sat in the car. I spoke then gulped the prescription.

"How was your trip?" she asked as she drove off.

"Fine. It certainly did me some good, I tell ya."

"Oh, I imagine your brother and his family were happy to see you."

"They were. They tried to spoil me, too. Had I not ran out of Lyrica, I might've let them do all the wining and dining they wanted. I just couldn't seem to feel better no matter what."

"Are you talking about physically or mentally?"

"Both. I have to admit, I thought a lot about Tempest, and that baby she's carrying."

"Have you decided anything?"

I sighed. "I think so. I suppose I'll be ready to have a talk with her when we get home."

"Um . . . she's not there, Ace. She and her girlfriends left for Cancun on Saturday. They're scheduled to back late this evening."

"Cancun?"

"It's not what you think, Ace. To be honest, Tempest was broken when she left. She said she needed to get away as well. She asked me to take care of the house and let you know where she was if you happened to call home."

"Hmph. Well, I hope she managed to have a real good time."

"You didn't say that like you mean it, Ace."

"Probably because I didn't mean it. Had I known she wasn't around, I might've cut my trip short. I enjoyed Chicago, but you know there's no place like home."

"I hear ya."

We rode the rest of the way in silence. Faith offered to cook for me once we got home. I wasn't hungry, but I did want a cup of coffee. I sat in the den, watching TV until it finished brewing. She brought the coffee to me.

"Anything interesting on television?" she asked, taking a seat next to me.

"Not really." I turned down the volume.

"Faith, can we have a serious talk?"

"Sure, Ace."

I sipped my Folgers then set it on the coffee table. "I'm going to have a talk with Tempest tonight. I'm not sure how it's going to turn out, but let's say it doesn't turn out the way I think it should. Would you stick around for me?"

Her eyebrows rose. "You mean in the event the two of you decide divorce, would I be yours?"

"That's exactly what I'm saying."

She huffed and puffed, squinted and squirmed, and then came close to tears before responding. "Ace, I love you so much."

"But?" I asked. "Somehow I feel there's a 'but' coming, so don't spare me. Tell me what's up."

"But . . . I know we can't be together."

I was stunned. "Why? What didn't I do for you, Faith? Ever since you came here, I've tried to show you I love you."

"Yes, you have, and I have no doubt you do. You know we've been wrong, Ace. I'm very afraid of reaping it."

"You mean because we've been closer than God would have wanted for the moment?"

She sighed then nodded. "I'll tell you something else, Ace. I can't help feeling like I'm part of the reason you'd choose to divorce Tempest. If I wasn't here, and had I not shown up in your lives, would divorce be as heavy on your mind given the circumstances?" I didn't answer. I had to think about it. "Or, would you consider counseling?"

I shook my head. "I don't know."

"I know you don't. I'm torn because I love you, but I don't want to be the deciding factor of how your story with her ends."

I nodded then grabbed her hand and kissed it. "You think you can be my friend no matter what I decide?"

She smiled then a tear fell. "Sure."

I reached to wipe the tear away. Just then, we heard the front door opening. I looked at Faith. "I thought you said later this evening?"

Faith shrugged then whispered, "Maybe she had her times mixed up. You know she got back early last time."

Faith stood then went to the foyer. I heard Tempest ask Faith if I had returned. The two of them said a few more things I couldn't hear then they retreated into the den. I looked up at Tempest as she entered. Her face wasn't swollen and as bruised as I remembered. Neither of us spoke. Instead, I picked up my coffee, sipped it and stared at the television as though she wasn't standing there. She began to slow stroll toward me, but I never turned to look at her. Faith was seated in a chair. I could feel Tempest looking at me, so I went ahead and turned to her. She was the first to speak.

"How're you doing, Ace?" she asked.

I nodded. "And you?"

She nodded. "Did Faith tell you where I went?"

"She did."

Everyone sat silent for a minute then Tempest turned her attention to Faith. "Faith, listen," she said. "I don't know how you're going to take this, but I'm very sincere. I can't tell you enough how much I appreciate you taking care of our home while we were away. We've had our disagreements and issues, but the one thing I can't take away from you is your patience and tolerance level. Any other woman might've left me high and dry after Ace went out of town, but you're one of a kind. Just let me say thank you."

Faith nodded. "You're welcomed, Tempest."

I picked up my coffee then stood. "Faith, I may call you later to take care of this cup for me. Tempest and I need to go upstairs to talk."

"No problem," Faith answered.

I stood then took Tempest's hand. She stood with me, and we headed to our bedroom. Once inside, she closed the door as I went to sit in my favorite chair. She sat on the bed and waited for me to speak. I was the one who said we needed to talk, so I led the conversation.

"Did the trip do you any good, Tempest?"

She shrugged then looked around the room, and then back at me. "It was alright. Lynette and Lemont are still having problems, so Lynette made things difficult by not wanting to do much, but Tracey was a lot of fun."

"Lynette didn't enjoy herself at all?"

"She tried, but for the most part, I could tell her mind was somewhere else. Truthfully, so was mine, but I made the best of the trip."

I sipped my coffee before responding. "So, did you ever find out how far along your pregnancy is?"

"At this point, I should be close to eight weeks," she answered, dropping her head.

I wanted her to look back at me so I could see her eyes, but she didn't. Staring into her lap seemed to be more comfortable than to look me in the eye with the truth. I finished off my coffee, trying to give her time to regroup, but she never did. I finally picked the conversation back up.

"Are you planning to keep this baby?" I asked.

She sighed. "What do you want me to do?"

"I want you to look at me as we talk right now. That's what I want you to do." She looked up. "Even though you're the one who put this obstacle in our way, I imagine you're hurting just as much as I am . . . because I'm sure you didn't mean to get pregnant, am I right?"

"No. I didn't."

"I figured that. I didn't call you in here to make you feel worse than you already do, because I don't want you to do that to me. However, I deserve your full attention, and I deserve the whole truth."

"I know. You're right, and I'm going to give you that."

"Good. Now let me hear you admit this baby belongs to Craig Dennison." She dropped her head again. "Un-un, Tempest. Look at me. You just said—"

"Okay . . . okay. Craig is the baby's father," she said, staring into my eyes. "Ace, I wanted him to use a condom, but he forced himself on me without one."

I sat up in the chair. "You're the Memphis woman accusing him of rape?"

"Yes," she answered, her eyes filled with water. "I dropped the case, thinking it was for the good of everybody. I had no business over at his hotel. I was there for no good reason, and I ended up paying for it. I never thought in a million years that situation produced a baby."

I couldn't believe my ears. Craig and my wife deceived me. "And college . . . you two were together behind my back like everyone said, weren't you?"

"We were young, Ace."

"I didn't ask you that? Answer my question."

"Yes. We were, but Ace I've told you I married the man I love."

By now my hands were on top of my head. If I had enough hair to grip, I would've pulled it all out. "Shut up . . . just shut up. I don't know if I want to hear any more." She was silent as I'd demanded. "And now you're pregnant with that man's baby. Am I supposed to accept that?"

"I asked you what you wanted me to do."

"I don't have an answer. I'm not going to have any part in your decision. You got yourself in this predicament, so you determine what's best."

She was silent for several minutes. I sat patiently until she was ready to speak. "Ace, I want my marriage."

"And you want this baby, too, don't you?"

She nodded. "I can't live with having an abortion, and I know I'd later regret adoption. I've wanted to be a mother, and

226

this is my chance. I know I'm asking a lot of you, but I want us to be the parents."

I reached over on the nightstand then picked up the remote. Tempest kept staring at me, apparently waiting for an answer. I clicked on the television and began flipping through the channels. She didn't budge. I don't think I've ever seen Tempest more patient. Had I been in her predicament, I would've thought I wasn't going to get an answer. I just didn't know what I wanted to do. I wondered if I could trust Tempest to change now that she saw everything we'd built about to be snatched from under her. That baby was proof of her infidelity. I could leave her and take mostly everything with me if I wanted.

When I looked back at her, she was still staring. "You should have the baby, Tempest. You've got a lot of hell in you, and I believe this baby would be the only reason you'd change. However, I don't know that I can comfortably raise Craig Dennison's child. It's not the baby's fault, but me staying would mean I'd have to deal with Craig for years to come and be reminded of what the two of you did to me."

"Then let's not tell him. He doesn't have to know I'm having his baby."

I shook my head. "I don't think I can do it, Tempest."

"Just think about Ace. Don't say no right now. Please, honey. Think about it."

I stood and picked up my coffee cup. "I'm going to the den to watch television. I don't want to be bothered because I've certainly got a lot to think about. We'll talk again in the morning."

I left her in the bedroom. After placing my cup in the sink, I went to the den to think. I didn't turn on the television at first. When Faith walked in to see me sitting on the couch with my head in my lap, she tried patting me on the back. I even begged her pardon and asked her for some privacy.

About an hour later, I was in the same position when I heard Tempest rolling her luggage from the foyer. I looked up and saw her peering at me. She seemed as if she wanted to say something but was unsure if she should. I dropped my head back into my lap, and then I heard her rolling the luggage away. I got up to turn off the lights, but I turned on the television. I'd done enough thinking for one day.

At some point, I fell asleep. I woke up around two o'clock in the morning hungry and erect. I dreamed that Faith and I had hot, passionate sex. It seemed so real, I was surprised to wake up and find it was a dream.

The television was off so I knew that meant either Faith or Tempest had come in and turned it off after noticing I was asleep. I went into the kitchen for a glass of water. I found a plate of food covered in the refrigerator so I pulled it out and heated it. Faith had fixed smothered chicken, scalloped potatoes, and broccoli. My stomach couldn't have been more pleased. After eating, I decided to pay Faith a visit.

When I opened her door, she lay in the dark, but she wasn't asleep. She watched me as I took off my shirt and pants then climbed into her bed. I slid close to her then kissed her forehead. That's when she began to push me back.

"Ace, I can't do this anymore," she whispered.

"Why not? We have proof my wife sinned against me. She doesn't love me, and she certainly doesn't respect me."

"I know, but I just feel so bad doing this in her house. Do you even know that she's asleep?"

"I didn't check."

"Ace, you don't even care. I can see it in your eyes, but I care if we get caught. I care that God may punish me for this."

I began kissing her lips. She moaned. "Just this night. You only have a few more days here. I won't bother you after this."

"Ace, please stop," she moaned as I rubbed between her legs. The more I fondled her, the wider she opened her legs. "Ace, you've got to stop."

"I need you, Faith. Don't turn me away. Please, baby. I need you."

I was wrong. I knew Faith would have a tough time turning me away. She gave in to my pleas and let me have her. I was in her room for more than half an hour, and I would've been in there longer had she not made me leave. I dressed then eased out of her room, making sure to close the door softly behind me. All of my cautiousness didn't make a difference because I was startled by Tempest in the hallway. She stood against the wall just inches from Faith's door. Her arms were folded and she wouldn't look up at me for a minute. I didn't know what to say. She started past me, toward Faith's room, but grabbed her arms, stopping her.

"No, Tempest," I whispered. "Take it out on me. Please. I'm the one you'd want to hate."

I expected Tempest to cause a ruckus in the hallway, alerting Faith to our presence, but she didn't. She gave me the how-dare-you look then stormed upstairs. I went behind her and closed our bedroom door. She threw herself on the bed with her back to me.

"So, now you don't want to talk?" I asked her.

She sat up in bed. "Yeah. I do, but what is there to explain?"

"How'd you guess I was in there?"

She slid out of bed then picked up a baby monitor. "I installed one behind her bed while she was cleaning the kitchen and you were on the couch asleep. I knew I wasn't the only deceiver in this house. Ace, you've been sneaking in the woman's room quite a bit, haven't you? What's up with that? She doesn't look like shit, and I have to beg you to make love to me."

"Okay, Tempest. You've given me your whole truth and now here's mine." Tempest looked as if she was about to faint. She eased up on the bed to listen. "Somehow . . . maybe it was fate . . . maybe it was something else, but somehow you managed to hire the first woman I've ever loved to care for me and be my aide." Tempest really did need to pick up her jaw. I continued. "Faith is . . . was my high school sweetheart. We didn't tell you from jump street because I wanted her to stay. I knew she'd be great company, and I knew she'd be the best caregiver. But, I swear to you, she and I never meant to take things this far. Faith has always tried to change my mind about pursuing her."

"Oh, I heard. Ace, she begged you not to bother her, but you kept going until she gave in. Why?" Tears came to Tempest's eyes.

I felt sorry for her, but I was angry at the same time. "Look how you've treated me. I lost respect for you a long time ago. 'Why?' Do you really have to ask me why I'd take interest in another woman—one you brought into our home in the first place?"

"Ace, tomorrow she's got to go. I've messed up. You've had your fun. Now I want to save my marriage. It's been a rough couple of months, but shit can't get no worse for us than what they already are. Please, Ace. Let's just figure out a way to move forward from here."

"You keep saying that, but it's going to take me more than a night to figure out if I can deal with your pregnancy."

"Ace, this baby could be a blessing to both of us."

"I hear you, but let me decide that on my own."

She began to sulk then she blurted out, "You love her, don't you?"

"She's not the reason we're having issues, Tempest. Don't even try it."

"I swear she's leaving here as soon as daylight hits, Ace."

"And I say she stays the few days she has left. I've told you: take whatever you want out on me, but if you so much as cause Faith's eye water to form, I'll make you sorry you did."

Tempest's face turned hard as she ogled me from head to toe. I could see all of the bitterness she once felt against me had returned. Common sense told me not to go back to sleep.

Tempest's silence was louder than her bark. Not only did I fear what she'd do to Faith when given the chance, but I feared my security as well. I decided that by morning, I'd put Faith up in a hotel—just to be on the safe side.

Tempest

26

___

I got out of bed around seven in the morning. Ace was dressed and walking around the room, seemingly preparing to go somewhere. I questioned his intentions.

"I'm going to find Faith a hotel room until you and I can finalize our divorce," he said.

I jumped out of bed. "What divorce? We're not getting a divorce, Ace. I thought we discussed we would work this out?"

"Then you must've been dreaming because I told you I didn't know what I wanted to do," he snapped.

"I don't care what you say. We're not getting a damn divorce. You can get that out of your vocabulary. I'll be damned if I go somewhere and let her have you."

"I guess you'll be damned then. I love her, and there's nothing you can do about that."

"You don't love me, Ace? After all we've built together, you mean to tell me you can't forgive me so we can move on?"

"Tempest, you've got a different sense of love. Nobody is going to take all your crap like I have, and then stick around and hope there won't be more to come. If you haven't figured out

I've stuck around because I'm the most patient man in the world, then something is wrong with you. I've waited and waited for you to express real love to me . . . be what a wife is supposed to be. I'm out of patience." He headed to walk out then turned to me. "I've asked Faith to stay in her room and finish packing. She's leaving. That's what you want, so don't go in there bothering her."

When he left the room, I repeatedly beat both my fists down on the bed. Had it been glass, I would've mutilated it. I pinched myself, hoping I'd find I was only dreaming, but I wasn't. My husband had just confirmed he was leaving me, and for the woman I first felt confident he'd never want. I had to stop him from divorcing me. I just couldn't let that happen. I began to pace, and I became more upset with every step.

I couldn't stay around the house and not have anything to say to Faith. I showered then dressed in one of my favorite teal-blue sundresses before getting out of there. When I got to the car, I put on my Armani sunglasses then took off. I had hoped a drive would calm my nerves. I stopped by my office first to retrieve the 357 Magnum I was permitted to have there for protection purposes. I needed to be ready in case Craig's friends were on the prowl again. I stuffed it into my large shoulder bag then got back into my car.

As fate would have it, I was listening to Soul Classics 103.5 FM when I heard the DJ interviewing a young man who stated he'd just hung out with Craig Dennison the night before at the Weston Hotel. *He sneaked his ass in town,* I thought. Instincts told me given that Craig hung out at the Weston, he was probably staying there as well—avoiding his regular hotel as an attempt to keep me from getting in touch with him in the event I discovered he was in town. I needed to talk to him, so the drive downtown was worth the try.

Upon entering the hotel, I spotted a restaurant. I wondered if I could block my number, change my voice and convince Craig to come into the restaurant if he was there. As I approached the door, I forgot my plan altogether because I heard a group of men laughing and Craig's voice was among them. I stepped inside and saw the back of Craig's head. A young woman walked up asking if she could help me, but I fanned her off then started toward Craig's table. The two gentlemen facing me saw me coming.

"Good morning, sexy," one of them said.

I stopped in front of the table just when Craig looked up. He quit chewing his breakfast. "Swallow, Craig," I said to him. The other men looked at him. "You really need to chew that up and swallow it before you get choked." I smiled. Craig remained silent and so did the other men. "It's not what you think. I'm not stalking you. I just need to speak with you."

He put down his fork. "We ain't got shit to talk about. You need to get the fuck out of here before I call security on your crazy ass."

I took off my shades. "Now, Craig. That's a jacked up way to talk to the mother of your child," I told him. One of his friends spit out some water. Craig's eyes traveled from my face to my stomach. "Well, you know after you *raped* me, I could've taken the Morning After pill, but for some reason, I really didn't think I would be pregnant." I reached into my purse and whipped out my discharge papers from the hospital. I pointed out the section that verified my pregnancy as I handed it to him. He seemed at a loss for words. I leaned across the table, peering into his face. "Now I suggest you get your ass up and come talk to me because I'm sure you're concerned about being tied to me for the next eighteen years."

His friends seemed just as stunned as he did. He got up and followed me out of the restaurant. I began rambling, but Craig shushed me because the lobby echoed.

"If you're not too scared, I'd like to take this up to my room," he whispered. "I don't need anyone in the middle of our conversation."

I thought about the steel piece in my purse then answered, "I'm not scared at all."

We got on the elevator then rode up. I tried to begin an innocent dialogue. "Is this place anything like the Madison Hotel?" I asked.

He looked at me but never answered. Once we got off the elevator, he led the way to his room. He closed the door then offered me a seat. "I'll stand," I told him.

"I thought you weren't scared," he said.

"Craig, I have a 357 Magnum in my purse. If you try anything foolish, I'm blowing your ass halfway across this suite." His eyes widened. "If you plan to be cool, then you have nothing to worry about."

He walked over to the bar. "May I fix you something to drink?"

"So you can poison me and my baby? I don't think so."

"You're really pregnant?" he asked, turning to me.

"Yes, and I don't appreciate you sending them big ass men-looking women to jump on me. They could've killed your seed."

"Tempest, you kept all of this shit going. And anyway, this is the first I've heard of you being pregnant. What is Ace saying?"

"He found out when I did—at the hospital. I've told him everything from beginning to end. He's not happy."

He dropped his head and sighed. "Are you planning to keep this baby?"

"Why do you and Ace ask that question?" Craig didn't say anything. "I know there are some options, but I'll tell you right now, I'm not having an abortion."

Craig nodded. "Are you positive the baby couldn't belong to Ace?"

"Without a doubt."

"Tempest, Ace is not going to stick around and be a father to my child."

"Trust me. He doesn't have a choice. He says he'll leave, but I won't let that happen."

"So now how am I going to be impacted? I know you're here because you've come up with a new game to play with me. Tempest, I've learned I can't beat you at your own game, but tell me all the rules anyway."

I shook my head. "I'm here for two reasons. One: I thought you should know about the baby, but Ace and I want nothing from you. Two: I'm ready to right my wrong."

Craig looked at me sideways. "What does that mean?"

"The last thing your butch friend said to me was that it wasn't over until I right my wrong. Whether you send them after me again or not, I now have a conscience about destroying your engagement. I'm through with the games. We both need to move on with our lives."

Craig scratched his head then pinched himself. "I'm sorry," he said. "This seems real, but repeat it for me one more time, please. I just want to make sure I'm not hearing things."

"I know what you mean." I paused. "Seriously. I want the games over. Now tell me what I can do to fix things."

Craig and I came up with a scheme to block the number in the hotel room and have me call his fiancée, pretending to be Tekeysia Houston. I put on my acting shoes and gave her a convincing story of how I falsified that health paper because I was angry Craig had turned me down. I also gave her Tekeysia's birth date, address as well as other vital information, and then told her to verify I was who I said I was. Our plan must've worked because I was there with Craig about an hour later when she called expressing her love.

I got up to leave as they finished talking, but Craig grabbed my hand, stopping me. He wrapped up their conversation then hung up. He stood looking at me with sympathetic eyes.

"Thanks, Tempest," he said. I threw up my hand then turned to leave. He stopped me once again. "Hey . . . are you going to be okay?"

"I'm going to be fine," I answered.

"Listen. I don't know what Ace is going to decide, but I just want you to know that if you'll do me a favor by keeping things anonymous, I'll gladly pitch in and do my part."

That made me feel good. I smiled. "Thanks, Craig. I'll let you know if we ever need you," I answered, rubbing my belly.

I walked out of the room, leaving Craig with a look on his face that said he still couldn't believe what all had transpired. Sure Craig had more money than Ace, but I never cared for Craig like I did Ace, nor had I built a life with him. Although both Craig and Ace had desires to move on with other women, I wasn't married to Craig. I could easily let him go.

As I drove toward home, I decided to call the house to see if Ace had returned. Faith answered on the second ring.

"Bynum residence," she said.

"Where's my husband?"

Her sigh was intense. "Hello, Tempest. Ace is out getting me some more boxes."

"Great. Now what were you sighing about. Did I say something wrong? Hell, he is my husband."

She released a loud huff. "Look. I don't want to argue. I just want to finish packing my things so we can be out of your way today." She hung up on me.

We? Did that bitch say, 'we?' I thought. Ace obviously had been back there, telling her he was moving out, too. He told me *she* would go until he and I could finalize things, not both of them. I was so angry, a migraine began to invade my head. As I began to speed home, my phone rang. I answered it with my blue tooth.

"Yeah," I shouted.

"Tempest?" the voice said.

"Who is this?"

237

"Lynette. I was calling to check on you. You sound pissed. Are you okay?"

"No, but I will be in just a few minutes. I'm almost home."

"Tempest, you don't sound well. What does that mean?"

"That means a certain, alien-looking woman at my address is about to meet a three-five-seven, and then disappear."

"Come on, Tempest. You can't be serious," Lynette said, giggling. I didn't say anything. When she heard my car door slam, she became concerned. "Tempest, are you home already?"

"Yeah."

"Where's Ace?"

"He's not home, and if he knew what was good for him, he wouldn't come home."

"Tempest, please calm down. You're scaring me."

"I love you, Lynette, but I have to let you go."

I hung up on her then darted into my house. I slammed the door, causing Faith to sprint out of her room to see what was going on. She stopped in the middle of the foyer with her jaw hanging to the floor. I gave her the hard-nosed stare as I passed her and went upstairs to begin unhooking all the phone lines. I made my way back downstairs and unplugged the lines in every room. I noticed Lynette's number on the caller ID as one ring came through the kitchen phone just before I snatched it out of the wall. Faith entered the kitchen, looking perplexed.

"Tempest, was that the kitchen phone I heard? None of the other phones seem to be ringing."

I immediately went into my purse and pulled out my gun. She jumped, dropping and breaking the glass candy dish she had in her hand. I stepped toward her.

"You knew my husband was your ex when I hired you, didn't you?"

"No, Tempest. I swear to God. I didn't know until the day I came to meet him."

"Why didn't you tell me then?"

"It was Ace's idea not to tell you. I didn't come in here to steal your husband, Tempest." She began to cry.

"Bitch, you're already ugly. Please stop crying." Despite my demand, she couldn't seem to dry her eyes. "Give me one reason I shouldn't kill you, and hurry up."

"I-I-I—"

"'I-I-I' my ass. I said hurry up," I yelled. She fell to her knees, still crying. "Do you really think I would let you move out of here and take my husband with you? Huh?"

Ace burst into the house and was in the kitchen faster than I'd seen S.W.A.T. take over a place. "Tempest, what the hell are you doing?" he yelled from a safe distance.

"If you don't want to find out, I suggest you take your ass back where you just came from," I told him.

He started toward Faith as she kneeled on the floor. I turned the gun on him. "Un-un, un-un," I said, shaking my head. "Don't go over there. Her ass is about to get blown away. I wouldn't be anywhere close to her if I were you."

He had tears in his eyes. "Tempest, if you kill her you might as well take my life, too."

This can't be right, I thought as I shook my head in silence. *Did I just hear him say that?* "You love her that much?" I yelled. I began stomping my foot. "You love her that much, Ace? So much that you not only despise life with me, but if she dies, you don't want life at all?"

"I never said I despise you, Tempest."

"No, but you can't tell me you love me either. I know you love me, Ace. You just can't tell me." I looked over at Faith. "How many times have you said the magic words to this thang over here?" I asked, waving the gun toward her. He wouldn't answer. "Was it that many?"

I took aim at Faith then cocked it. Ace yelled, "Tempest, don't."

"Faith, if you haven't been praying or talking in tongues already, I think it's time."

Ace ran toward me, screaming. "Tempest . . . no!"

The gun went off just as my hand was pushed into the air. I heard Faith scream. Ace and I hit the floor simultaneously. The gun flew out of my hand and slid across the kitchen about six feet from us. Faith wasn't hit, and had she not been busy screaming and covering her ears, she could've recovered the weapon before either one of us could. Ace and I scrambled at the gun. I broke from him, and then kicked him in the stomach. I knew he was through.

I made a dash for the gun then quickly got to my feet. Lynette burst into my house, screaming my name. When she made it to the kitchen, she looked as if she wanted to faint.

"Oh God, Tempest. What are you doing?" she asked.

Ace got off the floor, holding his stomach. "Tempest, I was willing to work things out with you," he said, panting. "But, I can't live with a woman whom I know can kill someone. Just do me a favor and take me first."

My heart sank, and at that moment, I lost all hope of ever having a normal life back with my husband. I turned the gun on myself, placing it to my head. Ace broke to his knees and cried like a baby. He was trying to say something, but his sobs were too strong to comprehend his words. I got the sense he didn't want me to kill myself. I began to cry as well. He caught his breath.

"Don't do it, baby," he said to me. His face was wet with tears and sweat. "I didn't mean to drive you to this." He gasped for air, released more tears then continued. "We're all hurting, Tempest. All three of us. You said shit couldn't get worse, but you turning a gun on us and then yourself *is* the worse. I love you, baby. I don't always tell you, but you know I do. I wanted to leave because I lost confidence in your ability to change. Rather than see you dead, Tempest, I will stay. Put the gun down, baby, please."

I looked around the room. Lynette was crying, and so was Faith. Ace seemed to be more broken than any of us. He hadn't cried so hard at either of his parents' funerals. I realized he had just given me what I wanted—to know he cared. I eased the gun down from my head. Ace got off the floor then came over and took the gun from my hand, placing it on the counter. He then pulled me into his arms and squeezed me tight. As I held him back, I looked over at Faith on the floor. She seemed as though she had lost her mind. She sat rocking and crying. Lynette went over to console her. Realizing what I had just done, I came to grips with something else. I needed psychiatric help, and I needed it fast.

I pulled away from Ace and looked him in his eyes. "Something must've snapped in me," I said. "I shouldn't have reacted like that. Ace, I think I need help. Will you help me?"

He kissed my forehead. "Of course I will. I'll stay right here, and I'll help you, Tempest."

Several hours later, Faith was finished packing her things and heading out of my house with Lynette's help. By the end of the day, she was no longer a resident of my home, but neither was I. Ace drove me down to Charter Lakeside Hospital for an evaluation. I was admitted without much hesitation. I asked to use the restroom and was escorted to the nearest one. Inside, I met up with a woman who clearly had it's a thin line between sanity and insanity written all over her. Although she looked vaguely familiar, I did recognize her. She was my reflection in the mirror.

Lynette

27

People could call Tempest Bynum what they wanted, but as for me, I labeled her human. She made a lot of wrong choices in her marriage, but since God could forgive her, so should all others. I've always tried to understand people rather than judge them. She and I were two women wanting badly to keep our marriages in tact, so I understood her desperation.

I recall when Tempest and Ace gave my husband a position at their bonding company and looked out for him like I know no one else would. They took a liking to us and befriended us during a time in our lives when we desperately needed structure and balance. Once Ace got sick, it was tough watching their marriage deteriorate as a result. Although our dilemmas were different, Tempest and I were the same in the sense that we didn't want to give up. I could never be as tough as Tempest, but her sternness kept me sober, and helped me realize that not all wives were as passive as me.

Tempest was admitted to the hospital on Tuesday, and by Saturday, I was permitted to see her. I picked up Tracey so she could visit as well. Vicki was home with Lem. I explained the situation to him, so he agreed to entertain Vicki until I returned. Lem still wouldn't give my phone back to me, claiming he had ordered a new one because our new mobile plan, minus his mistress's cell, called for the upgraded Blackberry. I didn't argue with him on it. I still had his business phone for emergency purposes. I dared not contact Parnell on it.

Tracey and I were shocked to see how well Tempest looked. She sat in a lounge-like area, wearing a black-and-white print halter dress with her head buried in the Bible as we walked in. Tracey stepped to her and felt her forehead.

"Who are you, and what did you do with my friend, Tempest?" Tracey joked.

We all laughed. "Don't play. You know it's me in the flesh," Tempest answered. She stood to hug us. "C'mon over here and have a seat."

"Girl, you look great," I said just after sitting. "I'm really happy to see you looking so well."

She frowned. "What? You thought I'd be in a straight-jacket with my hair all over my head or something?"

I giggled. "No. I don't know what I expected. Maybe something like a hospital gown."

"Oh, I would've been checked myself out of here if that was the case. I ain't walking around nowhere for days at a time with a gown on," she stated.

"So, I take it Ace has been here," I asked.

"Every day. How do you think I got my clothes and makeup here? He's really concerned about me, you know?"

"That's a strong man, Tempest," Tracey said. "He's sick himself, and after how you treated him behind his illness, it's a wonder he doesn't dish it back now that you need him."

"Tracey, what I'm going through is different. Ace doesn't have to do all the physical work I had to with him."

"Still, Tempest . . . don't take this as me rubbing this in your face, but the man found love elsewhere . . . and he hasn't turned his back on you."

There was a brief silence. Tracey's conversation made me nervous. I wasn't sure if Tempest could handle such truths. I tried to think of something to say during the silence, but I was blank. Tempest spoke next, and surprisingly, she was calm.

"You know . . . you're absolutely right, Tracey. On one hand, I want my marriage, but on the other hand, I can't say I deserve Ace. To be perfectly honest, I can't even say I won't get tired of him again. It does take strong individuals to put up with me. I have to admit you two are real friends."

Tracey placed her hand on her hip and said, "You're just now figuring that out?"

"No. I mean, y'all could've just brushed me off and said 'forget her—that bitch is crazy.'" She sighed. "But, you didn't. You're still by my side."

"Tempest," Tracey said, "I don't mean any harm, but we been knew you were crazy," she said, laughing. "If we were going to bail on you, it would've been long before now. Not when you need us the most."

Tempest was laughing, but tears formed in her eyes— happy ones I suppose. She marked a place in the Bible with a napkin then closed it. Although she had visited my church before, I don't recall ever seeing Tempest with a Bible in her hand. I was curious as to what she was reading.

"So what Book are you in?" I asked.

She huffed. "Matthew, but don't ask me what I'm getting out of it. I've got to get a Bible that will simplify things for me. This is the first time I've attempted to study the Word for myself."

"So, what led you to even pick It up?" Tracey asked.

"That Faith Winston," Tempest replied.

Tracey and I looked at each other then responded simultaneously. "Faith?"

"Yeah. I'm going to check myself out of here by Monday. I'm gon' need Jesus all up in me to keep me from finding her and finishing what I set out to do to her."

"Aw, girl, you don't mean that," I said.

"Yes, she does," Tracey interjected. "I don't know who that was when we first walked in here, but the real Tempest is back," she teased. "I was starting to think they had given you some type of medication that fixed your personality traits." We laughed.

"Ha, ha, very funny, Tracey," said Tempest. "No, seriously . . . I just know I need to do better."

"Well, I'm proud of you, girl," I said.

"Believe it or not, me, too," Tracey seconded.

We group hugged then chatted a bit more before leaving. It was good to see Tempest in great spirits. Tracey and I discussed how glad we were that we'd had the chance to visit her. We were also proud of Ace for standing by her in spite of all she'd done to hurt him.

I dropped Tracey at her house then went home. I saw an unfamiliar car parked in my driveway with a rental sticker on it. Lem hadn't mentioned he was expecting company, nor had he called to inform me someone had come to see me. I couldn't wait to get in the house and see what was going on. I had a notion that I should ease into the house, and so I did. I heard Lem and another familiar male voice chatting in the living room. I stopped just short of the entryway to listen.

"You're a man of the Cloth with a family of your own," I heard Lem say. "God expects you to do differently than what you're doing."

"Yes, God called me to preach, but what you have to understand is that I'm still a man," the company told Lem. I gasped because I recognized the voice to be that of Parnell.

"I hear you, but let me tell you that you're a man who could've gotten himself killed today. You're here because you thought it was Lynette replying to your text, inviting you over. Separated or not, Lynette is *my* wife, and this is still my house."

Parnell agreed. "I can't argue with that. My decision to come here was foolish, and I'm quite embarrassed to be

245

confronted by you. Just let me say that I'm here because I care about Lynette."

"No, tell the truth. You love her. Isn't that what you wrote in the texts? Even after she warned you not to send such messages, you still tried to be slick by sending texts that said: I AGAPE YOU. You didn't know I had confiscated her phone. Love, agape—is there really a difference when it comes to another man's wife? Call it agape if you want . . . you know what sin is."

"Brother Lemont—"

"I'm not your brother," Lem said, cutting him off.

"You are whether you like it or not. I realize I've sinned against you, so let me apologize."

"Apology accepted. Now leave my wife alone."

"I wasn't finished," Parnell stated. "I apologize to you, but I can't help that I want to be the one to show Lynette what real love is. I'm going through a divorce myself, and I intend to bring Lynette into my world soon."

Lem huffed and puffed then he spoke. "Look . . . did God really call you to preach? I'm asking because the man I hear, sitting before me doesn't sound anything like His Shepard."

"We all fall short—" Parnell started.

"Then you're short on a lot of things—character, integrity, substance, goodness and theology just to name a few. How do I know? Because the Bible clearly states in Psalms 37:23 the steps of a good man are ordered by the Lord. You can't sit here and make me believe God would have you come in and destroy my family. That's not at all the case because I've prayed to keep my marriage, and I know God is working on me. He's called me to be a better Christian and a better husband. I think perhaps you heard him wrong when He was calling you because surely He wouldn't place a man like you in charge of His sheep."

It took Parnell a few seconds to respond. "God sees potential in all of us."

"I believe that, but can't you at least understand where I'm coming from? I pray that your marital issues will be resolved so you and your family can stand. You should want that. I'm asking you to step back, so my marriage can have another chance. Lynette obviously thinks highly of you. Had you not been in the picture, I don't believe she would've ever filed for divorce. You're giving her some other kind of hope. Although she can't see it, I can tell it's not the kind of hope that God would condone. Yes, I've let her down many times before—even more recently than I think you know, but as I sit here today, my heart is bleeding for what I've done to her. I've already promised God that if He'd see us through this time, I'm going to do right by her." Everything went quiet for a minute. I was choked up and found it hard to hold back tears. After a couple of minutes passed, Lem added something else. "Wasn't it just you who said 'God sees potential in all of us?'"

"That's true," Parnell responded. "I did say that, and you don't have to say any more. I pray God sees fit that you can keep your family together. I know Lynette loves you very much. This time work harder at being good to her."

"Thank you," I heard Lem say, almost in a whisper. "Thank you very much. I *will* work harder."

I could hear them getting up from the leather couch so I opened and closed the back door hard as if I had just come in. I went into the living room just as Parnell was heading out. I called out to him.

"Parnell, what are you doing here?" I asked.

He and Lem looked at each other before he responded. "Hi, Lynette. Well, I thought I was coming to see you." He looked at Lem then back at me. "It's a long story, Lynette. I think it would be better told by your husband."

Lem and I stared at each other for a few seconds before I addressed Parnell. "Well, are you leaving so soon?"

"Yes. I really need to." He went to shake Lem's hand. "It was nice to meet you, Lemont. Stay prayerful."

"I will," Lemont answered. "You do the same. God bless."

Parnell waved goodbye to me then left Lemont and I standing, staring silently. After all I'd heard, I didn't know if I wanted to open up or allow him to go first. Lemont said so many things that seemed unlike him, and I didn't know how to accept he was being true. He sat on the couch and asked me to join him.

"Where's Vicki?" I asked, taking a seat.

"She's in her room watching Hanna Montana."

"Oh. How'd you trick Parnell over here?" I asked as if I didn't already know.

"I don't want to get into all of that," he responded. "You just need to know that I've asked him to step back so we can work on our marriage."

"Lem, that wasn't necessary. I know you read a few text messages, but neither of them said I would be with Parnell after our divorce was final."

"I know, but Lynette, I felt threatened by him. I don't need another man texting you the type of things he'd say while I'm trying to fix things between us."

"Why are you so confident things are going to work out?"

He took my hand into his. "Because when you discovered me back over to Tekeysia's place after I'd promised I wouldn't do that to you anymore, I knew I had lost you for good. I had to open up my heart and my ears to God."

"So what did God say?"

"First, He revealed to me how much pain you were in. Parnell sent so many texts between your trip to Cancun till now that I understood things perfectly. The woman I married, know and love wouldn't have ever built an emotional attachment with another man unless she was hurting. The wound must've been cut deeper than before. In reading Parnell's texts, I could tell he was like medicine. He made what you were dealing with comfortable and bearable. I began to feel awful knowing I was the cause of so much agony. Then, God reminded me of His Word—that I should love you as I would myself. I'm sorry, Lynette." Lem slid to his knees in front of me. "I'm begging you for one more chance. I've got a long way to go, but I promise I won't be anything like I use to be. God ain't through with me. We've had twenty-two trying years, but we've got that many plus more waiting for us to enjoy. Please . . . don't give up on me now."

Lemont had never seemed so sincere before. It had only been a week since I called and discovered him with Tekeysia, but I could see real growth. I thought about all the things he'd expressed to Parnell, including the part about God seeing potential. When I married Lemont, he was unsaved, but after noting the light in me, he got saved. Over the years, he back slid, fell down and got back up. We were in a period where I believe God allowed him another chance to get back up, so I decided not to give up on his potential either. His head was down in my lap. I raised his face then spoke to him.

"I can forgive you, Lemont Rapid, but know this is it. If you say God is speaking to you, then I'm choosing to believe it. Don't make me regret my decision."

"I won't, baby," he said, kissing my hand. "You have my promise. I'm ready to be the man God has called me to be."

Lemont's words were soothing to my soul. He sat next to me on the couch then wrapped his arms around me in a tight embrace. After several soft whispers of "I love you" in my ear, Lemont held the sides of my face and kissed me like he'd never see me again. God is real, and can't nobody tell me differently.

Ace

28

I had gone out to check on things at the office Monday morning, but once I returned, I heard Tempest's voice upstairs. She was apparently on the phone. I could also hear her moving and shuffling things. I went up to see what she was doing. I stood just outside the bedroom door and watched as she packed items into several suitcases while fussing on her cell. She was so into the conversation, she didn't even notice me.

"Well, I doubt very seriously, Craig, that Ace will be calling you," she said then paused. "Your friendship with him may not survive, but we all want one thing in common, and that's peace. What's done is done, and it's a new day."

She paused again then turned and saw me standing in the doorway. I waved then entered, taking a seat in my chair. She didn't seem very interested in her conversation with Craig anymore. In fact, she let him go.

"Look . . . Ace is here, and I want to chat with him a minute, so let me get back to you," she said. They were off the phone just like that.

ALISHA YVONNE

"Craig still cool with the idea of you having his baby?" I asked.

She sat on the bed then sighed. "I guess so. I think he's a little bit concerned about me moving to Detroit though."

I wondered if I heard her correctly. "Moving to Detroit?"

"Ace, let's face it. You don't want me here no more than Craig wants me near him in Detroit."

"Why are you putting words in my mouth, Tempest?"

"I'm not putting words in your mouth. It wasn't until I put that gun to my head that you expressed you still love me. I had to threaten to commit suicide just to hear the words I'd been longing to hear for months."

"Oh, let's not go there, Tempest. I don't want to get started on you."

"Go ahead. I'm not sensitive and you know it."

"How about I couldn't get no love from you until Faith came into the picture? You didn't think anybody else was capable of loving me."

"That's not true. I just didn't think Faith was even in the range of what you'd want. I never figured I was doing myself an injustice by hiring her."

"I guess you've learned strange things happen, huh?"

"You ain't lying." Tempest glanced around me to look at the clock on the nightstand. "Gosh, it's two o'clock already?"

"Do you have a flight leaving today?"

"Yeah, at five-thirty. I've told my mother and brother I'm coming. I need to get up from here and go have another look around this place before I leave."

"For what?"

"I want to be able to remember what it looks like."

"Tempest, quit playing, girl. You know you're coming back."

"If I thought you really wanted me back, I would."

She left the room then headed downstairs. I followed, calling behind her.

251

"Tempest, I'm talking to you. Don't walk away."

She stopped and turned to me. "Then walk with me," she said, cupping her arm under mine.

"You're making the decision to leave by yourself. You haven't allowed me any say over what's best for us."

"Well, we both know some time apart will be great," she said, opening the sliding glass door. She walked outside and stood in front of the pool.

I went and stood next to her. "So, we'll have our space, and then you'll come back, and we'll discuss our future."

She looked at me and shook her head. "Will you take me to the airport?"

"Yeah, but why are you shaking your head?"

She walked off and went into the house, making me follow her once again. "Don't forget to lock the glass door, Ace." She darted off, heading upstairs.

I secured the sliding door then made my way to her. She sat on top of one of the suitcases as she zipped it. I know she heard me enter the room, but she ignored my presence.

"Tempest, I don't have the energy I once had. Stop making me chase you," I said, taking a seat.

"Then don't chase me, Ace."

"Why were you shaking your head outside?"

"Because . . . you don't even realize how you just told off on yourself."

"Then explain to me what I did."

"You made the comment that we'll discuss our future upon my return. That tells me what I already know. You're uncertain about our future."

"I didn't say that."

"Ace, if you knew you wanted me, we wouldn't have to wait until I return from Detroit to discuss hope for our marriage." She zipped the other suitcase then lifted it. "The other one is lighter. You think you can carry it?"

"Sure," I answered.

I wanted to expound on her statement, but she was so determined to get to the airport three hours early that I decided to save the conversation for the car. We locked everything up then headed out. Tempest turned up the radio as soon as we got in the car. I turned it down.

"I want to talk, if you don't mind," I said.

She let out a deep sigh. "Alright."

"If you stay in Detroit, who's going to help you raise the baby?"

"Me, myself and I," she answered.

"Wouldn't you want a father in the child's life?"

She shrugged. "That would be nice, but in many cases, life isn't like that."

"Tempest, I admire you trying to be strong and everything. I can certainly respect your decision to have the baby, but the baby can't help any of our current circumstances. He or she shouldn't be made to suffer."

"Ace, you think I want you in our lives because you feel sorry for us? I would only want you in our lives because you really want to be there."

"So, let's have our space, and then we can decide things later."

She let out a loud tsk then said. "Forget it. I ain't coming back."

"Why? Tempest, you're being unfair to me. You're aware of all we've been through . . . you were a part of it. It's not fair for you to expect me to make choices right now. You said yourself space would do us both some good. Trying to decide right now could lead to bad consequences. All I'm asking is that we not force things, baby. Can you understand that?"

She turned to face the window. "How's Faith doing, Ace?"

I sighed. "I don't, Tempest, and Faith isn't the reason I don't want to make judgment on our lives right now."

She turned back to look at me as I drove. "What do you mean you don't know? Haven't you talked to her?"

I glanced at her. "No. When Faith left last Tuesday, that was it. I have an idea where her apartments are located because she told me the name of them once she had been approved, but she hasn't tried to call me, and I haven't tried to reach her."

"Wow. Why not?"

"I don't know, Tempest. It might have something to do with the fact that you pulled a gun on her, and I chose you over her that night. What do you think?"

She laughed. "Well, when you put it like that, I can imagine she wouldn't want to have anything to do with either of us."

I stopped for a red light then looked at her. "I'll be glad when I can find the humor in it."

"Ace, I didn't mean to laugh. It's not funny at all. That's why I'm trying to learn to be a better person. That's also why I'm going to file for divorce and move permanently to Detroit."

"What?" I couldn't stop staring at her.

"Ace, pick up your jaw and start driving. We have a green light now."

I continued driving, but Tempest's comment threw me off focus. "What are you saying, Tempest? You don't think I love you?"

"You said you still love me, but honestly, I don't think either one of us love each other enough."

I pulled onto the airport grounds still not sure I understood her. "Tempest, I—"

"Drive down to the Continental terminal, Ace. I need to get out there."

"Okay, but—"

"Listen. Don't fight me on this. You and I have shared some great years together. I'll always cherish them. Just let me have my share of the company or buy me out. It doesn't matter to me. You've taught me about the business to where I can start brand new in Detroit. My baby and I will be fine, plus Craig has promised to pitch in, so don't let my unborn be your excuse to hold on."

I pulled over at the Continental baggage terminal. "Tempest, I don't even know what to say."

"Don't say anything. If you feel I'm deciding for you right now, that's because I am. Ace, you're a wonderful man, and you deserve better than me. I just want to move forward with my child and a change of scenery. Let's end on a good note, okay?"

She leaned over and kissed me softly on the lips. I still couldn't say anything. She opened her car door and got out. That was my cue to get out, too, so I could assist her with getting her bags up to curbside baggage check.

After taking care of her luggage, she turned to me. "I'll do the filing. I still want my cars, and if I find I need anything else from the house, I'll be sure to let you know ahead of time when I plan to come down."

I finally had something to say. "Tempest, are you sure about this?"

She had a slight smile on her face. "I'm sure, Ace."

She wrapped her arms around my neck and squeezed. I held her tight as well. Neither of us could seem to let go until we heard a stern voice asking about my car.

"Who's vehicle is this?" the airport policeman asked.

"That's my car, sir. I'm getting ready to move it right now."

"Alright. Let's hurry it up," he stated.

"Yes, sir," I answered. I turned to Tempest and kissed her lips one more time. "You take care of yourself, you hear me?"

"I will," she answered, wiping lip gloss from my lips. "Now go find your woman." She smiled and then winked.

I winked back then stood, watching as she disappeared into the airport.

Faith

29

___

My new condo was a safe haven and a prison all in the same. The space was fine. It was the loneliness for nearly two months that had become more like a punishment than anything else. Ace had given me a large severance pay, so I didn't have to find work right away, and I used this to my advantage. I couldn't bring myself to do anything more than run out to get groceries, and then it was back into the comfort of my own dwelling I went. Depression had set in big time, and everything frightened me. *What if Tempest still wanted me dead?* I wondered. *How would I now react to seeing her in the streets?* I had definitely sinned against her, and no matter how many times I could apologize to her, my shame had me in a mental jail.

For the longest, my funk had me in no mood to unpack or decorate the place. One morning, I woke up and decided everything would change. I had the mind to finish the remaining boxes and make the condo feel more like home. After turning on the vacuum, it seemed as though I heard a bell chime. *Surely no one is at my door,* I thought. So, I kept working. I moved closer to the door as I pushed the vacuum across the floor. This time, when the bell rang, it was louder and more distinctive. Yes, someone was at my door.

I shut off the power then peered through the peephole. All I could see was a large spray of red roses. "Who is it?" I yelled through the door.

"Special delivery," the male voice on the other side said.

"Who is it for?"

"For the lady of the house."

My parents were the only ones who knew my address. I knew they wouldn't have given it to anyone, so I decided to shoo the man away.

"Listen," I said. "I think you might have the wrong door."

"Um, these flowers are for a Ms. Faith Yarbrough."

The hair on the back of my neck rose out of nervousness. Ace was the last person who had called me by my maiden name. But the man at the door didn't sound like Ace. I remembered Ace's masculine voice so well because he'd speak to me in my dreams every night. The delivery guy sounded more like the late, great Sammie Davis Jr. I wanted him away from my door, but not before quenching my curiosity.

"Sir, who sent those roses?" I yelled through the closed door.

"Um, it doesn't say. Look, lady, do you want 'em or not?" he questioned, his voice ending with agitation. I didn't answer. "Alright. Suit yourself," he said after my long pause.

I unlocked the door and swung it opened as fast as I could. "Wait," I yelled. To my surprise, the delivery man hadn't moved. He stood with about two dozen roses, shielding his face. "I'll take 'em," I said more calm now.

He slowly lowered the roses, and the sight of him made me buckle at the knees. "For you, my lady," he said in his own voice as he extended the roses toward me.

"Ace?" was all I managed to say.

"Hey, babe. May I come in?"

257

My stomach began to do all sorts of flips and turns. There Ace stood, looking even more handsome than I had remembered. Apparently, he hadn't let his illness get the best of him. This day, he stood tall and strong-like. He was totally debonair. A quick breeze swept his cologne up my nostrils, and then I became like butter, almost creating a puddle at the front door. I realized I still loved this man very much, but I hated him, too.

I couldn't move. He tilted his head as though he was trying to read me. I guess since he hadn't spoken to me in what seemed like forever, he didn't know how receptive I'd be to his visit. Little did he know, the poor imitation of Sammie Davis Jr's voice wasn't necessary. I would've let him in regardless. We needed closure. Or, at least I did. Perhaps that was the only way I'd stop dreaming of him nightly. I mustered enough strength to step back and allow him in.

"How did you find me?" I asked as I fastened the door back.

He gave the place a once-over. "Nice . . . very nice, Faith. I like what you've done here so far."

"I asked you a question, Ace," I said, standing firm near the door.

He remembered the roses. "Oh, these are for you." He stepped closer with his arm outstretched. I didn't take them. "Are you gonna let my arm fall off before you take them or what?"

I took the roses then walked over to the couch. "Thanks . . . I guess. I suppose the next thing you're going to say is we need to talk."

"Yes—that is, if you don't mind."

I motioned him over to the couch. His pace was slow. Now, this made me wonder if he was really feeling well, but I didn't question him. I watched him take a seat on the couch, and then it dawned on me that Tempest could've very well followed him.

"Ace, wait. You didn't answer my question. How did you find me, and what if Tempest followed you?"

"I watched you leave your parents house a few days ago, and don't worry. Tempest didn't follow me."

"How do you know?"

"She left me shortly after getting out of the hospital."

"Left you? What do you mean?"

"She filed for divorce, and it'll be final in about another month. She lives in Detroit now, but we talked before she left, and she encouraged me to come find you. I've waited all this time because I figured you needed some space. And to tell the truth, so did I. I had to be sure of what I wanted."

I sat next to him. "And what's that?"

"I want us, Faith."

"You have got to be kidding me," I yelled as I abruptly stood. "Do you remember the little show you put on in your kitchen the day Tempest put that gun to her head, Ace? Huh? Do you remember your reaction? Who do you think you're fooling? The history you have with her far exceeds what you and I could ever have. You love Tempest more than you love me, Ace, and you know it."

"Not so. I love you both . . . for different reasons, of course."

"Ace, why are you here? I don't think I can take any more hurt."

"I've told you why I'm here."

"Oh, yeah. You want us," I said, gesturing quotes as I said us.

"Do you still love me, Faith?" When I looked away rather than answered, he stood and stepped to me. "Look at me, sweetie. Do you still love me?"

I stared for a minute. He was so fine, it was hard to tell he had an illness. His skin was like dark chocolate as usual, but this day, it was his eyes that got to me. His eyes were sincere—very hard to ignore. I wanted to jump and wrap my legs around him, ʠueeze him, and hold him captive so he'd never get away. But then I remembered he technically belonged to someone else.

"You know I still love you, Ace, but in the famous words of Tina Turner, 'What's love got to do with it?' Have you forgotten you're still married?"

"But, that's over . . . well, almost."

"Then, I believe if you truly love me, you can wait until everything is final."

Ace couldn't mask his disappointment. "So what does this mean, really?"

"I love you, Ace. And I do want you. But true love waits, right?" I paused for his reply, but he only dropped his head. "I just want things to be right this time."

He slowly lifted his head then said, "Okay. I hear you." Then, he was silent. We both were. Who knew what to say next? Ace spoke up, "So, should I go now or what?"

My heart wanted to say no, but my mind led me to say otherwise. "Yes," I said, looking at the large bouquet. "Thanks for the flowers, but I think you should leave."

Ace headed for the door. I set the roses on the coffee table then followed close behind. He turned then kissed my cheek. "As soon as I get those papers, Faith, I'm scooping you from this place. I'm going to marry you, and you're coming home with me."

His hand rested at the small of my back. I wondered if my ears had deceived me. Ace wanted to marry me. *Could he really mean it?* I wondered.

"We'll cross that bridge when we come to it," I told him, trying to hold my composure. I really wanted to scream a hallelujah, but I played it off because I didn't want Ace to see so much excitement.

Ace kissed my cheek one more time then let himself out. I locked the door then headed back to the vacuum, feeling like a new woman. The man I loved had found me and proved he not only had been thinking of me, but he actually loved me, too.

I turned on the vacuum. After three good pushes, my home phone began to ring. I shut it off. "What now?" I yelled then headed to the phone.

The caller ID revealed it was a private listing, and the only other calls I'd received came from my parents who's number was public. I figured this had to be Ace.

"Don't tell me you somehow found my phone number, too, Ace," I said, fussing before picking up the receiver. "Hello." There was no response. "Hello," I said again.

This time the caller spoke. Her voice was plain and clear. "Roses are red, violets are blue. I only called because I see you." She laughed then hung up.

"What the—" I said, staring into the receiver. I placed the phone back on its base. It rang again. "Hello," I screamed just after pressing the talk button.

"Roses *are* red, aren't they?" she said then laughed. "Did you think the best woman had won? Well, think again, dear handsome lady. You can have my husband, but he comes with a price. It's game time. Are you ready?"

"Damn you, Tempest!" She let out an eerie laugh as I hung up on her.

The phone rang again. Tempest was definitely in the mood for games, and something told me, things would only get worse before they got better. I began to wrap my mind around all I might have to endure in the days ahead. It dawned on me that I was suddenly in the market for a gun.

RING RING RING

I should've known Tempest wasn't one to bow out gracefully, regardless of what she told Ace. No—she would have to be taken out. And I'd have to be the one to do it.

RING RING RING

Discussion Questions

1. What do you feel was the root of the problem in Tempest's and Ace's marriage?

2. Based upon what you know about love, which characters truly loved each other?

3. What is your overall opinion of Parnell Fender? Did your opinion of him ever change by the end of the story?

4. If you were Lynette, would you stay with your husband through it all? Why or why not?

5. Which characters did you root for and why?

6. Once Faith knew the circumstances of her job, should she have taken the position? Where and how did she go wrong?

7. Which of Tempest's actions were extreme?

8. Should Craig be reported for what he did to Tempest? Why or why not?

9. Can a man like Lemont change for the better?

10. Who was fooling who?

Acknowledgments

To God, I give all the Glory!

To Lillie Garrison, Rhonda and Charles Brown, Donald and Bobbie Smith, Donna and Maurice Brown, Peggy and Leonard Swift, Gregory and Shatrina Savage, Kendal and Eric Hubbard, Paul Tutwiler, Ronald Byrd, Deborah Tuggle, Lawanna Cox, Kay Sikes, Angela Bonner, Will Scott, Danielle Childress, Lajuanese Bradley, Mary Fluker, Kimberly Richardson, Melvin Edwards, Pauletta Thomas, Tasha Gant, Leroy Arnold, Penny Nathaniel, Tasha Parker, Gregory Johnson, Donna Harvey, Kim Anthony, Sherita Nunn, Pat Tucker, Keith Lee Johnson, Patricia Harris, Linda Johnson, Turjemia Robinson, Shamanda Griggs, Pamela Small, Teresa Mitchell, Jennifer Sanders, and all GFI of Memphis members . . . I thank you because of your continuous support, encouragement, and love. Again and again I say thank you!

To Anyone I may have forgotten: Please charge it to my head and not my heart. I appreciate everyone who has been a part of my success and endeavors.

About the Author

Playwright, Screenwriter, and National Bestselling Novelist, Alisha Yvonne is a native Memphian. She is the Essence® Bestselling Author of *Lovin' You Is Wrong* and *I Don't Wanna Be Right*. She is also nationally known for *Naughty Girls, The CleanUp Woman* and having contributed to the bestseller, *Around the Way Girls-3*.

Alisha continues to be prolific as she ventures into the nonfiction and young adult arenas. Look for her Hopeland High novels, *If I Were A Boy* and *Soulja Girl*. She is currently working on her next book.

Visit Alisha online at www.alishayvonneonline.com or email to: alisha@ebonyliterarygrace.com

22060567R00146